Saturday, the Twelfth of October

ALSO BY
NORMA FOX MAZER

I, TRISSY

A FIGURE OF SPEECH

NORMA FOX MAZER

Saturday, the Twelfth of October

DELACORTE PRESS/NEW YORK

Library of Congress Cataloging in Publication Data

Mazer, Norma.

Saturday, the twelfth of October.

SUMMARY: After spending almost a year
with cave people from an earlier time,
a young girl is transported back to the present
greatly changed, both by her experience
and by the fact that no one believes her.
[1. Space and time—Fiction] I. Title.
PZ7.M47398Sat [Fic] 75–8006
ISBN 0-440-05947-X

FOR RON,

WHO BELIEVED IN THE STORY

Saturday, the Twelfth of October

1

On an afternoon in October, walking home from school, Zan Ford played the eye game—her own secret invention, played for all it was worth. She couldn't take the game lightly, she couldn't take anything lightly. "You *vi*brate," Aunt Cici had told her. "If I was drawing you in a cartoon, I'd make little jagged lightning marks streaking out from you."

The eye game: Zan, walking down the sidewalk, looked straight into the eyes of a stranger picked out of the crowd. If eyes met eyes, if she was truly seen, then she had won. Her spirits soared. She had pierced the numbing anonymity of the street, if only for a moment.

You, she said silently to a man approaching, *you wearing the baggy blue pants, look at me.* His hands were in his pockets, his hair was thinning; did he have a daughter her age? Did he look at his daughter and see the real person? *Mister, look up. Come on!* But the man, his eyes filmed, passed by.

With one part of her she scoffed at herself. *City kid, do you really think that with the mere force of your mind you can make strangers open their eyes?* It was a game destined for failure—no one ever saw anyone on these hurried dirty streets. It was silly—it could even be dangerous—but she didn't care! With every person chosen, in that split second before passing, she felt a little catch beneath her ribs, as if something important and unexpected were about to happen. Yet she knew that even on those rare days when her glance was met and returned, when eyes talked and she felt an almost frightening shock of pleasure reaching from stomach to throat—even then, nothing would come of it. But still she persisted.

No one knew about the eye game, not even her best friend, Lillian, of the round blue eyes, the armful of dangling charm bracelets, the pearly pink polished nails. She would never understand about the eye game. Nor would anyone in her own family. Ivan, for instance, would make her life miserable. She could just hear him! "You're out of your gourd, Madame Koo-koo! Watch out for the funny-farm boys, they're coming to get you!" Years ago, she and Ivan had played together, had been friends and buddies. Now he sneered at her at every opportunity and went into choking giggling fits whenever she tried to say something serious.

Okay, next. You with the plaid beret and the duck walk. Hi, there! Hello! Hey—damn! Another one gone.

All right, the lady with the baby carriage. I'm looking at you, you've got a nice face, you're coming closer, closer. What are you thinking? Why don't you look at me? Quick, now, before you—gone! Forget this side of the street. Only losers here.

She ran into traffic, darting expertly between the cars. A horn blared. A man wearing a leather cap stuck his head out the car window. "Good way to die young, kid," he yelled furiously. Zan jumped onto the sidewalk, shrugging, smiling. The cars, like a pack of frenzied animals, raced on. And people, frowns cutting into foreheads, chins thrust tensely forward, surged past her, bumping and shoving. *Keep walking,* Dad always told her, *don't talk to strangers, don't stop for anybody, keep to yourself.* The way he saw things, the world, the city, the very street she was walking on, was crammed with perverts, creeps, and criminals. Oh, no! She couldn't believe it. She had to keep playing the eye game. It meant something to her. *What?* her father would say. *What does it mean?* I don't know. *Now, that's dumb.* She could hear his voice, see his broad face, that vertical cut between his eyebrows deepening as he spoke. He drove a truck for Consolidated Newspaper Service, leaving for work early in the morning wearing a nylon windbreaker and a cloth cap set at a jaunty angle, coming home late, his jacket crumpled, complaining that his job was ruining his kidneys. He worried all the time about his health, or people breaking into their apartment, or money.

Money, the root of all arguments. Like the one last night. "If you're going to buy, buy the · best," her mother had said, showing off the new electric broiler she'd bought. It was gleaming and beautiful, with all kinds of timing controls and dials. But her father had been mad; he wanted to hang on to their money. "How?" Bernice Ford had said. She was freckled like Zan, but bony, not an ounce of fat anywhere. "The money goes to pay bills like water down the drain," she'd said. "Every cent you make and every cent I make goes out as fast as it comes in."

"Sure! Because you're buying junk all the time," her father had said. "Buy, buy, buy!"

Zan's mother blazed right back; there was nothing meek about her. "You agreed we needed a broiler. The old one's been broken for months. Whatever I buy is for the family. I don't get one thing for myself. And you know that's the truth, Nate Ford!"

Her father had stuffed a cigarette in his mouth as if he were going to swallow it. "Okay! Okay! I can hear you. The neighbors can hear you. They can hear you all the way down to the corner!"

The rest of the evening her parents hadn't spoken to each other. Zan had escaped by going early to her cot in the kitchen, slamming the door to let everyone know that they had better stay out. She hated her parents' fights. She'd never get used to them! She had dug her diary out from under the mattress and got into bed, hunching beneath the blankets to write: "Why do they fight so much? Dad gets that tight look around his mouth, and Mom's neck gets as red as a turkey. And just because they're mad at each other, they act mad at us kids, too!"

Digging her pencil in to make the exclamation mark, she had broken the point. Disgusted, she threw it down on the floor. *Fair's fair, Zan. They don't fight all the time. They're not exactly beasts of Buchenwald.* True. Sunday mornings, for instance, were nearly always great. Her father hung around in his pajamas and didn't mind all the noise; and her mother cooked things like french toast or sausages and pancakes.

Flopping over on her belly, Zan had retrieved her pencil. She bit off the cedar to make a point and began writing again:

"I remember thinking when I was little that a-month-of-Sundays was the prettiest word in the world. Then Cici got divorced and she and Kim came to live with us. Cici would be okay all week until Sunday, when she'd get depressed because she said Sunday was the loneliest day of the week for her. I wonder if Cici is frustrated about sex. She's been divorced two years now. I don't think my parents do it much. Lillian's parents sleep in separate beds, which she says proves they don't ever do it. But that's childish. She just doesn't want to face the fact that her parents are having sex. When I was about 7 or 8, I used to think parents did it only when they wanted children, which meant to me that Mom and Dad had done it two times, to have Ivan and me. Now I know that's ridiculous, but still—I wonder. There are so many things I wonder about, sometimes I feel so stupid and ignorant, I think everyone knows more about everything than I do."

Sometimes Zan imagined talking to her mother seriously about the questions that crowded her mind, about her moods, about so many things. But it never happened. Her mother, with her job and the house, was up before anyone else in the morning and was the last to get to bed at night. If Zan had tried to talk to her about the eye game, she would say, "Honey, I haven't the time now. Maybe later. Eye game? Aren't you getting too old for games?"

Not for the eye game. But hurrying now through the crowds, her thoughts jumbled and quick, Zan felt less of her earlier exuberance. The faces swam toward her, wave after wave of blank faces. Not a smile, a nod, a chance glance, or even a furious glare. Sometimes mouths moved, silently speaking, but not to her. Only to themselves.

She began to feel invisible. If she were suddenly

snatched out of the crowd by a giant hand, would anyone even notice?

The next day, in school, she was still thinking about the same thing.

Visible. Invisible. Did anyone really see her? No. Not kids. Not teachers. There were waves, smiles. Hello! How're you? Automatic. Bright. Unseeing.

Then, at the end of the day, something strange happened in Mr. Oberdorfer's class. Mr. Oberdorfer, chubby and serious, talking about the past, evolution, missing links. Zan doodled in her notebook, half listening.

"For hundreds of thousands of years *Homo sapiens* —wise man, remember?—has roamed this earth. Today we live in a highly sophisticated, technological society. But we are connected to all those people before us, those millions back through history and prehistory, right back to the Stone Age man. Can anyone tell me what we have in common with those primitive people?"

Feet scuffled on the floor, there was a hum and buzz of talk, notes were passed around.

"Is anyone here interested in what I'm saying?" Mr. Oberdorfer demanded. He was a young man with manicured fingernails and monogrammed ties.

Zan felt sorry for him. He was just too sincere, and the kids were always having fun at his expense. Most of the time, though, he sort of asked for it by talking too much.

"We share a common heritage of basic human feelings," he said. He sat back in his chair, tapping a pencil against one of his manicured nails, and spoke rapidly. "Just like people today, people ten thousand years ago felt heat and cold, joy and sorrow. They didn't work in factories or offices, but they had their work of hunting. They probably lived in family groups, eating together, caring for their young, making love—"

That broke up the class. Suddenly they came to life, whistling, stamping, cheering. Mr. Oberdorfer's round pink face became even pinker. He smacked his hands on the desk, calling for attention. "Must you people show your ignorance? Are you so parochial that you think only people just like yourselves know the range of human activities and emotions?" More laughter. Someone burped. Someone farted. This produced roars of glee. Mr. Oberdorfer went on, his voice rising. "We are related to the past in the deepest ways. The past is part of us, yes, even the past of ten thousand years ago. The great Albert Einstein once compared time to a river, with the past flowing into the present, and the present into the future. Do you understand what this means? A river of time on which everything that has ever been, everybody who has ever lived, every moment of being still exists."

In the middle of a yawn, Zan sat up straight, suddenly alert. "That's crazy," she blurted. "It doesn't make sense." A river, on the banks of which swarmed, like a million trillion billion ants, all of human life?

Mr. Oberdorfer fingered his tie. "Why not?" He sounded bored.

"People die, they get buried . . ." Zan mumbled, feeling foolish, but she struggled on. "Cities die, too, you taught us that. Everything changes, nothing stays the same. Even if it did, how could everything and everyone still *be*? And on a river . . ."

Mr. Oberdorfer's eyes focused on her. He looked down at his seating chart and came up with her name.

"Try to think beyond your usual frame of reference, Alexandra. The river we're talking about is not a literal river, but a metaphoric river. Not a river of water, but of time and space. Clear your mind, open it! Stop thinking of time like squares of goods, as if a week, a month, a year, were solid things. Time isn't a thing. It has no boundaries, flows on endlessly. It's only we humans who label time, who perceive it as something to be measured and marked off. Do you understand me?"

"I don't know—maybe . . ."

"Imagine time as a curving ribbon in space, an infinite curve without beginning or ending." He turned to the blackboard and with the side of the chalk made a thick ghostly white curve that turned back on itself and ran off the board.

"Tell me that again," Zan said, dimly aware that she was speaking to Mr. O. as if there were no one else in the classroom and that he was looking at her as if he were aware of her for the first time.

"Time is infinite, only human beings make it finite. Perhaps because we die? Because our own lives have a period put to them? Infinite, remember, means endless, without measure, boundless. Almost by definition it's a term we can't understand. But we have to try. To comprehend infinite, endless time, a river is a useful analogy, but even this is limited unless you can imagine a river that never begins or ends, but simply *is*. That is the river of time. Now remember, it cannot move in a straight line because a straight line means from *here*, a beginning, to *there*, an ending. Are you following me?"

"Yes," she said, almost in a whisper, struggling to grasp what he was presenting. Excited, her mind floated, glimpsing a shimmering, dazzling river spilling endlessly through space.

"Time, then, if it has no beginning and no ending, *must* curve back on itself. And who is to say where we fit in, where the past is, where the future is? 'Past,' 'present,' 'future' are boundary terms, like 'start' and 'finish,' 'born' and 'die.' They mark beginnings and ending. But what if there is no such thing as the beginning, or the end. What if it's just our own imperfect vision that lets us believe in such untruths? What if there's only time, only that river on which nothing is lost? Do you know what this could mean? Someday, we are going to find the way to step out of our tiny tiny place on this river, step across, or into, all of that river of time." Mr. Oberdorfer's pink face glowed above his yellow shirt and monogrammed tie. "I believe this, I believe this very firmly, I have the notion that someday in the future, science is going to discover how to take that step. Imagine what that will mean! Imagine—"

Just then, the bell rang. The class stampeded for the door. Zan had time only for a smile in Mr. Oberdorfer's direction, then Lillian grabbed her arm and hustled her into the hall, saying, "He's so *queer*. He was practically slobbering he was so excited."

"Oh, he's all right, I like him, I really do," Zan said, holding back the excitement she had been ready to spill out and share with Lillian. She changed the subject. But Mr. Oberdorfer's words rang like bells in her head. She wanted to hold onto everything he had said, the images he had given her, so that later she could think it all over again. But in the process of leaving school, gossiping with Lillian, stopping to buy a candy bar—doing all those ordinary things—too much of what Mr. Oberdorfer had said slipped away from her. Now, as she neared home, smelling the smoky, fishy smell of Friday, she had to struggle to remember what it all meant.

Time without ending or beginning. This time? This moment? Clattering onto a boardwalk surrounding a construction site, she glanced at the heaps of debris, the half-demolished building. A steel ball on the end of a long, giraffe-necked crane cracked into a brick wall. Clouds of dust and ancient bricks showered to the ground; bits of filth swirled around her legs. Was this moment, which seemed no longer than the blink of an eye, fixed in that river of time? And the next moment, and the next, and every moment that had ever been? Were they all still there, frozen, happening over and over? It was an idea so momentous, so beyond comprehension as to be either sublimely profound or profoundly silly.

Halfway around the construction site was a tipsy wooden wall made up of old doors hammered together. Every door was thick with scrawls: *From the day we're born, we begin to die . . . Hilda, Jan. 2 . . . Buzz and Banana Boy and Lori and Grapes . . . Finley, he was here, yeah! . . . Today is the tomorrow you waited for yesterday . . .* Like epitaphs on tombstones, Zan thought, except all these people leaving their names and slogans were alive. She understood. She felt the urge to add her own name and, digging out a grease pencil from her book sack, she sprawled, "Zan, full of questions and no answers, was here on Friday, October 11." Not so original, but somehow satisfying. She thought about passing this way day after day and seeing her name, the mark of Zan, each time. Then she remembered that as the new building rose on the site of the old, the door wall would come tumbling down. All her life she had seen temporary walls rise and fall; seen buildings blank-eyed before their destruction, and new buildings sprouting on old sites. Her own family had moved three times from old buildings.

She remembered each one of the moves distinctly. She had hated each one, hated the change, the loss of coziness that came with knowing the cracks in the bathroom ceiling, which faucets dripped, where the furniture belonged, how the floors creaked. Whenever the family moved, things were broken or lost, her parents were tired and irritable, and it would take weeks for her to get used to the smells and sounds of the new building. Maybe that was why she especially loved the old boulder in Mechanix Park. Nothing, she was sure, would ever change that rock. She slowed down as she passed the park on J Street with its sagging wire fence, dilapidated swings, and the ancient boulder in a far corner. Blistered and bumpy, criss-crossed with crevices and cracks, at least six feet high and twice as wide, the boulder heaved blindly out of the earth. Years ago, someone had tried to dynamite it out of existence. A perfect round hole had been bored in one side, but the charge had succeeded only in splitting the boulder halfway down the middle. As a little girl, Zan had often scrambled to the top and peered down into the strange dark corridor in the middle.

Across from the park she cut through a narrow alley between brick tenements, a shortcut to her street. The stench of garbage seeped like dust from the faded walls. Two boys perched on overturned metal trash cans watched her approach, then unfolded themselves and blocked her way. Her heart began banging behind her ribs. The taller one held out his hand. "Your money, Freckles." He had blond hair cut straight at the shoulders and pale blue eyes. Zan looked past him to see if anyone was around to help her, but the alley was empty. Everyone she knew had either been mugged or knew someone who had been. Now it was her turn.

"Your money, dummy!"

The second boy, narrow-faced, wearing sharply pressed green trousers and a green and white checked shirt, kicked Zan's ankle with the toe of one polished boot. Pain traveled up her leg.

"Don't just stand there looking dumb."

She fumbled with her book sack. "I haven't any money," she said, although she had a five and two ones folded flat in her left sneaker. She didn't know why she lied, except that, hating her feeling of helplessness, she had to somehow defy them.

"Oh, come on, don't give me that shit." The blond boy jerked her arm behind her back, smiling a little.

Her book sack fell to the ground. Her arm was on fire. "Junk," the other boy said, kicking at the books and papers spilling out of her sack. He poked his hands into her pockets and turned them inside out. Her locker key, a crumpled note from Lillian, half a sticky Mars bar, twenty-five cents in change, and her jackknife were scattered on the dirty pavement. He picked up the knife, which she'd bought for around three dollars in the Tru Valu Hardware Store. "Nothing here except this cheap knife," he said disgustedly.

"Oh, she's got money," said the blond boy. "Everybody has money." He let go of her arm and, as she started to rub it in relief, he put both hands against her breasts and shoved her. As she staggered back, he shoved her again, harder, and she smacked down on the concrete flat on her back. She lay helpless, without breath. She felt as if she were drowning. The second boy grabbed her feet and yanked off her sneakers.

"What a liar," he said, stuffing her money in his pocket. He dropped the jackknife, uninterested in it now. "I could tell you were a liar." He spit toward her. The gob landed next to her, spattering her face.

She wanted to get up, but was afraid to move. She couldn't bear it if they touched her again. She hated them both with a hatred so ferocious that she felt it like fingers jammed down her throat.

"Come on," the blond one said impatiently to his friend, "let's go." Without another glance at her, they loped easily toward the end of the alley, disappearing around the corner.

2

Zan dropped her books on the telephone table in the little hallway of their apartment. "Aunt Cici? Are you home, Aunt Cici? I was mugged! I was mugged by two boys!"

"In here," Cici called from the living room. She was sitting on the floor, using an emery board on her nails. Her daughter, Kim, and Zan's two-year-old brother, Buddy, were playing with tiny model cars on the floor. "Did you say you were mugged?" Cici got up, putting her hands on Zan's shoulders. "Are you okay?"

"The creeps!" Zan said. She had planned to tell the story calmly, but now it came out in a spurt of furious words. "They got me in that alley near Mechanix Park. Oh, I was so dumb! I knew the moment I saw them—"

Buddy, two fingers stuffed in his mouth, staggered to his feet to lean against her leg. "Zan," he breathed. She put her hand on his headful of tight red curls.

"You should have seen them, Cici. This one boy had blue eyes, but not *nice* blue eyes—"

Cici's daughter, Kim, looked up alertly. She was three, a year older than Buddy. "They took Zan's money?"

"That's right." Zan's voice trembled.

"You are all right, aren't you?" Cici said. "They didn't—"

Zan shook her head. In her mind's eye, she saw herself lying helpless on the ground. "No, they didn't." "Then forget it, love! Just put it out of your mind. Okay?" Cici gave her a little shake and went to the mirror over the telephone table to examine her face and her hair. Her marriage to Neil Vinson had lasted almost two years. Now she said that she was looking for a good father for Kim. She was sick of being on her own. Neil was off in British Columbia living in a commune with a new girlfriend and hardly ever even wrote Kim. "The best thing when something ugly happens is— forget it," Cici said.

Zan shook her head. "I can't!"

"Take it from me," Cici said, "it's the only way I've been able to cope. Don't dwell on ugliness." She knotted a silk scarf over her hair and behind her neck. "Tell Bernice I won't be home for supper. I'm meeting Chris."

Nearly every day after school, Zan took over watching the two babies so Cici could get out to shop, do errands, or meet one of her boyfriends. Cici blew Kim a kiss and, humming, left the apartment.

"I really wanted to tell you more about the mugging," Zan said desolately to the closed door. Maybe Cici was right. Forget it. Pretend it didn't happen. Zan played with the kids, getting down on the floor so they could climb on her back, giving them rides around the living room. "Giddyap!" Buddy crowed, hanging onto her hair. She snorted and reared, making the kids scream. And all the time, she was thinking about the mugging.

Her mother came home, clutching a grocery bag, newspaper, her pocketbook, and a plastic-wrapped dress from the cleaner's. "Oh, those mobs on the bus!" she said as she dumped everything on the couch. She picked up Buddy for a moment, ruffled Kim's hair, looked sharply at Zan. "What's the matter?"

"Zan was mugged," Kim said. Coming from Kim, it sounded cute, not serious.

Quickly, Zan explained what had happened.

"Going into an alley—that wasn't using your head!" her mother chided, almost as if she were mad at Zan for getting mugged. Then she sighed. "I have nightmares about one of you kids really getting hurt. This city . . ."

She went into the kitchen. Zan trailed after her and began setting the table, feeling worse and worse. Her mother flipped on the radio, poured hot milk into the instant mashed potatoes. "Listen, let's not tell Daddy," she said, beating the potatoes vigorously. "You know how upset he gets about things like this." Zan nodded. She hadn't told her mother how the blond boy had shoved her, putting his hands on her breasts. She felt it would disgust and anger her mother and she might say something about it, after all, to Zan's father or in front of Ivan. "And don't worry about the money," her mother said. "I'll make it up to you. Between you and me, all right, honey?"

Zan nodded again, as her mother smiled at her. Suddenly, Zan wanted to lean against her and cry; she didn't know why; she didn't do things like that anymore —she was too big, too old. "I'll do the garbage," she said instead, taking the pail from next to the sink and carrying it out to the incinerator in the hall.

Later, when supper was over, the dishes done, and the family out of the kitchen, Zan pulled on her pajamas and got into bed. Fumbling under the mattress for her diary, for a moment she couldn't locate it, and her stomach jumped painfully. Then she felt the hard metal spiral and, drawing out the notebook, opened it to a fresh page: "Today I was mugged. Lillian and I are always talking about what we'd do if it happened to us. I couldn't do anything! It was awful. They could have beat me or raped me. Anything. I wonder, could I have a baby, if that happened—I mean, because of not having my period yet."

Outside, the wail of an ambulance, like a howling dog, cut across the steady *thug, thug, thug* of traffic, and then for several moments the rumble of a jet blotted out every other sound. "I told Mom about the mugging, and she was upset, she really cares, I know she does, but she doesn't understand how I feel inside. The same thing with Aunt Cici. She cares, but she doesn't understand. I wish I could kill those boys! They made me feel like nothing, like a piece of shit."

She looked at what she'd written. Her mother would be furious if she saw it—she hated that kind of language. But the diary was secret, private. Zan wrote everything in it, all her thoughts, questions, fantasies, her wonder and dismay at the world. She lay back, tired. The comfortable *tock, tock, tock* of the dripping faucet and the buzzing of the refrigerator were soothing. Her mind drifted and a line of poetry she'd read somewhere came into her head. *I'm twelve and leaking blood.* No poetry books at home, so she must have read it in school, probably in the Resource Center because no regular school book she knew ever mentioned anything about girls' bleeding. There was only the health class, in which cute little Mr. Franko had spent most of the semester so far talking about his new grandson and parading around with his shirt sleeves rolled up to show off his muscular arms. And, oh yes, a few words now and then about keeping yourself clean, about your body preparing itself for womanhood and manhood. Mixed class. Really wild.

Usually, Zan hardly listened. Most of the time she doodled stick figures, or wrote her name, "Alexandra Mary Ford," in elaborate script, or dreamed about dark-haired Steve Sykowski, who was a year ahead of her and blew the trumpet in the school band. *I'm twelve and leaking blood.* Zan was fourteen and still nothing. Every morning in the locked bathroom she examined her pajama bottoms, both relieved and upset when she found nothing. All her friends had their periods except her.

In the bathroom on the top shelf of the medicine cabinet was usually a small blue box of tampons. Instructions came in the package on a folded piece of paper. Zan had read it often with the door locked and the water running to cover the sound of the crisp paper. So she knew what to do when it started, though it all struck her as gross—sticky blood and putting those little cotton tubes into yourself.

A long time ago when she was in the fourth grade her mother had said, "Let me know when it starts," and had handed her a book, saying, "Read this, honey, it's all about the things you want to know. Some girls get it early, maybe you will." It had been night and her mother sat on the edge of Zan's bed, smoothing the tufted bedspread between her fingers. "I'm not much good at explaining things, honey, but I don't want you to be ignorant or feel that it's anything bad. It's natural, nothing to be afraid of. We used to call it 'the curse,' but girls today know better. You should be proud to be a woman, when you get the—when you get it, your time of the month I mean, that will show that you aren't a little girl anymore." And she had bent and kissed Zan's forehead very tenderly.

Since then, nothing. Five years almost, and nothing!

Yet, something had happened. In secret, her body had changed itself, and in secret Zan had thought often about the blood she sensed was waiting for the right moment to pour out of her. Sitting at her desk in school, she sometimes looked down at her feet, her stomach jerking, almost expecting to see a pool of sticky blood on the scuffed floor.

Zan hated the thought of her period; yet she also longed for it, so that all the waiting would be over, and she could be like everyone else. She felt excluded, as if there were a club she hadn't been able to join yet. Every month, Lillian stayed home for three days with cramps, whether she had her period or not. "Missing school is one of the good things about it," she told Zan.

On her cot now, Zan stirred, her eyes heavy, thinking she ought to shut off the light. Her mind floated into a corner of the room; there was something about a river and Ivan . . . The diary slipped from her unresisting fingers to the floor, and she groaned softly in her sleep as she thought again of the boy with the blank blue eyes.

In the morning, Ivan, wearing baggy gray sweat pants and a tee shirt, opened the refrigerator and stood in front of it for a long time, trying to decide what he wanted to eat. On weekday mornings he usually gulped down a glass of milk and then bought a doughnut on the way to school. But on Saturdays he liked to eat a real breakfast. He was famished because Zan, the pain in the ass, had slept late and nobody could come into the kitchen on Saturday morning till she woke up. Orders from above. "Cripes," he muttered in disgust. He could hear her out in the hall yakking on the phone.

He took a long drink from the plastic milk carton, then nibbled a handful of cold spaghetti, dropping a few strands on the floor. Nothing in the refrigerator looked interesting. "Corn flakes," he said at last, turning to the cupboard.

As he dumped sugar on the bowl of flakes, he hoped his mother wouldn't come in and tell him again that too much sugar was why he had pimples on his forehead. He shoved a spoonful of sweet, soggy flakes into his mouth and, from the corner of his eye, noticed Zan's diary on the floor, half under her cot. He stretched out a foot and toed the diary toward his chair. "PRIVATE. KEEP OUT." Big fat letters. Big fat deal! Ivan touched his forehead, feeling the hateful bumps. The thought of his pimples made him feel sorry for himself and mad at the world. Zan didn't have pimples on her forehead. He picked up the diary and read a page at random. Something about his sister's dumb dreams. She was always going on about her feelings this and her feelings that, and, oh, what a dream I had! It made him sick. He flipped to her last entry about the mugging. Oh, hot stuff, she used the word "shit." He snorted and riffled the pages, then, reading, his face got hot. Holy Cow. Ho-ly Cow! HO-LY COW! Wait till Billy and Carl hear about this.

Footsteps broke into his concentration. Zan was coming back. He started to throw the diary on the floor again, then changed his mind and hastily slipped it under his tee shirt. He'd just tease her a little when she noticed it was gone. He jumped up from the table and, grinning, held his arm pressed stiffly across his belly to hold down the diary.

"What's so funny?" Zan said, entering the kitchen. Then, "Phew! You sure are sweating. You need a bath, El Smello."

"Go to hell!" He walked out of the kitchen. It would serve her right to find her diary gone. Give her a good scare, the bigmouth, teach her to take better care of things that were so PERSONAL and PRIVATE. In his bedroom he dropped the diary into his top bureau drawer. His pimples felt as if they were on fire.

About an hour later Zan heard shrill guffaws leaking out from behind Ivan's closed door. His two friends, Billy Gold and Carl Whitman, had come over, and all three were in Ivan's room. For a while she paid no attention. She talked to Lillian again on the phone, then cleaned the front hall—orders transmitted through her mother's closed bedroom door—wiping up the floor, the woodwork, and the telephone table on which assorted odds and ends always accumulated. Then she went into the kitchen to make her bed. Folding her pajamas, she thought of her diary and slipped her hands under the mattress, but felt only bare steel springs. She worked her hands up and down the length of the springs, then bent to check the floor. Nothing but dustballs and a pair of sneakers. Then, from Ivan's room, she again heard Billy Gold snicker. She thought of Ivan's grin and his stiff-armed walk. "Oh, no!" She ran to his room and pushed open the door.

". . . don't know why I haven't had my period yet," Ivan was saying. Reading from her diary, he sat on his bureau like an Indian guru, legs crossed, feet tucked beneath his thighs. Skinny Carl Whitman and fat little Billy Gold were sprawled on Ivan's bed, choking with laughter. "My breasts are developed and I've got pubic hair . . ." he read.

"Ivan. Ivan!"

Ivan looked up, his forehead blazing, and instinctively tried to hide the diary.

"Give that to me," Zan ordered. "Give it to me!" As

she grabbed for the diary, Ivan tossed it to Carl, who, still laughing, curled up with the notebook under him. Zan dived for Carl, knocking off his glasses. "Give that to me. It's mine!" Tears of rage filled her eyes. It was yesterday all over again. She was being robbed and humiliated. She pummeled Carl with her fists.

"Ow! Hey, cut it out, you're hurting me."

"Give it to me, give it, *give it!*" She pounded on him, sick with fury and shame.

"She's going crazy," Billy said, with a touch of awe.

"*What's* going on here?" Mrs. Ford was at the door in her green bathrobe. "Zan. Alexandra Ford! What are you doing?" She pulled Zan off Carl.

"Ask him!" Zan tried to reach Carl again. "Ask Ivan! Ask him what he did."

Sweating, Ivan tried to appear unconcerned. "Aw, she left her dumb diary lying right out in public, in the middle of the floor."

"He took it, he read it, he read it to Billy and Carl. He read them my diary."

Mrs. Ford looked at Ivan. "Is there never to be any peace around here? Ivan, I'm ashamed of you, I'm ashamed of all you boys. Carl, give me that diary." She took the notebook. "Now, Ivan, apologize to your sister. Then I don't want to hear—"

"No! What good is an apology? An apology won't change anything." Zan pushed blindly past her mother. Cici was at the door to her room in her blue pajamas, her mouth pale.

"Zan? What's the matter?"

Zan ran out of the apartment, her mother's voice calling after her, "Come back! Don't be silly!" She ran down the stairs, down and down, aching, hurting, out the front door, into the street. She didn't know where she was going, only that she had to go somewhere, away from her brother, away from her mother who thought that saying "Sorry" made everything all right. Soon she found herself at Mechanix Park and knew that was where she wanted to be. Throwing herself down behind the boulder where the grass grew high and tangled, hidden from sight, Zan pressed herself into the earth and the shadow of the rock. Words leaped into her mind. Words she had written. Words Ivan had seen and read to Billy and Carl. Her skin felt as if it were melting off her bones. Then Ivan's voice rattled down the street. "Zan? Zan Ford. Zan, are you there? Hey, come out, come out wherever you are, I gotta talk to you."

She didn't answer. He was calling only because their mother had forced him. Even if it had been his own idea, she wouldn't have answered. She hated him now. She pressed herself against the boulder, longing to dissolve into the earth, into the stone. She pressed harder and harder against the stone, her face and body burning, her head, her arms, her whole self melting and burning. A humming grew in her ears, a distant humming like the humming of a hundred wires. It grew gradually louder, more insistent, and became a furious, shattering buzzing, as if the sky were black with a million insects. She didn't hear Ivan call her again. Her self was dissolving, coming apart, melting into the earth and the stone. "WHAT?" she cried. She wanted to stop this thing that was happening, but was swept up, her head filling and threatening to burst like an overripe fruit. "WHAT IS THIS?" she cried in terror. Then a storm of darkness descended on her, wings of darkness spinning and tossing her in a blur of silver and black. WHAT? HELP! HELP ME! HELP! Her mouth was filled with darkness. Her blinded eyes streamed silver. Silver poured through her arms and silver streams jetted from her nostrils. Silver flew from her body, streamers of black silver, black as the earth, black and silver as the depths of the earth.

3

She lay on the ground, crumpled, shaking, bones scraped raw. Behind her closed eyelids, stunning, needle-like flashes of black and silver pierced her skull. For a long time she lay there, shuddering, shaking. Gradually she became quieter; her body knit itself together; her flesh softened; her bones again became an uncounted, unfelt part of herself.

"What was it?" Her voice was a whisper. Her lips were swollen, sore. She groped for an explanation, a way of understanding the silver and darkness, a name for the merciless force that had flung and flayed her. Beneath her body she felt the earth still trembling from the—storm? Hurricane? Tornado? Yes, tornado. Greedily, she fastened on the familiar word, the possible explanation. A tornado was terrifying, but comprehensible. A raging wind whirling through the sky like a giant egg whisk, sucking her up into its black center. She had had no warning of its coming, no signal, no premonition, but that was understandable. Tangled in misery, she had been oblivious to everything but her need to get away from Ivan. A tornado, yes. A force of nature, a disaster, and she in the heart of the disaster. In her mind she saw rubble of toppled buildings, dust and smoke rising silently in a devastated city beneath a sullen sky. She pushed her clenched hands against her jaw, trying with the little ache of bone rubbing against bone to keep away terror. Her family. Her home. What had happened to them? She became aware of silence, sound unburdened by the rumble of vehicles, the rasp of machinery, the muted city roar.

Open your eyes. Don't be a rabbit. Face it. But the ominous silence, thick, almost palpable, seemed as threatening as the storm had been; silence poured over her like a deadly gas.

A loud buzzing filled her ears. She recalled the onset of the storm, and her eyes flew open. A swarm of stout metallic green insects with bulging black eyes beat around her face. They hovered vertically in space like tiny evil helicopters. She leaped to her feet, covering her head with her arms. "Go away! Go away, go away!" Instinctively she ducked lower and threw herself against the boulder. Behind her, the buzzing diminished, then disappeared. She raised her head cautiously and looked around. She was in the middle of a vast overgrown field. Above her the sky was shockingly blue, the sun blazed with a fierce purity, and everywhere grass, bushes, and flowers grew in lush, dazing, brilliant profusion. The wire park fence, the pigeon-spattered statue of James P. Mechanix, the scarred maples, the paint-flecked teeter-totters—all had disappeared. The buildings outside the park were gone. The streets, the cars, the people, the city itself—all had vanished. She put her hands to her eyes. Her mind felt as hot as the yellow sun, thick and boiling, uncomprehending.

In the distance, the sharp peaks of mountains shimmered like water. All around her was the silence—a silence unlike anything she'd ever known, deep and thick, yet not silence; for the air was rippled with the high, shrill calls of invisible insects, with wind soughing through the trees in the distance, and with strange hoarse bird cries.

She tried to remember her geography, to relate stray facts to the physical landscape around her. The storm had snatched her and set her down—where? Could she have been flung so fast and so far that she was now in a distant part of the country? Or even another country? At the thought her heart thumped painfully. Unbidden, then, her hands wandered over her face, touching eyes, cheekbones, lips, as if in this confusion and terror her physical self might, somehow, have been altered. She looked down the length of her body, stretched out her arms, flexed her fingers, rose on her toes. Her relief was silly and real. She was all there, intact, unchanged, still Zan. Her clothing, too, was unchanged—sneakers, jeans, shirt, all limp and familiar. She felt a sudden fondness for her clothes—they had come through this with her!—and with the same feeling of gratified fondness she took out and fingered each object in her pockets. Her jackknife, a white button, a crumpled tissue, a safety pin, two linty Lifesavers, her school locker key. She stared at them as if they contained answers, then put them carefully back into her pocket.

She cupped her hands around her mouth. "Hello. Anybody here? Hello. Anybody around?" Only bird-calls, insects, and wind answered her. She pushed up the sleeves of her shirt. No reason to panic. There were explanations for everything. She had only to find a house and people. Then everything would not seem so strange and ominous. She turned to the boulder, touch-ing it quickly, for luck. Her own ugly beast of a boulder! A wave of emotion swept her, but at once chilling reason struck it down. How could this rock be *her* rock when Mechanix Park was gone, the city was gone, and she was *somewhere else?* Besides, she had never seen anything bloom on her boulder's tough hide except smashed soda bottles. This boulder blazed with red and blue lichens, clumps of green moss, and clusters of vivid, tiny blue flowers growing in every crevice. Then, too, there was no perfect round dynamite hole, no long secret shaft down its middle. She had only thought it was her boulder because she wanted so desperately to touch something known and familiar.

She stepped into the field, waving her arms to drive away the swarming insects, and pushed her way clumsily through the shoulder-high growths of grass and flowers. Astonished, she saw bright emerald butterflies as big as birds skeining the air, and others, jet black, as small as bees. She pushed aside the grass with swimming motions of her hands, fixing her eyes on the distant trees. Thick tangles of bushes choked her steps. The sun beat down on her head, and the high grasses swayed in front of her eyes. The field seemed to go on and on. The trees looked as far away as ever. Her arms were welting from the coarse grass, and she began kicking it aside with her feet. Her tongue clicked dryly against the roof of her mouth. She longed for a cold, moist can of soda. Bees and flies, attracted by her sweat, buzzed maddeningly around her.

She sank to the ground for a rest; it was cooler there, the stalks of the plants forming a dim, cave-like place. She brightened, enjoying the feeling of a hideaway, the shadowed little clearing close to the earth, just the sort of place she'd loved when she was small. But soon she got up and moved briskly forward again. Turning, she saw her path behind her, narrow, twisting, bent through the field. She continued on. As she neared the trees, her steps slowed, faltered, then stopped. Before her she saw a massive forest stretching impenetrably in every direction.

The trees were enormous, a race of giants of incredible height and girth. Vines, creepers, and thorns grew thick and tangled over blackened scabby trunks; wind creaked through massive, grotesquely twisted limbs; and long rays of greenish-black light filtered from the forest roof like murky water. Zan had to tilt her head until her neck ached to see the tops of the trees.

Several times in the past years her parents had taken her and her brothers to the state park forest, a two-hour bus ride from the city. The air in the park had smelled piney sweet, and her mother, relaxed for a few hours, had recalled the times in her childhood when *her* parents had taken her and Cici to the country. Each time they had brought a picnic lunch and, after eating at one of the wooden tables, they had gone walking in the forest, along trails marked with little red plastic circles stuck on trees. The trees had been trim and straight, growing in neat pleasant rows. But that forest had about as much relationship to the forest before Zan as did a glass of water to a raging ocean.

A thick, sweetish odor assailed Zan's nostrils. The wind carried unidentifiable clattering and barks and screams from the dark trees, making the hairs on her arms stand up. She could never go in there. Never! But the field was bounded on every side by forest, and there was no other way out. Blindly she veered in another direction, then in another, propelled by despair.

Suddenly the sky darkened. Overhead, thousands upon thousands of huge birds blotted out sun and sky, light and warmth. Curved necks extended like snakes, long blue legs dangling strangely, wings beating the air, they shrieked like a convocation of demons and devils. Ai-uuuhhh! Ai-uuuhhh!

Zan's own cry was drowned in the birds' sound as she plunged back through the field, pushing aside the whipping grasses and ending up, finally, against a rock. Only when the last, demonic call had faded did she see that the boulder she had been so furiously hugging was the same one she had left behind her. She had made a complete circle.

She slumped to the coolness of the ground, putting her head against the stone, remembering how Ivan had called down the street after her. If she'd answered him, if she'd gotten up and gone home, would she be here now? For a little while she went over again all the events of the morning, almost forgetting for a few moments where she was. After a while, she got to her feet again, and made a megaphone of her hands. "HEL-LO? HEL-LO! HEL-LO!" She turned, yelling in every direction. "IS ANYONE AROUND? DO YOU HEAR ME? HELLO! HELLO! ANSWER IF YOU HEAR ME. ANSWER ME!"

Her voice disappeared into the field like a pebble on a beach. It was stupid to stand there and yell. She struck out again into the field, in another direction. She sweated through the field, temples throbbing, thrusting down the grass and flowers, sidestepping the thorny little bushes, making another path.

Unexpectedly she came upon a small sandy clearing with scrubby grass and a shallow pool. Nearby, the forest again. Throwing herself down on her belly, she stuck her face gratefully into the pool, gulping down the warm water, splashing it over her steaming head. Drip-

ping, she rolled away and lay on her back, arms flung
across her face. She was exhausted, her mind blurry.
Colors and swarming shafts of light played behind her
eyelids.

She jerked suddenly to alertness with the conviction
that she was being watched. Her scalp prickled. She sat
up, looking uneasily into the watery gloom of the forest. The sense of being watched heightened. She turned
slowly round and saw two bright, bulging black eyes
with yellow centers staring directly at her. An animal as
big as she, furry, tawny, with long splayed-out, dan-
gerous-looking feet stood on its hind legs on the limb of
a tree, gripping another branch above it with one hand.
Its tail, thick and striped like a raccoon's, curled over
its upraised arm. It had an almost human look, calm
and appraising. Zan's belly jerked spasmodically. She
tried to make herself small. Then, with a squawk that
seemed like a derisive laugh, the animal leaped to another tree and disappeared into the forest.

There was a metallic taste in Zan's throat. An idea
gnawed at her; an idea that had been burrowing secretly
into her mind from the moment she opened her eyes to
that mad yellow sun. Something awesomely out of the
ordinary had happened to her, something so bizarre, so
incredible . . . She sprang to her feet, pushing away,
denying, her thoughts. Her head swam dizzily, but in
her stomach there was a leaden weight. She bent over,
sweating, and vomited bitter bile into the grass.

She rinsed her mouth in the waterhole, rinsing and
spitting till she felt clean again, then sank back on her
haunches, feeling hollow and fragile as a reed. She
hugged herself, shivering despite the sun. Over her head
three vulture-like black birds circled in the brilliant sky,
circling lower and lower till Zan could clearly see their

long hooded hangman's heads, their cold white-ringed eyes. They circled in slow, smooth, sinking circles, and Zan's heart seemed to circle and sink with them. She had wished violently to be somewhere else. Anywhere. And she had been given her wish. But it was awful, terrifying. She shaded her eyes against the shocking light of the sun and once again searched the landscape for something familiar. Anything. Anything at all.

Sweating and chilled, she cried out. "Hello! Hello, oh, hello, won't somebody answer me? Hello! Is anyone here? Anyone? Anyone?"

4

Zan was sleeping on the ground, dreaming of a vomit-colored bug walking on the kitchen ceiling. The bug's large eyes swiveled and stared straight down at her. Sickened, she backed away, bumping into the kitchen table, then into her cot. The bug scuttled along the ceiling, following her, staring at her. She couldn't escape. She woke with a start, sitting up and rubbing her cheek where it had pressed into the ground. Her eyes were hot and dry; there was dirt in her mouth, gritting between her teeth. She was stunned afresh by the jarring brilliance of the meadow, by the immense, empty sky, and most of all by her aloneness.

She went to the waterhole and, sucking up a mouthful of water, sloshed it around between her teeth, then spit it out. She splashed her hands and her face and swallowed enough water to temporarily fool her stomach into believing it had been fed. She remembered the Lifesavers and popped one into her mouth, sucking it slowly. Finally, feeling better, she squatted on her heels, considering her situation. She needed to make a plan, to do something sensible, not go on wandering back and forth in this field, yelling pointlessly and swinging crazily between tears and laughter. She could go back to the boulder, but what would it gain her? To find people, she had to leave the field. She had no choice. There was the field, there were the mountains, an incalculable distance away, forbidding and foreign. And there was the forest. She had to go into it, through it, and out.

Do it. Don't think.

She moved briskly to the edge of the trees. Branches creaked, an animal squawked harshly. She took a step forward, another, and another, passing from sun into shadow. The forest rustled with the scurrying and scuttling of unseen creatures. She peered into the dimness, her skin damp with apprehension. Wind creaked through massive limbs hung with thick tangled vines. She scuffed forward uncertainly. She snapped a branch to mark her trail and told herself to move forward in a straight line. Behind her, something thudded to the earth. Her heart pushed heavily against her ribs. "Oh, Mom," she whispered.

Staring into a dense tangle of limbs and leaves and vines, Zan wondered what creatures lived there and if they were watching her. She picked up a stout branch and held it in front of her like a spear. With each step she took, her nostrils flared uneasily and she looked in every direction, tense, poised for flight. Every creak and rustle alerted her senses in an ancient fear response: antennae quivered from every inch of her skin; the back of her neck prickled; up and down her arms the fine hairs stood erect. Warning! Danger! Her tongue was dry in her mouth. All at once she knew she was being watched: eyes were peering at her from a hidden place. "Who's there?" she shouted. The back of her head was icy. The conviction that she was being secretly observed became stronger, impossible to ignore. She whirled, clutching her stick, and forgetting everything she had planned, she veered wildly off to one side, stumbling and tripping over roots and fallen trees. She almost fell, caught herself, and banged into a tree.

Now mosquitoes appeared in clouds, whining around her ears and biting her arms and legs and face. This, finally, drove her back to the meadow. But even there, out in the open, the sense of being observed refused to fade. Hot and sweating, irritated because she would have to work up the nerve all over again to venture into the forest, she chewed furiously on a blade of grass.

She spoke aloud for courage. "Okay, you're going into the forest now." This time it was going to be straight on, do or die, no tears, no running away, no fear about being watched, just GO. If she moved fast and straight and resolutely, she was sure to find something—people, a house, some sign of life. As she thought this, a troop of tiny, deer-like animals appeared in the grass, heading toward her, their hooves beating like raindrops on the ground. She stared at them in wonder. Small as cats, with golden coats, they had two curved horns springing from between their ears and a third horn, like a tiny polished knife, jutting from above the nose. The lead animal, scenting her, froze. A moment later, the entire herd turned in a blur of gold and was swallowed up by the high grass.

Zan ran after them for a few yards, then stopped, her mind quivering with questions to which she had no answers. Miniature deer with three horns . . . the crushing immensity of the forest . . . butterflies as big as birds, and birds flying in such incredible numbers . . . And no airplanes, or telephone wires, or distant sounds of traffic. No people anywhere. Nothing but strange, buzzing, shrilling silence and the fresh smell of grass and the blazing sun in that fierce blue sky. From the corner of her eyes she saw movement at the edge of the forest. Her shoulders tensed for flight or fight. Then, in a stunning moment of disbelief, she caught a glimpse of long tangled hair and bare brown shoulders. A girl, her face in shadow, was peeking around the side of a tree. For an instant Zan was so startled she simply stood and stared back. Then an exhilarating wave of relief sent her running, yelling and laughing, toward the girl.

"Hey, hello, hello, hi, hello!" She waved her arms exuberantly, leaping high in her joy. "You're beautiful!" she cried. And the girl disappeared.

Dumbfounded, Zan crashed around, peering behind trees, calling, "Come back. Why did you run away? Please come back." Leaves clapped like leather, branches swayed and creaked, and in the deep shadows there were fleeting movements. "Are you there?" Zan called hopefully, straining to see into the watery gloom. Had she imagined the girl? Wanted so desperately to see another human that she had hallucinated her into being? Was she going crazy?

She ran back to the waterhole and, kneeling, scooped water to splash her face again and again, at last sinking back onto her heels, damp but sane. She had seen a girl. She had seen a real, living, breathing person. But somehow she had frightened her away. She crushed a handful of grass. If only the girl hadn't gone too far! If only she was still in the forest, secretly watching Zan. Hope gave way to conviction: the girl was nearby; was going to come back. Zan had to believe it. She took a deep breath to calm herself, then folding her grass-stained hands in her lap, she sat down cross-legged on the ground.

"Come on out, please. I guess I scared you with all

that dumb screaming and shouting, but I won't do that again." She spoke in a calm, conversational way, hoping the girl was listening. "Are you watching me? Was that you watching me before? Why don't you just peek around a tree again? I'll sit here nice and quiet, okay? No acting like Frankenstein's monster. Honest! Hey, what's your name? My name's Zan, and I'm really okay. It's just that I need someone to talk to. I really do. Come on back, please. Please?"

Flies droned around her ears, several large black ants crawled up her jeans, and an enormous red grasshopper leaped across her leg. Single-mindedly, Zan stared at the spot where she'd seen the girl. She had been like one of those tiny strange deer, appearing for an instant and then, startled, disappearing in a flash.

For a long time Zan sat very still; gradually, she fell into a half-waking state, her mind touching blurrily on all that had happened to her. Perhaps she was even falling asleep. Her head sagged sideways and she made a queer, throaty noise that startled her into sitting up very straight. She felt confused, as if a lot of time had passed, and for a fraction of a second she couldn't remember why she was sitting in the grass that way. Then she looked up and the girl was there.

"Hey," Zan said softly, without moving. "Hi. I'm so glad you came back. Don't go away, okay? I really want to talk to you." Then she saw that there were two of them, a girl and a boy.

Zan stood up carefully. She felt shaky and queer. They both appeared to be about her age, but she had never seen anything like them. They were naked except for woven belts around their waists with little flaps hanging from the front. The girl had narrow, shiny shoulders, a small blunt nose, and round, small breasts with very pink nipples. Her long tangled hair was tucked behind her ears, and she gazed unblinkingly, almost greedily, at Zan.

The boy's mouth was soft, half open, his head cocked at an angle. His thick eyebrows met over slightly tipped eyes. He, too, was staring at Zan. Like the girl, he wore necklaces and anklets made of beads and shells. His skin was smooth and hairless. Both wore some kind of long nets hanging from the backs of their heads and down over their shoulders, like capes.

"Who are you?" Zan said. She took a step toward them. The girl shrank back, the boy turned toward the trees. "No, don't go away!" She forced herself to stand quietly. After a few moments they both came very slowly toward her, chattering to each other. She couldn't understand anything they said.

"Where am I?" She appealed to the girl. "Can you tell me where I am? What is this place? Did you have a storm, a hurricane, or a tornado, too?"

The girl touched Zan in a tentative way, putting her forefinger on Zan's shoulder. She peered at Zan as if checking her reaction, then slid her fingers rapidly back and forth across Zan's cheek, as if trying to rub something off. "What are you doing?" The boy, too, bent toward her, flicking at her nose with his thumb. They spoke to one another softly, but in a strange language. The boy, tongue jammed between his lips, picked doggedly at Zan's nose. Zan realized he was trying to peel her freckles, as if they were paint, or dirt. As if he had never seen freckles before.

Both smelled strongly of sweat, sun, and earth, a not unpleasant smell, but one so unfamiliar to Zan that, combined with their nakedness and their strange actions, she became acutely alarmed.

They lost interest in her freckles and turned their

attention to her clothing, fingering, sniffing, and tasting everything she wore. In her astonishment at the sight of two kids down on their hands and knees, licking her dirty old sneakers, Zan was torn between a belly laugh and a wail of pure despair.

"Look, I'm lost. I want to get back home. Can you help me?"

They had pulled the laces from her sneakers and the girl was tying them around her neck, while the boy sniffed an edge of Zan's shirt. "I—don't—know—where—I—am," Zan said, speaking distinctly and spacing her words. "I am—lost. LOST! Listen to me!" She forgot to be calm, and pushed away the boy and snatched her sneaker laces back from the girl.

Biting her fingertips like a rebuked child, the girl stroked Zan's hair, speaking, but again Zan could understand nothing. The boy started to crawl around in the grass, parting it with his fingers and overturning stones. Loonies, Zan thought, her throat tight. Loonies! Crazies! But even as the thought came, she rejected it: there was another explanation, one from which her mind darted in terror.

Yelling triumphantly, the boy snatched something up from the ground and returned. He took Zan's hand and dropped a large iridescent purple beetle into her palm. She jerked her hand away, dropping the creature to the ground. The boy chattered at her, his eyes wide. Then, snapping off the head of another beetle, he popped the body into his mouth and spit out the wings with an expert flick of his tongue. White juice squirted from the corners of his mouth. Swallowing, he wiped his mouth with the back of his hand and went off again to search the grass.

Feeling slightly queasy, Zan turned to the girl. "My name is Zan." She waited. The girl smiled, but said nothing. Zan thumped herself on the chest. "Me, Zan. Me, Zan!" She could hardly believe she was talking that way, but she repeated it, trying desperately to make contact. "Me, Zan. Who you? *Me, Zan.*"

"Meezzan?" the girl said slowly. She poked Zan on the chest. "Meezzan?" She smiled, showing small, milky-looking teeth, and touched herself on the left breast. "Burrum," she said and, pointing to the boy, "Sonte."

"You're Bur-*rum*," Zan said, touching her. "And he's *Zon*-tee." The boy turned around at his name, and he and the girl laughed delightedly, pointing to Zan and slapping their legs as if she had done something terribly clever. Then the girl grabbed Zan, hugging her hard, rubbing her hands up and down Zan's back and arms. Zan stiffened with surprise at the long close embrace. Even in her own family they hardly ever hugged, and only pecked one another on the cheek. The thought of her family made Zan go still and aching. For an instant everything stopped; not even the cry of a bird could be heard. And in that frozen moment of stillness, with the ache hard and cold inside her, Zan felt a terrible longing come over her. *She wanted to go home.* Why was she here in this strange place with these strange kids? Why was this girl squeezing her? Why didn't she understand anything Zan said to her? And why didn't she help Zan, or else go away, just go far away and leave her alone!

As if sensing Zan's thoughts, the girl released her, said something to the boy, and the two of them moved swiftly toward the forest. Stunned, Zan stared after them. They were leaving her. "Wait! Wait for me." She ran after them. "Wait! I can't stay here alone!"

5

Early that morning, squatting by a rock as the sun came up in the east, Burrum had felt on her feet the warm touch of her body's water as it sank into the mossy earth. The honey smell of its wet warmth had made her think of the tall flowers that grew in Meadow-with-Watering-Hole. Were those honey flowers blooming? After they bloomed, one could name the moons till the Season of Rains came.

Thoughtfully, Burrum put up the fingers of her left hand. "Grass Moon," she said under her breath, pushing down her little finger. "Moon of the Long Night." Another finger down. "Egg Moon. Bird Flight Moon. Fire Moon." All the fingers were down now. After that would come the Season of Rains: Rain Moon and Moon of Tears. Then Miiawa's flowers, those tiny red flowers with petals like little drops of blood, appeared everywhere in the forest. And then—oh, then!—the Sussuru for all the girls whose blood had come down for the first time.

The Sussuru, the beautiful festival of Miiawa, she whom Burrum loved as she loved the forest itself. Aiii, the Sussuru! The wild joyful dances, the chants and songs that worked themselves into one's very bones!

How sore Burrum's belly felt as she thought that she had been left out once again! But until her blood came down she was still a girl—a child!—though she had her breasts and the sweet body hair that marked the difference between girls and women.

Standing, she felt the soreness in her belly again, flashing like a little fish, and she rubbed her belly soothingly. "I want to go there, to that meadow," she said aloud. If those tall honey flowers were not yet blooming, there would still be many moons till the next Sussuru. Surely, during one of those moons, her first blood would come. Sighing, she glanced down at herself, at the softness covered by little curls of crisp hair, and pulled her mingau into place.

Later, after she had gone to the river to wash and swim, she met Sonte, who said he had a craving for Ahera, the sweet root that grew near the white Pashuba trees. "Let's go together to gather those sweet roots," he said. "We haven't eaten them in a long time."

But Burrum, who usually liked to do whatever Sonte wanted, shook her head. "No, I am going to Meadow-with-Watering-Hole, to see if those honey flowers are blooming." She had just then realized that it was Miiawa herself who wanted her to do this. "Miiawa of the forest came to me in my dreams. She came to me in the night. I saw her!" Yes, she had seen Miiawa's flowing green hair, had felt her presence, like wind on the skin, and heard her voice, soft as the voice of night birds. "We'll find the Ahera tomorrow." She threw her arms around Sonte and hugged him. "I promise." She ran ahead of him, calling him to catch her. She had always run faster than he.

When they were very near Meadow-with-Watering-Hole, Sonte left the path to gather some Aspa nuts, while Burrum went on alone. Moving from the shade of the forest into the open field, she saw a girl running clumsily through the meadow. Burrum had never seen the girl before and knew at once she was not of the People.

Hurrying back into the forest, whistling like a bird to call Sonte, she ran to the Aspa tree. "Sonte, Sonte, come down from that tree!" she cried. Then in her excitement she climbed up to tell him about the girl.

"This girl—you must see her! A girl with mingaus all over her body!"

Sonte burst out laughing. "You have been sleeping and have dreamed another one of your dreams."

"Oh, you make me so angry," Burrum said, but she laughed, too, knowing that she had seen what she had seen. Something wonderful, frightening, and strange! She tugged at Sonte as he stretched out along a limb. "Come down, come with me, perhaps she has already run away." She slid down the tree trunk.

"Yes, yes, I'm coming," he said. He shook another branch vigorously, and Aspa nuts rained onto the ground. Burrum loved the small green nuts. Any other time she would have scooped up handfuls. "Oh, hurry, Sonte, my friend, my cousin, hurry," she implored.

Wrapping his arms and legs around the trunk of the tree, Sonte slid to the ground. He picked up a handful of nuts, tossed them into the air, and caught them. "Now show me this girl, this spirit," he teased. "Show me that you were not sleeping and dreaming!"

Taking his hand, Burrum led the way back to the meadow to the very spot where she had seen the girl. But the meadow was empty. Sonte slapped his thigh, saying that he would tell everyone about her wonderful dream when they went back to the caves. "Mingaus all over her body, even on her legs," he said humorously. He put his arm across her shoulder, nuzzling her neck affectionately. "What good dreams you have!"

Just then, Burrum saw the girl again on the other side of the meadow, near the watering hole. "Look!" In her excitement, she pinched Sonte's arm. He had also seen the girl and his mouth fell open. Burrum snorted with pleasure. Sonte was always so sure he was right about things—where the Ahera grew, how to find the best Buitiri fruits, and if the honey flowers were in bloom—so sure, and often right. But this time he had been wrong, teasing her as if she were a little girl who still pissed down her legs. "Come!" Burrum said. Sonte, she noted with satisfaction, followed her without protest as she led the way through the cover of the trees toward the waterhole.

Hidden, they peered out at the girl. She was covered with spots like a salamander. And she wore not just a small, neat mingau over her genitals, as was necessary and proper, but mingaus on her shoulders, her breasts, her back, her legs, and even her feet. In his astonishment Sonte whistled through his teeth like the Minhaw bird.

"Sss," Burrum said reprovingly. She was afraid the girl would hear them. Hastily, she climbed into a tree, followed by Sonte, and there, while the sun moved through the sky, they sat watching the strange girl. Never had Burrum seen anything like her spotted skin. Never had she heard anything like the meaningless cries that made the hairs on the back of her neck stand up in alarm.

Through the screen of trees, Burrum never took her eyes from the girl. Aii, what a story she would have to tell that night around the fire! For most of her life,

Burrum had been unaware that there were others in the world besides the People. She had been young and stupid! Now that she was nearly a woman, she listened more carefully to her grandmother, to the other old ones, and to Mahu, the Teller. From their stories and songs she learned that Beyond-the-Mountains other beings did, indeed, live. And, in fact, long ago when her father's mother's grandmother had been only a small child, a man of the Others, Niben, had come among the People.

"Yes, my grandmother told me of him," Burrum's grandmother had said. "She was one of the children who found the stranger fallen down near a stream." The stranger had been sick and weak. The People had cared for him and refreshed him. When he was well and strong, the stranger, Niben, had talked in a loud voice, and grabbed the food that others had gathered. Around the fire at night he sang no songs, but told instead how his people chased animals with long, sharp sticks. "Yes! They drove those sharp sticks into the animals' bellies, so they could eat the flesh of the animal races," Burrum's Auuhmaa said, recalling his words. He had talked like a man with fever, saying things that could not be. He had said that when hunger came among his people, when they could not drive sticks into Bear or Boar, they ate their old ones, and also the infants. "That man said bad things. He made our people unhappy," Burrum's Auuhmaa had wailed. And in a trembling voice, the old woman had chanted the Song of Niben. *He came from Beyond-the-Mountains, His voice was the voice of Thunder, He came from Beyond-the-Mountains, The sun died, The mountain fell, Aieee! Aieee!*

"Aieee, Aieee," Burrum hummed, sitting in the tree

close to Sonte. Suddenly the strange girl came crashing into the forest. Burrum and Sonte went still as tree frogs, made themselves part of the bark and the leaves, breathed as the tree breathed. Ignoring the path, the girl flung herself about, stumbling, nearly falling. She snatched up a stick and, holding it in front of her, ran about aimlessly, making loud sounds. Was it some sort of ritual of her people? Astonished, Burrum watched as the girl ran headlong into a tree, dropped her stick, and bolted back to the meadow.

Touching Burrum on the arm, Sonte made a sliding motion with his hand and pointed his chin toward the girl. Burrum dipped her head in silent agreement. They left the tree and crept soundlessly to the edge of the forest. Being so close to the girl, Burrum was overcome by curiosity and, forgetting caution, she peeked out. The girl saw her. For a moment they stared at one another, then the girl came leaping and shouting toward her. Startled, frightened, Burrum and Sonte turned as one and scrambled up a tree. "Perhaps she is dangerous," Sonte whispered. "She might be one of the Bear People!" He wanted to go back to the caves.

"I am not afraid of Bear People," Burrum said bravely. She had often watched bears fishing in the river in their own place. She had stood on Cliff-of-Bear, looking down into the white tumbling waters, and had seen the bears, sometimes on all four legs, sometimes upright. Bears had the power of spirits in them; they could walk like the People. Some said they could speak the language of the People, as well. At night, every night, fires burned in the caves. It was said that, otherwise, Bear might come and demand the cave for his own. Even so, Burrum would not be afraid if this girl was one of those Bear People. No, not even if she met her at night in the forest, she thought, her belly contracting at the very idea.

"You go back to the caves," Burrum whispered to Sonte, her mouth close to his ear. "I will stay and watch this girl." Miiawa had sent her feet to Meadow-with-Watering-Hole so she would find this strange one, this girl of the Others. She would not leave now.

"Mother Olima, today you are disagreeable," Sonte grumbled, but he did not leave her.

After a while, when the girl was sitting in the meadow, twitching and moving, not ever still, but at least not uttering her frightening calls, Burrum and Sonte once more left the tree and gradually approached her. Then, looking into her eyes, Burrum saw that the girl's soul, her Ta, was neither unfriendly nor dangerous. Therefore, she went up to her, greeted her, and touched her.

As they looked the stranger over, Sonte asked many questions that Burrum could not answer. "Is this a girl or a woman?" he wanted to know. "Why is her skin spotted? What are those sounds she makes?" And so on. Finally he asked, "If we take her back to the caves, with whom will she stay?"

"She will stay with me," Burrum answered quickly and firmly. "She will be my companion. I tell you, Miiawa has sent her to me."

Burrum sniffed happily at the girl's skin. Had not Miiawa come to her in her dreams? Yes, Miiawa had wanted her to find this girl and keep her. Surely, if she did as Miiawa wanted, her blood would come down in time for the Sussuru. And she would sing and dance and become a woman.

6

Trees. Everywhere, trees. Enormous, overwhelming, trunks rising straight into the air, huge columns, or twisting grotesquely. Surrounded on all sides by trees . . . living trees . . . dying trees . . . dead trees . . .

The whine of insects . . . sound of her own stumbling footsteps, crunching branches and leaves . . .

Underfoot, decaying logs . . . thick tangled roots . . . flowers, little pale things . . . a dead stump covered with orange mushrooms big as severed heads . . .

Zan shuddered and plodded on. Her thoughts came and went in abrupt spurts. Walking . . . following those two. Burrum? Sonte? Queer names. Everything so strange. Going where? No way out. Difficult to breathe . . . the air, thick . . . heavy . . . what if a tree fell?

Fall on me. Smash me. Where are they taking me? Hate this forest. Who are they?

Her eyes blurry with sweat. Stepping ankle deep into slime . . . scraping it off with leaves . . . pushing on . . . She was so tired. Ahead of her, the boy and girl leaping like deer over every obstacle . . . talking . . . jabbering . . . grubbing with sticks, digging up slugs, or twisted rooty things . . . eating them. Every time, Zan's stomach lurched.

Her head swollen, throbbing.

Following them like a dumb sheep. Dumb sheep go to slaughter. Naked people are savages. Cannibals . . . What am I doing? Stop. Think.

She slumped against a tree.

Mistake following them. Too trusting. What then? Back to the meadow? Safe there . . . but—no food, no people. Okay, stay here, just stop, don't follow them! Alone? Animals. No water. No food. I'll die. Oh, Mom!

Somewhere, an animal or bird tapped ferociously, a forest jackhammer. Zan's heart beat in ferocious accompaniment.

Follow them. No choice.

Ahead, the boy and girl were fading out of sight, blending into the foliage, showing only patches of skin, like bits of sun on leaves.

Zan's legs were leaden. Dwarfed by the trees, she felt insignificant, an insect easily crushed.

Tree coming down? I'll run. Fall on me, anyway. Spatter me. Nothing left.

She moved a little faster, looking up, over her shoulder, to each side. Everywhere, dead, swaying trees waiting to fall and break her like an ant smeared underfoot.

Her heart was beating up into her throat. She ran. Sonte? Burrum? Gone! "Anhhhh!" Sweat filled her eyes. Shouting, crashing into trees, calling the girl's name.

An answering shout. From behind her? She whirled, yelling again. The sound of her voice echoed, filled her ears. Which way had she come? Which way had they gone? She turned round and round helplessly. Then again, she heard her name. "Meezzan." She followed the sound. They were perched on a rock, the boy chewing on something, talking casually to the girl as if nothing at all were wrong. She wanted to scream at them.

They must have gone ahead of her on purpose, thinking it funny that she was frightened sick. She hated them both.

They went on again. Not looking where she was going, only following the bare backs ahead of her, Zan stumbled against a pointed rock embedded in the earth. Her toe throbbed with pain. Now the way was steeply uphill, trees thinning, sun splattering on the face of the towering rock outcroppings. She was breathing with her mouth open . . . too much effort to keep it closed . . . her heart pulsing in her throat . . .

Sonte and Burrum stopped, turned, sniffed the air with faces raised and noses wrinkled in concentration. What now? Too tired to care, Zan sank down on a log, arms and legs weighted. Her heart was beating in great heavy thumps—da-BUMP da-BUMP da-BUMP. *Maybe I'll die right here. Heart attack. Nobody will ever know. The worms and animals will eat me, just my skeleton left. Poor old white bones, white tones, singing off tune like always, Dad says I couldn't keep a tune if my life depended . . .*

"Meezzan."

Go away. Don't bother me. My eyes are closed, can't you see? She flopped her head into her lap.

"Meezzan!"

Quit that! Stop shaking me. I'm not your prisoner. I'm resting.

Leave me alone . . . leave me a bone . . . what was that about bones?

Muscles in her legs twitched and jerked; her arm flew out. She sat up, dazed. She must have fallen asleep. Behind her, the sound of someone, something, snuffling or snorting, a heavy, wet sound. Then, crashing noises. She jumped up. She was alone. They had left her again.

The snuffling and crashing came closer. "Burrum!" she shouted, and at the same moment a huge animal completely covered with long shaggy yellow hair came into sight and slowly lumbered toward her. Her bones grew fragile. Not an elephant, but almost the size of an elephant. No tusks, no fangs, but monstrous, terrible, huge enough to crush her with one swipe of a foot. She stared, horrified, at the long curving nails on its feet. Then her arms were grabbed, one from each side, and she was hauled into the air. For an instant, dangling painfully above the ground, she couldn't understand what was happening. She was jerked upward, and her neck snapped back. Above her she saw Sonte and Burrum in the tree, both of them flat on their bellies, slung over branches, their faces reddening with the effort of lifting her. They hauled her into the tree and dropped her like a sack of potatoes into the crotch of two limbs.

She clung to the tree, trembling, as the animal, its head nearly on the level with her feet, gouged up great swathes of vegetation, passing leisurely through the spot where she had been standing only moments before. *Sloth*, she thought suddenly, like a coin going into a slot. Breathing in the ripe, sickening odor of the animal, she felt other words drop into her mind like bits of ice. *Primeval . . . savage . . . extinct . . .* Slowly the mammoth beast passed out of sight, leaving behind it a trail of crushed earth.

Burrum and Sonte climbed down out of the tree. In a daze, Zan followed, scraping her legs against the rough bark, slipping, and then thumping to the ground awkwardly. As they set off again, she stuck close to them, sniffing the air herself, eyeing each tree for the one that would be easiest to climb.

Stopping at a stream, they drank and washed their faces. Zan threw water over her hot head again and again. They crossed the stream on a broad log, overgrown with fungi. The trees were sparser now; tufts of grass grew underfoot, and sun splashed down in long fingers of light. When at last they broke into the open, leaving the forest behind, Zan felt as if a weight had been lifted from her head.

They were in a narrow field situated between a mountain and a valley that spread below as far as she could see. Hills, meadows, and a river flowed between dense green banks. She could see for miles. Everywhere was that thick green carpet over the earth, broken only by the broad shimmering blue band of the river. She thought surely they would go that way, down into that greenness, but they turned upward and climbed a well-worn path. Huge tumbles of gray and pink rock everywhere, like crumbled buildings that had once housed giants. Caves pocked the side of the mountain and the smoke of many small fires puffed into the air. Zan had never seen anything like it before. Miles and miles of nothing but trees and meadows, and then the river, like a piece of blue glass. It was all calm, peaceful, soothing, like quiet music on her jangled nerves.

Burrum pulled Zan toward a cave beneath an enormous overhanging shelf of rock. Nearby, a fire burned within a ring of stones. Zan shrank back. Burrum grasped both of Zan's hands and pulled harder. Again, Zan resisted. The cave mouth yawned black, frightening, secret. She thought of bats and slugs, of white eyeless creatures, and a damp slimy darkness. She shuddered and dug in her heels. Burrum's arms were wiry, strong, but Zan had the strength of desperation flowing through her. "Auuhmaa," Burrum shouted. "Auuhmaa!" And

Zan, thinking the girl was calling for help to drag her into the cave, resisted more fiercely.

An old woman appeared at the mouth of the cave and came slowly toward them. She wore nothing but the same sort of little apron flap that Burrum wore. Necklaces of shells and acorns hung on long breasts as flat as two pieces of leather. Her eyes were deeply sunk into her bony head; one was black and keen, the other covered with a white growth like a thick pearly shell.

"Auuhmaa!" Burrum cried, breaking into an excited stream of talk. The old woman, nodding, smiling, showing bare, toothless gums like a baby, patted Burrum's arm and shoulder. Then she reached out suddenly and took Zan into her arms. She had a strong smell, dry and spicy. Zan felt as if she were suffocating as that ancient, leathery body pressed her and the pungent breath blew into her face.

When the old woman released her, a boy appeared, with a naked child sitting astride his shoulders. The boy stared unabashedly at Zan, his dark eyes large and wondering, but the child, screwing up his face, broke into loud fearful sobs and hid his eyes in the boy's curly head. Other people began to appear, some climbing up the mountain, others coming out from caves higher up, calling to one another and running down the rocky slopes. Children of all sizes appeared as if conjured up from the air. More and more people, all half naked and babbling incomprehensibly, crowded around Zan.

Burrum kept a firm, possessive grip on her. "Meezzan," Burrum said repeatedly, tapping Zan's shoulder or touching her on the breast. "Meezzan. Meezzan." People repeated the word, "Meezzan," pulling their lips flat and wide, then slapping their thighs and roaring with laughter as if at the very finest joke.

"Meezzan," a man said, reaching out and pinching Zan's arm. A woman tugged at a strand of her hair. A child scratched her jeans with his fingernails, his forehead creased in concentration. Almost at once, others surged in, surrounding her, touching her, poking her hair and her face, probing and plucking and sniffing.

Hands were on her everywhere like insects. Zan's hair was pulled, her arms smelled, her neck tasted, her fingers grabbed and stuffed into mouths. Her skin seemed to shrivel on her bones. She was afraid to move, afraid to slap away the hands, afraid to claim herself from the crowd. Afraid that they might become savage and turn from poking at her arms to poking out her eyes; turn from scratching her skin to clawing it off her bones.

She was grabbed, shoved, touched, her back and arms rubbed vigorously, then released, only to be grabbed again. "Leave me alone," she moaned.

She threw her hands over her head, her arms before her face, and sank down on the ground, hunched and shaking among the forest of dusty bare legs. A cry stirred through the crowd and people sank down with her, sitting on their haunches, laughing and nodding their heads.

Go away. Go away. GO AWAY. Their faces, their voices, their teeth, white in alarming smiles, mocked her. Their jabber pierced her head like little knives. They wouldn't leave her alone. They kept touching her, pressing her, breathing on her.

A fist was thrust in front of her face, a fist holding a mouse, its tail hanging out like a banner, its eyes bulging above the thumb. Then another fist appeared, holding another mouse with bulging eyes. Two small children, entirely naked, a little boy with dark curly hair and a girl a bit bigger, stood above her, laughingly pushing the imprisoned mice toward her. The shining, terrified eyes of the mice seemed ready to pop out of their heads and spill into Zan's lap like wet marbles.

She struck out blindly, shoving the children away from her. She hunkered closer to the ground, her knees encircled by her arms. She felt her heart beating through her body like the ticking of a bomb and held herself tighter. She felt that she might fly into a thousand separate pieces. In her throat the ticking went on; her ears ticked, and in her arms bombs ticked. People began to drift away. She understood. They heard the bombs ticking in her body. Tick, tick, tick, TICK, TICK, TICK . . . She would run from herself if she could.

After a while, after a thousand thousand ticks, they were all gone. All but Burrum, who squatted near, eyes fixed on Zan. Her watchdog? *Run away, watchdog, run before I explode!* Mad laughter swam into Zan's throat. Oh, what a joke had been played on Zan Ford! The laughter became a scream of protest, fury, helplessness, that ought to have stopped worlds, reversed time, shattered the nightmare. But tendrils of smoke from the fire in the ring of stones still rose. And Burrum still watched Zan, her face stiffened with something unreadable. And Zan was still there.

She closed her eyes. Closed herself away from the noise, the smells, the sounds. Closed herself into her head. Away from everything. Unreachable. Untouchable. Closed.

7

Throwing chunks of wood into his mother's fire, Sonte whistled softly through his teeth. What a funny face Burrum had made earlier in the day when he asked if Meezzan was a girl or a woman. Did Burrum think he wanted someday to sit in the circle of stones with Meezzan? Sonte snickered in his throat like a frog, but his good humor faded quickly.

He and Burrum had been special friends since they were tiny children. She could always make him laugh. When he was with her, there was so much happiness in his belly. Even when he was a very small boy, not yet wearing the mingau, he had believed that they would be life mates. But this was not to be. No! That ugly Hiffaru would come to live with her in her mother's cave. Sonte had known this for a long time, but he could never think of it calmly. He still remembered the day his mother had told him, saying, "Do not be sad, my son, my beautiful son. In time there will be a fine widow for you." But his mother's face had been dark like the sky when Thunder Beings spoke. Seeing her unhappiness and feeling his own misery, poison like toads' eggs had hatched in his belly.

Though he wanted Burrum to be happy, he was secretly glad that her blood had not come down and that she was still a girl. Only women sat in the circle of stones and lay in the forest with their men.

"Why are you grunting?" his mother, N'ati, asked as he threw another chunk of wood onto the fire. "You sound so fierce, my son. Does he not sound fierce, Yano?" Sonte's aunt smiled and spit on a shell, then rubbed it against her mingau to shine it.

"Perhaps you have bellyache?" his mother said solicitously.

Sonte scowled. "My belly is good, Mother!" He stared into the fire.

Farther down the mountain, Burrum sat near her family's cave, her hand protectively on Meezzan's back. It had been frightening when Meezzan screamed, but Burrum had not left the girl, though Auuhmaa had cried at her that she must come away. From a safe distance, the old woman had called out that the Anouch'i were surely burrowing into that daughter of Others like worms into fruit. Why else had she screamed? "Come away from her, my child," the Auuhmaa urged. "Come sit with me."

But Burrum hadn't left Meezzan's side. One must listen, of course, to the wisdom of the old ones. In this respect, as in others, Burrum was dutiful, but she did not believe that the Anouch'i had burrowed into Meezzan. Miiawa had sent her this girl; therefore, was not Miiawa protecting her? Burrum rubbed her belly thoughtfully. In the belly, one felt everything: all happiness, all sorrow, all fear, all joy. "Beware the times when the belly is hard." That is what Burrum's mother had taught her. She was a wise woman. In sorrow, fear, or anger, the belly must not stay hard for long, or else the bad spirits, the Anouch'i, come and drive out Ta, one's soul. Aiii! If only one could see the Anouch'i. But they could shape themselves into anything—a puff of wind, a tree, a stone. One never knew where they were!

Again Burrum clasped her belly. If the Anouch'i had crawled into Meezzan, wouldn't she feel the fear in her own belly? But her belly was quiet, her belly was happy.

She rubbed her hand up and down Meezzan's arm. "Perhaps you come from people who don't eat, but only drink water? Is that possible?" Burrum remembered how the girl had let the delicious beetle Sonte had found slip through her fingers, and how she had turned her face away from all the food they offered her. The girl blinked and blinked, but said nothing.

"Meezzan," Burrum whispered to herself, making her mouth go all wide and tight to make the ugly sound. There were so many queer things about the girl, including her name. Meezzan. What did that mean? Nothing. "Zzzz," Burrum said, giggling softly. Again she felt the strange garments the girl wore. Mingaus on her legs and feet. No wonder she was so tired! How could one run, swim, or climb trees wearing extra feet? Or feel the earth and the waters of the river? Burrum wondered if all the people of this girl wore such things. Was it possible they thought their entire bodies, not just their genitals, vulnerable to the Anouch'i? Burrum considered this idea with astonishment that gradually turned to amusement. Snorting, she looked around for someone to share this rich joke, but only her little brother and one of her small cousins were nearby, racing back and forth with sticks in their hands.

"Why aren't you out gathering the Bihaw berries?" she called out. They looked over at her a bit uneasily. Very good! One had to continually remind children in just this way that soon they, too, must do a bit more than play all the time. "Lishum! Are you ready to help build the stone dams?" she said to her little brother. He had a small round belly, which she often nuzzled playfully, driving him into fits of wild giggling. "You know those stone dams in the river to trap the big fish? That is what I mean, little brother." His mouth fell open. He had thick black curls and eyes like little silver fish. "And you," she said to her cousin Ai'ma, "you will have to pound the bark with heavy stones!"

"I won't pound that bark till I can wear the mingau," Ai'ma said spiritedly in her unusually deep voice. Whenever she spoke, the adults laughed. Still, she was only a small girl, not yet old enough to wear a tantua on the back of her head. Burrum hid a smile and continued to gaze at both children for several moments. Of course only the strongest men and women made the stone dams and pounded the bark to break down the fibers to make into a soft cloth. But it was her duty to her cousin and her little brother to put serious thoughts into their heads. They continued to stand there, staring at her, waiting for her to dismiss them.

She waved her hand. "Go. Go back to your playing, children." She herself went back to contemplating Meezzan, who sat slumped with her head down on her knees. Her eyes were dull, almost like that bad eye of the Auuhmaa. Thinking of this, Burrum held her belly protectively. She loved her Auuhmaa and dreaded seeing her other eye get lost behind a milky shell. When the eyes left, then the soul, the Ta, soon followed. Burrum's mother, Farwe, had told her that her own mother died this way. It had been so sad! Farwe still talked nearly every day of her mother, and how she would someday see her in Place-of-Night-Sun.

"Aii, Aii," Burrum sighed, just as her mother often did. Then her natural gaiety drove away the sad thoughts, and she smiled hopefully at Meezzan. "Soon you'll feel better, my sister." She leaned toward the girl, nuzzling her neck as she would nuzzle Lishum, or any of the little children, or her mother and father when she was feeling sleepy and tender, but Meezzan didn't respond. "One doesn't know where you came from or how long your journey was, but surely it was long and tiring," Burrum said.

As if in answer, the girl's eyes closed heavily. In moments, she was sleeping deeply, her eyelids twitching. Burrum gently pushed her over onto the ground so that she lay more comfortably on her side. The girl moaned, but continued sleeping.

Dusk was falling. Burrum sniffed. Up and down the mountain and across the plateau, fires were being fed. That was a good smell, the smell of warmth, comfort, safety. That was a smell as good as the smell of her mother's milky breasts. People passed, going to their hearths, calling greetings, and asking after the strange girl. Burrum's family, too, were gathering round the hearth in front of the cave. When Sun went to sleep, one wanted always to be near one's own blazing fire. Her mother threw sticks of wood into the hungry fire.

"Come over here, daughter," her father called. "Leave that girl now, don't stay so long with her. She is not one of the People. Come over here and sit with your father."

Her father's hair was turning gray, his face was heavily lined. He had seen many moons come and go. He had seen many things. He would soon be an old man, Burrum thought, and standing by him as he knelt before the stone-lined cooking pit, she put her hand on his head. He blew on the fire in the pit, threw in some more sticks, and squatted back on his haunches, his arm affectionately around her legs.

Lishum came running up and threw himself onto his mother's lap. His mouth was smeared with red juice. Burrum's aunts and uncles and their children also gathered around the fire.

"Daughter, I have here those white ants you like so much," her father said, pointing to several packets of leaves on the ground. "They were just about to grow wings, so you know they are very good." When the stones in the cooking pit were red hot, he would place the packets of leaves on them, cover them with more stones, and then cover all with earth, allowing no smoke or steam to escape. When he judged enough time had passed, he would rake aside the earth, pry out the top stones, and take the packet of cooked ants from the pit. "Sit down and share these ants with me," he said. "I have here salt from the ashes of the Gimba tree, so those ants will taste truly delicious."

"Sonte and I found butterfly grubs today," Burrum told her father. "Those long smooth ones with no hair. But they were not ready to eat. When they're no longer green, Sonte and I—"

"Sonte, Sonte, Sonte," her aunt Ainu interrupted, throwing down an armful of wood next to the fire. "After your Sussuru, you will not be with that boy Sonte all the time. You won't go alone into the forest with him then!" The adults laughed, Aunt Ainu louder than all. Sitting down, she put her hands beneath her belly as if she carried something very heavy there, although it was only a little belly, round like a Tamasini melon. It would be many more moons before the child dropped from her.

Burrum could feel her face getting hot like fire. Everyone looked at her and laughed. Even her father laughed at her discomfort, as Ainu teased her again about Sonte. That was the only bad thing about Miia-wa's Festival. After that, although she and Sonte could be together with others, she would be a woman and to go alone into the forest with a man would not be seemly. Those who had sat in the circle of stones went into the forest and lay together beneath the trees. Her mother and father went into the forest together still, and Aunt Ainu went with her man. That was right. But Burrum would not go alone again with Sonte and would no longer be free to be with him whenever she wished.

Of course they would always be friends! He was her dear friend and companion, yet it was Hiffaru who was promised her, and Sonte who would have no woman. It was so sad! Someday he might sit in the circle of stones with a widow, but what if she could no longer give him children? Would he get children from one of the younger families? Or perhaps Burrum could give him one of her babies! There was something so pleasing in this thought that Burrum decided she would tell Sonte the moment she saw him. Then his face might not get dark like a storm sky every time he was near Hiffaru.

She sighed. Someday when the time was right, when at last she had had her Sussuru and had grown altogether out of her child's bones, she and Hiffaru would sit in the circle of stones. Their parents, holding blossoming Desabi branches, would chant over them: *You who sit here in the middle of the world, you who will bring new life, you who are sister and brother to the wind, the stones, the trees, and the fish, you who honor your mother, you who honor your father and your father's mother, you who feel the winds of life blowing through you, you the children of Olima and the children of Miiawa . . .*

Yes, someday she would lie with Hiffaru and he would honor her when babies dropped from her body like new little moons. She thought of Hiffaru with his one large normal eye and one tiny eye, which was buried so deeply in his skull, yet seemed to see everything. A ripple of distress crossed Burrum's mind. Then she was cheerful again, for she could never stay unhappy for long. One side of Hiffaru's face was ugly, creased; therefore, when he came to her mother's cave to live, Burrum would try to look always at the other side of his face, the side that was normal and pleasant. Yes, that is what she would do. And when she had babies, she would have many of them, enough for herself and for Sonte, too.

8

A thin white curve of moon was rising slowly in the night sky. Up and down the mountain, fires had been banked and people had gone into their caves. Zan was on the plateau, alone. Holding her jackknife, she sat against a stone, her head flung back, staring at the dark clouded sky pierced here and there with pale stars. She looked up, searching for the Big Dipper, the only constellation she had ever known even vaguely. Once, on a clear night, long ago, her father had taken her up on the roof of their building and pointed out the Dipper to her. "You see the cup," he said. "Follow the last star in the cup with your eye and you'll come to the first star in the handle of the Little Dipper. See it there? See that one? That's the North Star. It's a good thing to know the North Star. Do you see it, Zan?" Yes, she had said, although she wasn't sure, but she had seen the Big Dipper, seven clear, large, sparkling stars. And her father had put his hand briefly on her shoulder, saying, "If you can pick out the Big Dipper, and then the North Star, well, you'll never be lost."

Now she thought that if she could only see the Dipper again, it would be something to hold on to. It might, somehow, make bearable all that was happening to her. But dark clouds passing slowly across the sky obscured most of the stars. She couldn't find the Dipper. Was it the clouds? Or was everything, even the sky, unrecognizable?

Far away, an animal howled. The call was answered, then taken up in every direction. Long tremulous howls shattered the air, and an answering howl of terror blazed in Zan. No, nothing was the same. It was all strangeness and horror.

As abruptly as it started, the howling ended. Shivering, Zan pushed herself closer to the rock behind her. She stared toward the cave, at the little flicker of firelight from within that only made the darkness around her deeper. *They* were in there, together, while she was out here, alone. Her hand was sweaty on the knife handle. The blade was open, sharp, dangerous. She peered into the night. She felt her lips drawn back in a snarl of fear. Then, for an instant, she saw herself as she would appear to a civilized person, and she pried her fingers loose from the knife, letting it fall to the ground. But instantly fear seized her and she fumbled frantically for it in the dark. The knife, the knife, she needed the knife! She found it and held it as before, jerking around at the smallest sound.

She tried to remember how things had been for her only twenty-four hours before, but it was hard to make anything seem real except the terror and sadness that came over her in waves. What was she doing here? She wanted to be home. Home. If she thought of home hard enough, long enough, would all this turn out to be only a dream, a nightmare? Would she wake up and find herself where she belonged, in her own time, her own real life? *Home.* She let the word repeat itself in her mind, home home homehome homehomehome . . .

chiming like a demented clock, homehomehomehome-home . . . till it became a single tone chant: ome ome ome omeome oohhmm ooohhhmmm ooohhhmmm . . . and she slept for a few minutes.

She opened her eyes. Above her, the dark sky. Beneath her, the cooling ground. Home, she thought again, dully now, and the word seemed to be only a thick, meaningless sound. Her hand was cramped around the knife, her knees and thighs ached. She lay down, curling herself into a tight comma, knees bent to her chest.

Through the night she lay there, the cold ground seeping into her bones, sometimes overcome by a silence so profound that she thought only she existed in the universe. Other times she found herself trembling uncontrollably at the secret whispers, cries and calls of night creatures. Tigers with burning eyes, bears with muffled sinister roars, shapeless creatures of evil prowled her mind, while the real creatures rustled around her. She heard the tac . . . tac . . . tac . . . felt them breathing in the dark night air and expelling it to turn the night inkier; whispering, breathing, scuttling, tac . . . tac . . . tac . . .

She was certain her eyes never closed against the dangerous darkness, but suddenly she was rigidly awake, aware of time having passed. In the dark she heard the splash of urine on earth, smelled its pungent odor. Then she heard the bare whisper of unshod feet as someone shuffled past her toward the cave.

She slept again, moaning, dreaming that her bones were cracking, that animals crawled into her mouth, that she excreted a camera, a tape recorder, records, all of them flattened, white, colorless, yet still looking like animals.

When she woke it was not quite dawn. Her dreams were sour in her mind. Her mouth was pressed against the ground, her arms bent beneath her. She was cramped in every limb, chilled, aching. The knife lay nearby. Below her, the valley was covered with mist like thick white fur. All that had happened to her passed through her mind in a moment. She sat up, her heart pumping in terror behind her ribs, her teeth grinding like stones against each other. She was lost, abandoned; she would die here, and no one would ever know. She threw her hands over her head in despair.

The sun came up, blurrily splendid, burning away the mist, splashing onto trees and stones, warming the earth. But nothing could ever again warm her chilled bones.

A man came out of the cave, yawned, and glanced at Zan. She shrank back, breath hissing between her teeth. He raised his arm and slowly, thoughtfully, scratched his armpit, then squatted in front of the stone hearth, his naked back and buttocks to her. Blowing on the ashes, he raked scattered leaves and bits of sticks and bark with his fingers into the fire. Thin tendrils of smoke curled along his arms. Burrum appeared and hurried to Zan, patting her hair and her back. Another woman came over, squatting down to stare into Zan's face and to poke at her arms. It was starting again—the poking, the prodding, all of it. No! she screamed in her mind, and she began to build a wall against them. She saw the wall in her mind, beautiful, curving, solid, a glass dome thick and unbreachable, guarding and protecting her from Burrum's voice, from the woman's fingers, from noise and smells, and from the unbearable thought of where she was.

A child left the cave, peeing in a golden arc. For a

moment, something familiar touched her. He was little, like Buddy, with curly hair and a round potbelly. Then she pulled the wall around her again. Soon, others came out, yawning and scratching, chewing on bark or leaves, talking softly, squatting around the fire. A little girl, sniffling, hands clasping her shoulders, chin cradled on crossed wrists, stared at Zan. But Zan was safe inside the glass dome, safe from all of them. She could see out, but no one could touch her. No one could reach her. And the screams of terror that kept crawling into her throat like worms—she was safe from them, too. Safe. Safe from everything.

9

Farwe, whose name meant Place-of-Night-Sun, toiled up the mountain toward the cave of Diwera, the Wai Wai of the People. It was a fresh clear morning. Farwe had been awake for a long time, even before Sun, going over the amazing events of the previous day. In all her life she had never seen anything like that girl her daughter had found in Meadow-with-Watering-Hole. Had the girl come from Beyond-the-Mountains? In Farwe's mind, Beyond-the-Mountains was a vague unknown space, vast, misty, fearful. All that was good, all that was safe, lay within the mountains, here in the caves, and in the forest, and in the fold of the river, the world of the People.

The day before, she had gone forward eagerly to see that girl, to touch her, to smell her hair, and taste her skin. Had no one else noticed the taste of fear like sour fruit on the girl's skin? As she moved steadily up the mountain, Farwe remembered that taste and spittle collected in her mouth. And thinking of that taste and of her man's mother, the Auuhmaa, she turned her head and spit delicately.

The moment she woke up, Farwe had begun thinking of Meezzan—how strange her eyes were, how Burrum had talked in her sleep about Meezzan. She had still been thinking when the Auuhmaa prodded her in the buttocks with a bony finger and told her to go to Diwera. The Old Mother could not wait for anything. Of course, she had no choice but to go at once. For when the old ones speak, one has to listen and obey.

Diwera was the wisest of all the People. She saw what others did not see, she heard voices no one else heard, she knew how to cure the sick and bury the dead. Everyone respected her, even the First Old Ones who were, themselves, so respected. And yet Farwe did not care to have much to do with Diwera. Before Diwera's steady gaze, Farwe always felt her belly tremble, as if she were a child again! Yet it was the Wai Wai's own son, Hiffaru, who would one day come to live in Farwe's cave, to be her daughter's man, to share fire and food. He would be Farwe's new-son, and she and Diwera would address each other as sisters. Yes, she and the Wai Wai!

"Aii, Aiii," Farwe sighed, picking a bit of grass from between her teeth. She would have preferred a perfect new-son, not one with but one good eye. After he and Burrum sat in the circle of stones, that other eye, that sunken unblinking little eye, would always be watching Farwe, peering out from deep inside his skull.

Stopping near Diwera's cave, Farwe looked back down the mountain, her eyes unerringly picking out the tiny figure that was Meezzan. The other tiny figure was her daughter, Burrum, who had gone to that girl as soon as she woke, not even going first to the river to bathe. If, as the Auuhmaa said, the Anouch'i had entered into Meezzan, then it was they who were telling her not to eat, not to drink; it was they who made her eyes look without seeing. Farwe breathed in sharply. Her belly was hard. Might not the Anouch'i slip from the breath and skin of that girl to the breath and skin of her daughter?

"Aii! Aiii!" Diwera must come to see that girl. She must drive away the Anouch'i, or drive away the girl! Farwe knew this was so. This was what she had been thinking since she woke. This was why she had come to the cave of the Wai Wai. She fingered the necklace of Curzon seeds she wore. It had taken many days to collect these seeds. To make such a necklace was not a thing for a child! It was fine and beautiful, and Farwe hoped Diwera would admire it. Then she would take it from her neck and lay it over Diwera's head, saying, "It's yours, it's nothing, only a trifle. Keep it, you will make my belly happy. It means nothing to me unless you receive happiness from it."

When she gave the necklace to Diwera, she would tell her first what the Old Mother said about Meezzan. And then about her bad dream. Aii, what a bad dream that had been. Farwe spit vigorously once more. Ppfuu! In her dream she had seen her mouth stuffed with poisonous toads' eggs. Long ago she had seen a child thrashing and screaming with pain after eating those eggs. The poor little thing had died. In her dream those poison eggs had filled her mouth and were spilling out of a hole in her chest. Waking, she had felt such fear in her belly! She had been shivering and her man, Raaniu, had put his arms around her and breathed his warm breath on her. She knew the dream had something to do with that daughter of Others, that Meezzan. All alone, the girl had stayed outside in the darkness! Night was the time when the souls of the lost dead wandered, calling and knocking on trees! Tariana, with eyes of fire!

Kneading her belly thoughtfully, Farwe turned her feet into Diwera's cave. Entering, she waited a moment just inside, and called out, "Farwe has come. I have come from my hearth to your hearth. Do you want something of mine? Tell me what you want, I am here to give you something."

As she finished speaking, her eyes found Diwera sitting cross-legged in front of her fire. Her hair, in two thick plaits, hung over her shoulders, swaying as she ground a plant between two stones. Little bunches of herbs and plants were scattered all around on the floor and were drying on ledges on the walls. Farwe stared respectfully at all this as she waited for Diwera to return her greeting. Now that she was looking into the steady brown eyes of the Wai Wai, she no longer felt that fear in her belly. She knew that Diwera would make everything right again.

10

Greeting people, Diwera moved leisurely down the mountain path. Near Farwe's cave she climbed into a tree and sat among the branches to observe the girl, Meezzan. The girl sat with her knees near her face, her arms around her legs, rocking back and forth like a child in its mother's lap. Back and forth. Back and forth. From her perch Diwera saw that the Ta was gone from the girl's eyes. Diwera pulled at her lip. Everything about this girl made her belly tighten uncomfortably—her skin, the unpleasant way her body was covered, and most of all, those empty eyes. And what was that thing in her hand? Not a stone, as she had first thought, not anything she could name. Diwera's heart quickened, for she knew there were people Beyond-the-Mountains who had their own ways, their own magic. She had heard of them in the stories of the Teller. She gazed for a long time at the strange brown object with the bright shining tongue that Meezzan held so tightly. Diwera did not like the way the shining tongue glittered and hurt her eyes. The skin on her arms tightened, and saliva gathered in her mouth.

When she left the tree at last she did not return to her cave, but went into the forest by a path known only to herself, letting her feet lead her. Diwera listened to the birds and the insects; she listened to the trees, the animals, and the stones. Each one spoke in its own voice to her. Their voices were part of her, as she was part of them. She knew how it was to be a rock, a bird, a tree. There were no secrets between her and all else. She belonged to all that she saw, all that she smelled and heard. She was the world and the world was her.

Now she sought a certain plant, the tiny, white Abena that, growing in the shade of the Mai bush, secreted a mysterious milky fluid. Only the Wai Wai knew its secret. She had not often sought the power that Abena granted; now she needed it to know the way with this stranger among them.

Yooria, the old Wai Wai, had taught Diwera the power and mystery of Abena. It could light the darkness of night with colors and rainbows, with soaring tongues of color that burst into fire and wisdom behind the eyes of the seeker. "But let the seeker beware," old Yooria had instructed. "The power of Abena is great."

Yooria, Night Woman, had taught Diwera this and all that she knew, the secrets of plants, and the language of animals. She had been as much to Diwera as her own mother. She had been wise and the People loved her. When she died, the Keeper beat the Death Drum for many days and nights. The People wept without stopping. They were bereft without Yooria, as children are without their mothers. For many moons after Yooria died, Diwera had been restless in her sleep. Her mother, her father, Yooria, all were gone to Place-of-Night-Sun. Her brothers lived with the mothers of their wives. She was alone. Yet she had not wanted a man.

Long before, when she had fasted and dreamed in

the Sussuru hut with other girls of her age, she had already known that she would have a different life from her friends. She had dreamed of a huge bird flying around her head, its wings touching her hair. She had trembled and cried out. Then the bird had said to her, *Do not cry, I come from the Bird People. You shall be our sister. You shall speak our language. You shall learn about birds, and herbs, and healing.*

All that the dream said had come true, and learning from Yooria, Diwera had been satisfied. She had felt need of nothing and of no one else. Yooria had lived and died without a man, and so would she. "A man draws the power from the Wai Wai," Yooria had told her. "When a woman has a man she does not want to leave him to search for roots and herbs. She thinks more of him than of the ones she must help."

"I will not have a man," the young Diwera had said. But after Yooria died, she was too much alone.

One night Yooria came to her in her dreams, chanting a song Diwera had never before heard. Waking up, she rolled close to her fire, hearing that song far away in her head and feeling great longing in her belly. The song called her out of the cave. Her feet led her into the forest. Night birds whistled and sang from all sides. Perhaps they were not birds at all, but spirits whistling, calling her? She had heard of those spirits in the shape of men who enticed women away from the paths, and only after seducing them revealed their true identities by snatching out their hair.

Thinking of this, Diwera faltered in her steps. Then, ahead of her on the path, she saw a black shadow, huge like a bear, but in the shape of a man. "Go!" she shouted bravely, although she trembled in fear. "You will not seduce me and pull out my hair! Do you hear me, you with the shape of a man?" She gathered saliva in her mouth to defend herself against the spirit. Then it spoke, and she knew the voice. But still she tested it. "If you are not a spirit or a bear in the shape of a man, then tell me at once why you are here."

"I do not know," he said. "I woke and left the cave to make my water, and then I felt the moon calling me."

Diwera's belly throbbed strangely. She knew this man. She had often smiled at him. He had a woman; if not, perhaps she would have thought differently about taking a man. Still, she tested him again. "Tell me now the name of your mother's grandfather, he who is happy in Place-of-Night-Sun."

The man answered at once, "His name is Tofu, Large Hand. He has visited me in my dreams often."

And now she knew that he was himself, not a spirit. "I saw you from afar," she said then. "I thought I was dying, but now I live again." It was the greeting the People gave when they came upon one another far from the caves.

She reached out her hand and, clasping it, he returned the greeting. "Until I saw you, I felt thirsty and hungry. Now my thirst has been quenched, my hunger has been satisfied."

So they spoke together, and as day always follows night, so did one thing follow another, and they lay together beneath the trees. They parted before Sun came back.

Diwera never spoke of that night to another, but soon she knew her belly was full with child. The spirits ceased calling to her, and her sleep was deep.

Diwera had made her birth bed near the river. Her daughter came easily into the world, sliding into the waiting hands of the women attending her. "Look at this child," they cried. "Look at her, she is so beautiful." Her skin was the color of honey, she had lips like fresh fruit. Diwera named her Akawa, Gift of the Forest.

The women pressed down on Diwera's stomach to bring out the afterbirth. Instead her son came screaming into the world. The women cried out joyfully at this bounty, then their cries turned to lamentations. "Aii! Aiii!" Old Mahu, into whose arms the newborn son had slid, dropped him to the ground, moaning fearfully through her teeth. "Do not look at him," she warned Diwera.

Diwera raised herself on her elbow. "Let me see my son." There was blood on her thighs. The child screamed on the ground. Diwera gazed at him, saying nothing. One side of his face was perfect with the closed eye of the newborn. The other side of his face was crushed, as if a foot had stepped upon the fragile flesh, crumpling it like a dry leaf. Deep within that crumpled side, a tiny eye, open and lidless, peered at the world. On both hands, the fingers were joined by a web, like a duck's foot.

"Do not take the child into your arms," old Mahu said. "Turn away your eyes! Close your ears to his cries! We will take him to the forest and do what must be done."

There they would lay the child on the ground and put a log on his neck. All would stand upon the log till he was still. They would shed their tears upon the tiny body and lay it in the branches of a tree where an animal would soon find it and consume it. Only the bones would be left, and these would become part of the forest.

Diwera understood. Perhaps if she had already felt

the joy of the infant girl pulling at her breast, she
would have listened to the words of old Mahu. But the
other women were passing the beautiful girl baby from
arm to arm. "Give my son to me," she said, but as no
one wanted to touch him she gathered him up herself
from the ground. The child stopped screaming. His tiny
eye looked directly into Diwera's face. Leaving the girl
to the others, she bit off the birth cord and washed
away the slime and blood on the child. She examined
her son minutely. Her flesh did not shrink from the
infant, from his strange face and webbed hands.

She opened his fingers, spreading them wide, and cut
between the webbing with a sharp stone. Then she put
bits of wood between the fingers, tying the wood firmly
with strong grass so the fingers would remain separated
and not grow together again. She named him Hiffaru,
Duck's Hand.

When the children were infants, there were always
women who would help her with the girl, but the boy
was left to her. After she took away the bits of wood,
his hands grew normally, but nothing could be done for
his face. Diwera soon grew used to it. Even when he
was tiny, he had a way of looking at her with that
small, deepset eye, as if he and she were forever linked.
She loved him intensely, perhaps more than her daughter. If he had been a girl, she would not have hesitated
to teach him the ways of the Wai Wai. He was alert,
willing, clever. From one side, he was quite beautiful.
She had made sure that he would have a woman.

But as for Akawa, the girl refused to think about a
man. "You did not, Mother, why must I?"

"But I am the Wai Wai," Diwera answered each
time, and each time she hoped her daughter would say,
"Well, then, I will be the Wai Wai, too. You must

teach me everything." But her daughter only looked at her from her long eyes and smiled her secret smile.

The girl was a sadness to Diwera. She longed for a girl to teach the secrets of the forest, the ways of the Wai Wai, the hidden paths, the herbs that could cure, the chants that were beautiful and sacred. She would not forever be strong and healthy. A Wai Wai must come after her. But who would it be? Bahii was too timid, Em'Fadi too quiet, Burrum must be her son's woman, and Noomia and Naku, those two big girls, sisters, wanted to do nothing but paint in Cave-of-No-Name. Most useless of all was her own daughter, who cared only for ornaments and her own beauty.

Thinking of all this and of Yooria, the old Wai Wai, Diwera flung out her arms, calling as she had not called in many moons, "Yooria! Yooria! Here I am, doing the things you taught me, searching for the Abena plant."

Her feet led her farther into the forest. She followed a shallow stream, then stopped abruptly by a tree, watching a group of Llachi drinking. They were called the Deer with Skins the Color of Morning Sun. Three times as large as the largest man of the People, they had great branching antlers jutting out from their heads. Taken by surprise, they had been known to be dangerous. One looked up, saw Diwera, and huffed uneasily. Diwera remained silent, still. In the way of the Wai Wai, she grew into the trunk of the tree, breathed with the tree, the juices of the tree rising in her body. Wind passed through the tree, passed through Diwera. A female Llachi shook her long head from side to side, glancing toward Diwera. Soon, the animals moved slowly away. After they had gone, just where they passed from Diwera's sight, she found the Abena plant. Kneeling, with the sweet odors of the earth rising to her nostrils, she carefully snapped off several stalks, turning them upside down in order not to lose the precious fluid.

In her cave again, she gathered twigs and brush to build up her fire. The smoke curled upward, then drifted out, leaving a low film near the ceiling. She squeezed the precious drops of milky Abena juice into a large leaf, and when the fire was blazing brightly she placed a flat stone in the middle. Laying the leaf on the stone, she built the fire higher. Soon, the edges of the leaf blackened and curled inward. She fed the fire, staring into its depths. Sparks leaped over the stone, burning little holes in the green fabric of the leaf. Smoke poured from inside the leaf and then it burst into flame and was consumed, leaving only a small pile of ashes on the stone.

"Ahhh," Diwera sighed softly. Wetting two fingers of her left hand on her tongue, she dipped them reverently into the ashes and brought them to her mouth. Soon she would have dreams and visions and be given much wisdom. She would learn what she had to fear from that daughter of Others, and what she must do to protect the People against her. Closing her eyes and throwing back her head, Diwera began to chant. She felt the ashes slide down her throat and enter her belly, and the mysteries began to flower in her blood.

11

Zan, under the glass dome: eyes unfocused; breathing carefully; thoughts turning slowly; holding the knife. Important knife. Must not let it go. Safety.

Next to her, Burrum squatted, hands outstretched, rubbing Zan's arms, rubbing Zan's head. Something was on Zan's head. It lay there lightly, so lightly perhaps she didn't feel it at all? She considered this for a long time. Yes, something was on her head. She felt it, yet she didn't feel it. Because of the glass dome. Inside the dome, no feelings. Only safety.

Carefully, she raised her eyes enough to see a large leaf on Burrum's head. To keep off the sun? Was there a leaf on her head, too? The sun was high, hot. The morning mists were dissolved. The people were gone, like the mists. Perhaps the people had never existed? Untrue thought. They existed. She existed. They were existing together, at the same time. *Their time.*

Phrases flitted through her mind like insects: *their time, her time, the same time . . . time is a thief . . . beyond space and time . . . how many times do I have to tell you? . . . time and time again . . . don't waste time . . . this time I mean it . . . time enough for that*

*another day . . . what time is it? . . . time flies . . . not
this time you don't . . . the time has come . . .*

She slept. Or did she simply go away, eyes open,
mind frozen inside the glass dome? Focusing again, she
saw Burrum to one side and, squatting in front of her, a
woman with two thick braids hanging over broad
shoulders. A woman with her nose flattened as if someone had pressed a thumb into the fleshy part. Zan remembered her. Earlier she had seen her sitting in a tree,
staring. *I saw you, sitting like a monkey in a tree. I saw
you watching me. I remember you.* The others had
slipped into a blurred mass in her mind, but she remembered this brown-eyed woman who gazed at her
straight on now, trying to tunnel into her mind. *Stop
that. Stop!* The eyes were trying to shatter the glass
dome. But Zan was smarter than any naked savage who
lived in a cave like an animal. Her neck trembling
under the impact of that brown gaze, she built up the
glass dome, made it thicker, stronger. No one could get
to her through it. No one.

Peering at Zan as if to pluck secrets from her heart,
the woman spoke: "Meezzan. Meezzan." Zan had to
lower her eyes to defend herself. *Go away. Leave me
alone.* The knife was solid in her sweating hand, the
glass dome high, shiny tight around her, keeping her
safe.

The woman began singing softly. "Hau . . . auu . . .
hauu . . . auuuu . . . hau . . . hau . . . hau . . ."
Gradually her voice grew louder, less varied, less
melodic; louder and then louder still, till she was shouting, raving, crying out in a strangely thrilling voice, like
a challenge, "Hau! Hau! Hau!" Sweat dripped down
her face, her voice did battle with an unseen enemy.
Zan, inside the shell of herself, trembled at the on-

slaught. She was unable to drag her eyes from the
woman's face, from the mouth, crying out that single
sound that twanged and plucked at Zan's gut. Moaning
softly, Zan held her stomach. Burrum patted and
rubbed her; but the woman said something, and
Burrum drew away.

All at once the woman snatched a handful of hair
from Zan's head, yanked it straight from her scalp.
"Uhhh!" Zan cried.

Rolling the hair in one hand, the women turned and
took a live ember from the fire. She dropped the ember
into the nest of hair, which flared up, crackling, and
burnt in her palm with a penetrating acrid odor. Spitting into her palm, she mixed the ashes and saliva with
a forefinger. Still chanting, she rubbed the mixture of
spit and ashes across Zan's forehead and down both
cheeks.

Stupefied, Zan strained to stay inside her glass dome.
The woman's voice fell away to a whisper, then
stopped. The silence grew as the woman's eyes held
Zan's steadily, unblinking. "Meezzan," she whispered.
She waited. "Meezzan." Her voice rose. "Meezzan."
The call was louder, more demanding. "Meezzan!"
Zan's neck muscles strained with the effort not to re-
spond. "Meezzan! MEEZZAN!" Still she didn't re-
spond, and inside the glass dome she felt her victory.
She was safe.

The woman blew up her cheeks, pursed her mouth
and, craning her neck forward like a huge bird, spit
straight into Zan's face. Zan's stomach lurched. Calmly,
nodding, the woman smeared her saliva over Zan's face
and neck.

"You pig!" Zan cried, speaking for the first time.

The woman sat back on her haunches. She touched

her left breast. "Diwera," she said. She touched Zan's left breast. "Meezzan." She waited.

Zan watched the woman warily, her body shuddering with revulsion. The shock of that wet slimy saliva smeared over her flesh had cracked the glass dome. Everything was coming through now. *All right, your name is Dah-wara. So what? Go away. You spit on me. Animal! You're all a bunch of animals.*

The woman sat there, eyes as calm as water. No getting away from those eyes. She repeated, "Diwera— Meezzan," and waited again, as if she had all the time in the world. *Her eyes won't leave me alone. Go away, Dahwara. If I say your name, will you go away?* Barely opening her mouth, Zan muttered, "Dahwara." The sound emerged sluggishly, but she had said it.

And Diwera had heard it. She slapped her knee. "Ahha!" She smiled, the merest lifting of the corners of her mouth, a tiny reward for Zan.

Now go away.

But Diwera had no intention of leaving. She began all over again. She named herself, then nodded at Zan, and waited for her to reply. She picked up a stone, said a word, a sound, waited. Zan stared, mulish. *Go away. I don't want to play.* But the woman sat there like a rock and, holding out the stone, made the sound again. Then she put her hands to Zan's mouth as if to coax the sound from her lips.

The touch of the hands that had smeared spit on her struck Zan with fury. "Don't touch me," she cried, pushing away Diwera's hands. "Leave me alone! I don't care about your stupid stone and your stupid words—" Aghast, she broke off. With each word she had widened the crack in her glass wall, splintering and shattering it. Now it was gone. She was no longer protected, safe, unfeeling. Her stomach clamored for food. Her tongue clicked dryly against the roof of her mouth.

Diwera held out the stone, coaxing from Zan the repetition of the sound she had made. Then, "Eno!" and Zan knew she was being praised. In the numbness that still pinched her mind, she couldn't help feeling a little stir of pleasure. But what did it matter? What did any of this matter? She was here, trapped, and all she cared about was getting away. *Do you know the words for that, Diwera? Getting away. Escaping. Going back. Returning. Teach me those words, teach me how to do that, and I'll say Eno! to you.*

Diwera picked up a charred stick. "M'nup." A strange sound with a tongue thump in it. Grudgingly, Zan repeated it, unable to manage the tongue thump. Prodded by Diwera, she repeated it again and again, till she managed a fair approximation of the sound. But when, after this, Diwera picked up the stone and looked questioningly at her, Zan had forgotten that word and had to start all over again. Annoyed, humiliated, she repeated in a hard, furious voice every word Diwera said. Then, under her breath, she repeated it for herself. In this way she learned the words for stone, fire, stick, hands, mouth, feet, and earth.

But she was tired, her mind dull, her legs and back aching from sitting so long. Her head sank down and she refused to say anything else. Diwera called out to Burrum, who went away and returned a moment later holding a large bony-white fruit. Laying the fruit on a flat stone, Diwera tapped it sharply with another stone, lopping off one end as Zan might have removed the top of a boiled egg.

Clasping Zan's hands around the fruit, Diwera brought it up to her mouth, forcing her to swallow. A small amount of the thick, murky liquid dribbled down her throat. It was unlike anything she'd ever tasted, dark, acid, earthy. A violent fit of trembling seized her, a spasm of hunger and thirst. She seized the fruit and drank the contents without stopping.

12

Zan, who had never been a follower, followed Burrum around for the rest of that day, still in something of a daze, still trying to absorb her new situation. She washed her hands and face in a stream and combed her hair roughly with her hands. Cautiously, she ate a few small greenish fruits that Burrum had shaken down from a tree. Wherever she went, people eyed and touched her curiously. Once, she spotted the boy who had been with Burrum in the meadow. Seeing his slanting eyes and thick eyebrows, Zan felt something strange happen: it was as if she had come upon an old friend. "Hello!" she shouted, and gave a smile that for a moment washed through her misery like a stream of clear water. But mostly she still felt wobbly, tired, hungry, and her head whirled with protest. *This is crazy. What am I doing here?* Then, remembering the dizzying intensity with which she had wished herself *someplace else*, she knew she had brought this on herself.

Toward evening, as the sun was setting, Burrum, carrying an armful of dead wood, led her back up the mountain. Zan was exhausted. Her legs ached. She had to stop often to rest. Mountains! Up and up and up, and up some more. No comfort now in looking back down on the green, spreading valley.

When she saw again the cave with the overhanging shelf of rock and the fire blazing in the middle of a ring of stones, it seemed to her a very long time ago that she had built herself into the glass dome. She sank down on the ground, stretching her legs out and slumping against a tree for support. People were gathering around the fire. The sun was sinking, and the light of other fires flickered on the side of the mountain. In the clear air, sound carried—laughter, snatches of song, bird-like whistles. At Burrum's fire there were men, women, and a cluster of little children. They were all eating with satisfied grunts, shoving stuff into their mouths, licking their fingers.

Between bites Burrum talked and talked, as if Zan could understand. She could hardly keep her eyes open. The fire, the talk, her empty belly, the attempts to figure out who was who and what was going on, the need to be on guard, all of this exhausted her. And then, she had slept very little the night before. And half the day she had been in that crazy state behind the glass dome. She dozed off and was dreaming at once. *I'm sorry,* Ivan said. *I'm sorry, I never meant* . . . He was so agreeable, so sweet. She smiled at him, loving him. Her brother. She wanted to hug him. But the phone rang, short and sharp-shrill, and she thought, *Gotta hurry!* and woke up, still smiling about Ivan. But it was Burrum laughing into her face. In the darkness the girl's teeth shone, sharp, feral. The dazed feeling came over Zan again. She trembled with fatigue.

Standing up, Burrum stretched out her hand to lead Zan toward the cave. Remembering the lonely terror of the night before, Zan had no will to resist. She passed under the broad ledge and into the cave. For the first moments she saw nothing but their own gigantic shad-

ows cast on the walls by the light of the fire burning
near the entrance. Gradually, her heart slowed down
and her eyes adjusted. She was in a large irregular room
with curving, chunky walls. The fire threw a feeble glow
back into the darkness. People drifted in, talking and
laughing. A man wrestled with two small children, taking on one with each hand. A woman braided another
woman's hair, and a mother suckled her baby. Not far
from the entrance hearth, in one corner of a mass of
leaves and branches, the old woman with the bad eye
was curled up, looking like nothing so much as a giant,
wrinkled insect in a nest. A nest it was—a nest for all
of them.

Lying down near the old woman, Burrum patted and
smoothed the place next to herself, calling Zan. Other
people were settling themselves, leaning back on their
elbows, or curling up with one another. "Meezzan!"
Burrum called again. But never, never could Zan lie
down among them and sleep with an easy heart! She
had slept on the ground the night before, she could do it
again.

She lay down on her side near the fire, tucking her
hands between her drawn-up knees. "Aii, Meezzan!"
Burrum called, getting up and coming over to her. She
lay down by the fire, too, but in a moment, poking Zan
to make sure she was watching, Burrum began to grunt
loudly, as if very unhappy. She turned and twisted on
the ground as if it were impossible to find a comfortable
position. Finally she jumped up, climbed onto the mass
of branches and leaves, lay down and sighed deeply
with exaggerated satisfaction.

"Terrific performance," Zan said, clapping her
hands. This amused everyone, and the baby, who'd
been concentrating on her mother's breast, looked up

and clapped her hands, too. A babble of talk broke out.

Zan closed her eyes. She was tired enough to fall asleep instantly, but instead she became more and more wakeful. Her hand went to her pocket and she fingered the odd things there, her knife, the key, the safety pin, the button. An odd, silly collection, but comforting. She brought out the shred of tissue and wiped her nose. They were all watching intently. A feeling of unreality seized her. Here she was, lying on the floor of a firelit cave, her every move observed by half-naked savages. What could they make of a yellow tissue that had come from a gold-stamped box purchased in a supermarket with a dollar bill? What could she make of it? What was real? What unreal?

Zan tried to take firm hold of her thoughts. *Floor under me is real. Fire is real. Cave. Tissue in my hand real. Old woman snoring, that's real. And the safety pin, the knife. My world. This world. Both real. River of time . . . everything going on at the same time. I'm here . . . am I there, too?*

Stop thinking. No use! Be quiet, sleep. But the floor beneath her was hard and the fire on her face was hot, while the rest of her was chilled and aching. She moved, shifted, tried to get comfortable. She really needed to sleep. Everytime she moved, they laughed. She was a whole circus by herself. Furiously, she turned onto her back, staring up into the darkness above her. A half dozen bats, hairy little monsters, hung upside down from a ledge, their wings folded around their bodies like capes, their eyes open, reflecting tiny points of firelight.

Panic threatened. Her stomach rolled.

Don't! Want them all to see you're scared?

She pitched over onto her belly, laying her head on her folded arms. Pebbles, bits of debris, poked into her legs and arms. Overhead, the bats squeaked.

What if they fly down, attack me, tangle in my hair . . . Something, an animal, whipped past her into the darkness beyond the fire. Zan squeaked like a bat. The laughter swelled. She had to laugh herself. Idiot, if you're afraid of the bats, get away from them.

Zan got up, brushed herself off, and went over to lie next to Burrum on the common bed. She would never sleep, though. The smells, the sounds, the very thought of all the bodies around her . . . She stared, open-eyed, into the flickering darkness. Burrum snuggled next to her, her arm over Zan's waist, whispering in her ear. Soon, though, Burrum was quiet, breathing deeply, and the others, unbothered by their own groans, snores, and mutterings, slept like healthy animals.

The night slowly wore on. Zan dozed, only to wake and stare again into the darkness. *I'll find that meadow again . . . try to make it come again, that storm, or whatever . . . must be something to do with the boulder . . . find the same spot . . . see what happens . . . try, all I can do is try . . .*

A spasm of fear shook her. Try. What a little word. How insignificant compared to what had happened to her. She hadn't *tried* to make that storm happen: how could she *try* to undo it? She pressed her fingers to her mouth. Yet, what else could she do except believe that somehow, someway, she would restore herself to her own time? *I am going to get away from here. Back where I belong. I'll cross that time bend again.*

13

Zan was dreaming. Her feet on the blade of an upright shovel, hands lightly gripping the handle, she bounced as if on a pogo stick, across a street, over a car, higher and higher, over a building, leaping and bouncing. A wonderful feeling! She was as light as air, flying. She *was* air. My balance is perfect, she thought with satisfaction. This is a marvelous invention, I must show it to the class. Smiling, she woke up and saw where she was. All around her people were sleeping, curled up with each other, snoring, or sighing and muttering softly. A feeling of incredulity gripped her and she became aware of a desperate need to urinate, to empty her bowels. She felt filthy. Despair threatened, a dry bleakness forcing itself into her throat and behind her eyes.

Fighting it, she scrambled to her feet. The cave was dim, the fire smoldered, sending up thin wisps of smoke. She stumbled toward the entrance, seeing the green of trees, and far away the glint of water. Outside, the sun was rising, the air rang with strange birdsongs that sounded like chimes and bells and guitar strings. It was an incredibly fresh, lovely morning. She had never before been present at such a morning.

"Meezzan—" Burrum was at her elbow, eyes smallish with sleep. She yawned and took Zan's hand, led her across the plateau into a wooded area. What time was it? Zan wondered. How long had she slept? What day was it? Sunday. No, Monday. "Monday," she said out loud. "It's Monday morning." Burrum smiled. The words hovered in the air like foreign sounds, meaningless. Monday morning.

Burrum stopped at a fallen log and, sitting over it, relieved herself. Zan followed her example. Afterward, Burrum covered what she had done with leaves and dirt thrown up with a stick and, wordlessly, Zan did the same. They left the grove, moved down a hill, through more trees. The river came into view below them, morning mists still on its surface. Zan scrambled down the bank after Burrum and dipped cold clear water to wash herself and to drink. Then she was really awake and feeling better, able to smile in response to Burrum's chatter. She walked along beside the girl, putting in a comment now and then, simply to hear the sound of her own voice. "You don't say." "Fan-tas-tic!" As Burrum spoke, her hands made shapes in the air—sign language —but Zan understood no more of this than the spoken language.

They entered a boggy field full of tangled, lush green grasses and tall, thick ferns. "Her" meadow? Zan wondered, but no, this meadow was flatter, wetter, and there were no boulders anywhere. On hands and knees, Burrum crawled slowly through the tall grass.

Carefully, she showed Zan a bird's nest deep in the grass, filled to bursting with four green speckled eggs. Burrum's eyes sparkled. Taking an egg, she tapped it across the top with a little stone, cracking it, then tipped back her head and sucked out the contents. She threw aside the shell, and seeing that Zan hadn't taken an egg she made a face of astonishment and put Zan's hand firmly into the nest.

Eat one, Zan's stomach ordered. *Raw?* her head protested. But she was hungry. The egg, warm and smooth, filled her hand. She tapped at it with Burrum's little stone, and knocked the top right off. The white began to spill out. Quickly before she had time to think what she was doing, she brought the egg to her mouth. It tasted more delicious than almost anything she could ever remember eating. She reached for another egg, but Burrum grabbed her hand, bursting into a flood of words. When she had found another nest, she permitted Zan a second egg, while sliding one behind her into the net bag she wore from her head.

With food in her stomach, Zan felt slightly more confident of what the day might bring. She was alert again, and as they moved on she saw no reason not to think that they might come upon the meadow with the boulder. Then—well—she would see. Something would happen, surely!

Burrum stopped in front of some tall bushes loaded with tiny blue fruit. She motioned to Zan to start picking. The berries were tart, but Zan was ready to pick and eat till her stomach was full. Burrum moved on a short distance, until she found a dead stump blanketed with closely packed white mushrooms. She broke several open, exposing firm pinkish flesh. Sitting down to eat them, she gestured to Zan to join her. But Zan's belly was now beginning to ache a little, possibly from the berries, and raw mushrooms didn't appeal to her at all.

By now, she had no idea where they were. Her sense of direction was obliterated. Stones, grass, hills, trees, swamps—all looked the same. How did Burrum know where they were? Where to turn? Which way to go? Zan's stomach pitched crazily. If Burrum walked away from her now, she would be hopelessly lost. As lost as if she'd been abandoned in the middle of the forest.

When Burrum had eaten all she wanted of the mushrooms and gathered some for her net bag, they moved on again. In this way, eating, throwing things into her bag, Burrum gradually led Zan back to the caves. There the net bag was raided by a swarm of children. The eggs, however, she took to the old woman, squatting next to her to watch as she drank them.

Later, when the sun was high and hot, they went back to the river. Zan dipped her face into the water and, taking off her sneakers, waded around in the shallows. Other people were there, men, women, and children, some swimming, some sunning, or playing on the banks. Burrum joined a group of boys and girls who were leaping off a high rock into the deep water. Zan was astonished to see a baby tossed into the water, where it bobbed, laughing, to the surface and paddled like a sleek little seal.

The heat, the voices of the people, the sun reflecting off the water made Zan sleepy. She lay down under a tree. Above her, a child sat on a limb and sang. Zan thought of Buddy, of Kim, of her family. Were they grieving over her disappearance? She imagined them sitting around the kitchen table, heads sunk into hands.

Two days since I ate breakfast at home and fought with Ivan. Two nights since I slept in my own bed. It seemed longer. It seemed forever, as if everything she had known existed on another plane, in another dimension that might not even be real. Madness! In her own life these people around her were shadows, shades of shades, dust. "They are dead," she whispered, but without belief. No, they were real; living, breathing human beings. And her home, her family, did they truly exist anymore? Or was their reality only in her mind? She knew she was dangerously close to numbing self-pity. She couldn't allow it. She couldn't withdraw again into that crazy little world of the glass dome.

Jumping up, she slapped her hands over her head, remembering second grade and Mrs. Marks with the purple hair who used to regularly lead the class in Simon Says exercises. "There's nothing like a little exercise to clear the head and get the blood working," she would say.

Simon says, do this. Jump, feet apart, hands clapping overhead. One. Two. Three. Four. Five . . . In moments, Zan had several small imitators, including the little boy with silvery fish eyes whom she thought was Burrum's brother. Having an audience cheered her. "Okay, kids, Simon says, do this!" She galloped in place, lifting her knees high, pumping her arms up and down. Giggling, the children followed. She jumped faster, higher, clapping her hands swiftly, calling out her Simon Says commands in a loud voice, a manic energy infecting her.

Abruptly she stopped. What was she doing? How stupid. How meaningless! The "class" hopped around expectantly. "Forget it!" she said disgustedly and sat down with her back to them all. The misery she'd been dodging all morning swept over her, and this time she let it come, waves of fear and self-pity, knocking her groggy, drowning her, leaving her gasping for breath. When the storm subsided, she was exhausted and slept on the ground.

Much later, when she was with Burrum and some other young people in the forest, Zan suddenly walked away from them. Why put it off any longer? She had to find the meadow. Within moments she was out of sight of the group. Sounds all around her, but none human. Whistles . . . hoarse trumpeting . . . creaking of branches . . . rustling leaves. Mammoth trees everywhere. Two, three, or four trunks, each one enormous, twisted into the air from a single base. Dead trees stood like knotted gray giants or, fallen across other trees, seemed to be held up by their living companions. Humility and terror touched Zan. She felt that the trees were looking at her. Or was it the eyes of hidden animals, dangerous and full of anger at her crashing progress through their territory?

She ran, breathless. From the trees there was a constant stirring of leaves and bits of wood falling, sifting through the branches. Surely, Burrum and Sonte had passed this way from the meadow? Or, was it through that little grove . . . ?

She was lost. She turned back the way she thought she had come, looking for something she recognized. But now every tree looked like every other tree. She brushed ants and insects off her arms and neck. Her heart pounded. She began to sing loudly, off key, "John Brown's body lies a-moulderin' in his grave, John Brown's body lies a-moulderin' in his grave, John BROWN'S BO-DY lies A-MOULDERIN' IN HIS GRAVE!" She paused, catching her breath, her hand to her chest. Someone giggled. "Who's there?" she cried. "Burrum?" Above her, she saw two children sitting in a tree, looking down at her. Behind their hands, they laughed softly.

"Oh boy," Zan said. She sat down at the foot of the tree, leaning her head against the trunk, waving limply to the children. They scampered down from the tree and she followed them, stopping when they stopped, moving when they did, feeling ridiculously, humbly grateful to them. Yes, she would have to be patient, stay close to Burrum till she knew her way about, or till Burrum went back to "her" meadow. It could happen any time, any time at all.

14

A day passed. Another day. Then another. And yet another. A week. Time obsessed Zan. What time was it when she woke in the morning? What time when she ate? When she lay down to sleep? If only she knew the time! She saw the sun·rise, she saw it set, saw it blazing at its zenith. But without a clock or a watch she felt as if something were missing from her life, from her very self. Often she seemed to hear ticking and would turn quickly as if expecting to see a clock sitting on a rock, or perhaps perched in a tree. "You're crazy," she told herself, and thought of all the timepieces in her life. The old-fashioned wind-up clock on her mother's bureau. Her father's square-faced wristwatch with the shiny, elasticized band. The little watch in a round, gold case on a gold chain that Cici kept in her jewelry box and said she would give Zan on her eighteenth birthday. The red-bordered electric kitchen clock on the wall above the stove. The big blank-faced school clocks that loudly marked the monotonous minutes, exploding every fifty minutes into an ear-numbing shriek. She thought of clocks, and then of radios and of television and of all the things she knew; the way she had been brought up, with buildings and machinery, with math

and science, with movies and books and cars and washing machines and men landing on the moon. And what
did these cave people know? Nothing! Nothing at all.
Thinking of it, she wanted to laugh; then she wanted
to cry.

One night it rained and in the morning, while following Burrum down the mountain, she slipped on the
mudslicked trail and fell, striking her mouth against a
stone. It was a little injury—her lip puffed up and there
was blood on her tongue. But suddenly, the self-posses-
sion she had worked so hard to maintain was completely
undone. For the first time she cried. Once started, she
couldn't seem to stop. Rapidly a crowd gathered—
Sonte was there, Burrum's little brother Lishum, the
pregnant woman who lived in Burrum's cave, a tall girl,
a boy with a mutilated face. All of them pressed around
her, rubbing her arms and her back and her head, patting and soothing her, crying as she cried. "H'chau . . .
h'chau, Meezzan . . ." Zan had noticed that they were
always touching one another, patting, rubbing, stroking.
Now they did it to her, too, as if she were one of them.
The same. She wasn't. She never would be! She wiped
her face, but still they hovered near her, watching her
mournfully till, at last, she forced a smile. "Okay. I'm
okay now." They smiled, too, laughed, and patted her
some more.

She ought, by then, to have been used to their attention. People were always watching her, laughing at her.
Everything she did was of the greatest interest, the
highest amusement to them. She had never thought of
herself as a comedian, but she had only to go into the
water with her clothes on, for instance, and there were
roars of laughter. They giggled when she made clumsy
attempts to say a word in their language, chuckled

when she turned away from a worm or an ant offered her as food. Everyone, even the old, one-eyed woman, laughed as easily as a child. Deep, easy, rich laughter that seemed to well up out of bellies, or from the soles of feet. Infectious laughter, and Zan always ended up laughing with them. At herself, most of the time.

Only Diwera was different. Several times Zan had seen the woman watching her, not smiling, not laughing and chatting like everyone else, not soft, easy, pleasant. Diwera was apart from the others, she was never part of the groups that went everywhere together—to wash, to fish, to bathe, to dig up roots and gather eggs and fruit. When Diwera came among people, Zan saw that they stood back a little, their voices dropped, their faces smoothed out respectfully. Diwera was Somebody. She had some kind of power. Zan couldn't forget that the woman had seen her behind that glass dome, had spit on her, had brought her back into the world—this world. Diwera filled her with an uneasy respect and fear.

On the day she injured her lip, Zan made a calendar, scratching into a sturdy branch a mark for each day that had passed. Six scratches, then a slash across all six, and a week was marked. Six more scratches, another slash, and a second week had gone. She rubbed her thumb across the slashes, thinking of the days behind her. The days ahead of her. She had done things she had never believed she would. Slept with all of them, eaten raw eggs, used the woods for a toilet, scrambled into trees for food, or to get out of the way of animals. She had done all this!

She thought of these things at night, lying on the common bed, and she thought of other things as well: how everything in a civilized world was done behind closed doors, quietly, circumspectly. Here everything was done openly, participated in, shared. Was there anything personal, anything private here?

Early one morning while Zan was squatting by a tree to urinate, she heard a soft rustling and saw a large green and black snake almost directly beneath her. Carefully, holding up her jeans, she rose and took a delicate step away, then another, and another, every moment expecting that narrow head to leap forward, the teeth to strike hotly into her leg. But almost before she could fully comprehend her fear, Burrum, who had been squatting companionably nearby, came running, swinging a thick branch. She brought it down across the back of the snake's head and held it prisoner. The snake's mouth opened wide, and the thick body whipped up around the branch. Her face screwed up with loathing, Burrum held the snake fast, crying out in a high-pitched voice. Moments later, several people came running, Sonte among them, all armed with stones. They rushed up and in a swirl of sweaty fear and flying arms pounded the snake till it was a bloody mash.

Shaken, Zan considered the violence with which the snake had been killed. Of course she was glad they had done it—but still, it was strange! In the beginning, she had been terrified of these people. Then she had begun to think them as harmless, even childlike. They laughed so much! Now she had seen something else. She turned these thoughts around in her head, but sometimes there was too much thinking, too much pondering over who these people were, where she was, why, what it meant.

In the meantime, Zan added marks to her calendar. Every day she and Burrum went to the river. There were always dozens of people there. Down to the small-

est child, they swam with grace and confidence, spending hours in the water. The younger children were always chewing on something. Zan had seen a baby with
nothing to eat poke its fingers into his father's mouth,
extract a crumpled wad of vegetable matter, and pop it
into his own. As for Zan, she ate what she could.

Eggs and fruit were the mainstay of her diet. The
roots and tubers Burrum foraged were sinister-looking,
sometimes wormy and covered with dirt. The mushrooms Zan mistrusted heartily, and the slugs, bugs, and
insects were impossible for her even to consider as
food. But in trees, in fields, under stones, and in
marshes, Burrum, with Zan eagerly helping, searched
out the nests of birds and egg-laying snakes. Zan
couldn't stomach the round white snakes' eggs, but developed a true taste for birds' eggs. Some were mild,
almost sweet, some strong to the point of being gamy;
and one tiny, deep blue egg from a funnel-like nest in a
dead tree left a peppery aftertaste. Sometimes, while
holding an egg in her hand, not hungry, simply warming
it, turning it round and round, Zan was startled by a
surge of unexpected pleasure.

She used her knife to tap off the top of the eggs, or to
punch a small hole from which she sucked the contents.
Whenever she brought out the knife, Burrum and
Sonte, or whoever else was around, eyed it avidly. Sometimes, to amaze them, she flipped it into the air so that
it plunged straight back into the ground. Or simply
opening and closing the knife blade seemed to have
an equally startling effect on everybody. Not only her
knife fascinated them, but her button, the safety pin,
and the locker key. She had only to take out these
things to draw an immediate audience. Except for
the knife, they were all useless to her, yet with every

day that passed, they meant more. They meant home.

Often, when she felt herself sinking, she took out the key or the button. They opened her to memories— playing with the buttons in her mother's straw button box, the key hanging on a nail in her parents' bedroom, and the times long ago when she and Ivan had piled into bed with her parents on Sunday mornings. These were things she hadn't thought of in years.

Sometimes Burrum tried to touch the key or the button, but Zan pushed her hand away. Not to be selfish, but because she felt that if she once let them out of her possession, they would be lost. Burrum would give them to Sonte, and Sonte would give them to someone else, and that would be that! She would never see them again. She had noticed how these people gave away things, their necklaces and bracelets, food they foraged, or wood they'd gathered for their own fire. So whenever Burrum reached out her hand, Zan said, "Mine!" shaking her head and frowning. And she would put away the key or the safety pin, explaining further, "They're from home. Listen, if you were away from your home, you'd do the same thing."

She talked to Burrum all the time, the way Burrum talked to her. If not, she would have gone crazy keeping all her thoughts inside herself. It wasn't that they understood each other, it was just the relief of talking, letting off steam, hearing her own voice speaking a normal, sensible language. And then, sometimes, Zan even felt that in a funny sort of way they *did* understand each other. That there was a kind of unspoken sense or sympathy seeping from one to the other. And yet, if that were true, why hadn't Burrum picked up what Zan wanted more than anything—to go back to the meadow, to find the boulder again?

Every day she followed Burrum into the forest, to swamps, fields, across streams, up hills, and along the river, always hoping they would chance upon "her" meadow. Then at night, throwing herself down on the bed, her body twitching with weariness, she would feel a growing fear centered somewhere behind her ribs, a fear that she was losing her identity, that she was changing so much she would no longer be Zan Ford. Zan Ford? Why not face it! She wasn't Zan Ford. She was Meezzan, dummy, stranger who couldn't understand anyone, or make anyone understand her. Yes, she had picked up a handful of words and phrases—she recognized the morning greeting, she knew some names, she recognized the chant that was used before eating anything alive. But for the most part, the language was a mystery to her. She lived as if deaf, often impatient, more often frustrated. She wanted Burrum to lead her through the forest, back to the meadow where they had met. A simple wish, a simple request, but impossible to make. She didn't know the words for it, or how to put them together.

One day when they were in a group in the forest, Zan wandered off alone, pretending to look for eggs, but hoping that by some miracle she would suddenly come upon her meadow. Being alone in the forest still awed and frightened her, but how long could she go on this way? She had to break away, she had to *do* something! Underfoot, leaves and rotting vegetation were thick, a deep carpet in which small pale flowers and violently hued fungi grew profusely. There were insects everywhere; she brushed them off automatically. In a little while, she knew she'd gotten herself lost again. Fear rushed, sour, into her stomach. She flung up her arms and tried to retrace her steps, berating herself without mercy. Was it so hard for her to accept that she could no more find her way alone in the forest than Burrum, set down in the streets of Zan's city, could have found her way? *Stupid! You are supposed to be smarter than them! Use your head, dummy!* Burrum's voice calling to her cut through her self-abuse. She called back and waited meekly for the girl to appear.

Zan had wished for a miracle. Now she saw that it wasn't going to happen, and that day she began to work at learning the language, repeating words, phrases, trying to make her tongue fit around the clicks and thumps and throaty frog sounds. She listened in a new way to the voices, the talk, the calls, not letting her mind drift off, but working out what was being said. Sometimes it seemed so hard, impossible, even futile, that she became convinced she would never be able to make sense of their gabble, never be able to make Burrum understand that she *must* get back to the meadow.

On one of those days when she felt low and miserable, she sat on the river bank while Burrum swam and dived among her friends. If only, Zan thought, she could enjoy the water the way they did. Swimming with her clothes on was awful. She always felt as if she were going to sink, then afterward in her dripping heavy clothing, she would shiver and feel horrid until she dried out. Now the water, fresh and sparkling, beckoned her. Why was she, alone, out of it? It was so dumb, really. Who cared if her body was covered or uncovered? No one, not one single person, except herself. Within moments she had pulled off her clothes and jumped into the river. The shock of the cold water on her bare skin was exquisite. She swam out, the water curling over her arms. Her body felt weightless. The river stretched endlessly and the far shore was a blur of green. Her sadness lifted like morning mist off the river.

Later, when Zan came out of the water, Burrum combed Zan's hair with her fingers, then brushed it with a little evergreen whisk. Insects whined in the grass, birds called. Burrum's hand on Zan's head was warm, the sun was another warm hand on her head, and even the ache of hunger in her belly was, in its way, pleasant.

In a little while Burrum stood up and whistled for Sonte. The three of them went off to find fruit, berries, and eggs. Zan pointed to the nest, to an egg, to a hawk circling in the sky, listened carefully, repeated what Burrum said, till she had got it right.

Later that same day, Burrum handed her a fruit and, hardly thinking, Zan said, "Habuiti feuoi, Burrum." *My thanks to you, Burrum.* Hearing herself, she broke into a huge grin.

"Ahhaa, Meezzan," Burrum cried. She and Sonte hugged Zan and made her repeat the phrase over and over, each time their faces breaking into smiles as proud as those of parents whose infant has said its first words.

15

O n the horizon, a pale new moon rose slowly. Up and down the mountain, fires flickered in the darkness. Zan sat cross-legged near the fire, Burrum on one side of her, Burrum's grandmother nodding on the other side. "Auuhmaa," Zan whispered under her breath, reminding herself of Burrum's name for the old woman. She had finally put names to all the faces in Burrum's family. Besides Burrum's grandmother and parents, Zan had identified her little brother, Lishum, plus two aunts, three uncles (one so young Zan had first thought him to be an older brother), a baby, and a small girl named Ai'ma. However, she still had to work at things, pausing to remind herself that the pregnant girl who walked around with her hands clasped under her belly was Burrum's aunt, Ainu. Or that Burrum's mother, with the missing teeth and the tips of two fingers on her left hand also missing, was called Farwe.

Trying to pick up the gist of the conversation, Zan bent forward. Ainu, who had a big horsy laugh, was saying something about Burrum and Sonte. The other aunt, Mai'bu (it sounded like My Boo to Zan), who was plump and usually quiet, threw in a few words. Zan caught Sonte's name, plus the word "Sussuru."

Then there was a burst of laughter and Burrum dropped her head on Zan's shoulder, giggling and trying to hide her face. The talk swung to the Bihaw berries that Burrum's father, Raaniu, had found earlier in the day. Zan remembered picking them once. They were hard and very green, but surprisingly sweet. She caught the word "run." Or was it "walk"? She could rarely keep the two straight: walk was tsi; run was walk-walk, tsi-tsi. Usually, by the time she had figured out whether it was either walk or run, she'd forgotten if she'd heard one tsi or two tsi's. Now, always a couple of beats behind, she realized that a bear had also been picking from the Bihaw bushes and had made Raaniu run.

Standing up, Raaniu made paws near his chin, hanging his head so that his neck thickened and growling ferociously. Lishum squealed and ran into his mother's lap, making everyone laugh again. He grabbed his mother's breast and sucked noisily. Two or three times a day he would do this. Lishum was a little older than Buddy, but full of the same mischievous sparkle. Often Zan would squat down, trying to talk to him, rub his curls, or draw pictures in the dirt for him.

"Meezzan, you come over here by me." Zan looked up to see who was speaking to her. It was Farwe, and Zan had half risen to her feet in response before she realized that, for the first time, she had grasped a complete sentence without having to work it out slowly in her mind. At once she doubted her ears.

Farwe smiled, showing the gaps in her mouth. Delicately, she picked a bit of matter from between her front teeth. This done, she called again, "Meezzan, you come over here by me, daughter." Once again, the words fell clearly on Zan's ears.

"Farwe," she cried. "Farwe—!" She wanted to tell

the woman what she felt, the excitement, the joy that made her heart rise and fall behind her ribs like a balloon. *She had understood.*

She sat down next to Farwe who gave her arm several little affectionate pinches. "Farwe—" Zan said. "Ah, Farwe—" She struggled among the ragbag of words and phrases she had painfully accumulated. The woman looked at her, smiling, waiting. Next to Farwe, Keyria, Ainu's man, also leaned toward her, his large, soft eyes fixed on Zan as if she were about to say something important. "Farwe . . . Farwe . . . Farwe, here I am," she said at last, triumphantly. There were howls of delight. It was the first real sentence she had spoken in their language.

After that night, the language began to fall into place. It was as if Zan had been standing at the bottom of a well, trying to hear what the people at the top were shouting down to her, but catching only muffled, blurred sounds that sometimes made a little sense, but more often drove her into a frenzy of frustration. Suddenly, she was up there almost at the top of the well, and she could hear and understand things that had mystified her only days before. The more she understood, the freer she felt, as if she were bursting out of confining walls.

But, to Zan's dismay, she discovered that understanding was easier than being understood. She continued to mangle words so that half the time she simply amused people, while the other half she was misunderstood. "Please—you take me—to the meadow," she said to Burrum, this being the purpose of having learned the language. Burrum readily agreed, but later Zan found herself following her around the perimeter of a bog while Burrum searched for a plant whose name was pronounced almost like the word for meadow. When that was straightened out, Burrum took her to three different fields on three successive days before Zan found the words to pinpoint the meadow she meant.

"Meadow-with-Watering-Hole!" Burrum said. "Yes, I will take you to that place. What will you do there, Meezzan? I want to see if those honey flowers have bloomed yet."

"Flowers?" said Zan, who had understood almost everything. "No flowers. I want—to run—home." But as the word for home was the same as for cave, Burrum was puzzled by this response.

"One does not go to the caves in Meadow-with-Watering-Hole."

Zan tried again. "I want to run—go!—away. A far place. My home. My mother. My father. My brother like Lishum."

"But that is Beyond-the-Mountains," Burrum said. She squeezed Zan's arm. "Do not go there. Do not go away from me. My belly is sad to think you will go away from me. I will cut off a finger if you leave me."

Now Burrum was talking nonsense, or perhaps Zan had misunderstood. In the morning, however, after swimming and washing, Burrum finally agreed they could go to Meadow-with-Watering-Hole; she was in no hurry as, indeed, she never was, and stopped often to gather nuts and dig roots. Coming up on a spreading patch of small, satiny-leaved plants in the forest, Burrum knelt down and began digging. "My mother will be so happy when I bring her these M'wa roots," she said, lifting a short slender root resembling a little white carrot from the earth. She brushed off the dirt and bit into it, then offered Zan the rest. But Zan couldn't eat anything. She felt like a needle, hard, shining, sharpened to a point of expectation that was nearly excruciating. "Please—hurry, come!"

For weeks Zan had been dreaming of the moment when she would return to the boulder in the meadow. She had imagined in great detail how she would go to exactly the spot where she had first opened her eyes, how she would sit down just as she'd done in Mechanix Park, her back against the stone, her eyes squeezed shut, and then—at this point she usually skipped over "It."

She had begun to refer to that shattering, bone-shaking silverstorm as "It"—as if this would somehow encompass the awesomeness, the ferocity, the terror. "It." Not the "storm," or the "force," but the mysterious, all-encompassing "It." In her mind she let "It" blur and visualized herself immediately home. The greetings. The questions. The tears. The amazement and joy and relief. Her parents' tear-stained faces, the wonder they would feel that she was home, alive, unharmed. What they must have gone through! There was a fist squeezing behind Zan's ribs.

She followed Burrum through the forest, not even trying to focus on the path. If all went well, she wouldn't be coming back again. She linked arms with Burrum.

"I think those honey flowers will be in bloom now," Burrum said. She held up one hand, fingers spread wide, and singsonged, "Grass Moon, Moon of the Long Night, Egg Moon, Bird Flight Moon, Fire Moon, Season of Rains, Rain Moon, Moon of Tears." She smiled. "Meezzan! Then the Sussuru, the beautiful Sussuru!"

"Yes, the Sussuru," Zan said vaguely. She knew it had something to do with girls. She wished Burrum would walk faster. Was it possible that once she had hardly been able to keep up with her?

"Shall I tell you a story?" Burrum said. "Meezzan, listen, I am going to tell you about the spirit Miiawa and the Hera Hera Hutumy. This is a very great story, a story my mother told me long ago. She was told the same story by her mother, who was told by her mother. And I will tell my daugher this story, also." She peered into Zan's face.

Zan nodded, even though she only partially understood what Burrum was saying. "You will like this story," Burrum said firmly. "Long ago Miiawa lived in her forest, this very forest we are in now, and she was happy. Everything in this forest was then white, green, black. Birds, plants, animals, all were white, green, black. That was the way things were.

"One day the Hera Hera Hutumy came. These also were spirits, like Miiawa, but from another place far far away. Perhaps from Beyond-the-Mountains. Certainly not from such a fine place as this forest! Therefore, when the Hera Hera Hutumy saw how fine everything was in Miiawa's forest, how birds, plants, and animals all praised Miiawa, they were full of envy. 'You think you are the best,' they taunted Miiawa, 'but you are missing something we poor Hera Hera Hutumy have.' Miiawa said, 'Tell me what it is.' But the Hera Hera Hutumy climbed into the trees and refused to speak. Miiawa was very upset. She said, 'I must know what they have.' So she changed into the shape of Bear and stood on her hind legs, growling and putting out her great, sharp claws. To drive away Bear, the Hera Hera Hutumy made rain fall on the forest, so much rain that the forest became a lake. Miiawa changed herself into a huge bird and flew over the heads of the Hera Hera

Hutumy. 'Stop this rain,' she cried, but the Hera Hera Hutumy only screeched to each other, 'Get that noisy bird away. The waters are rising. Quickly, make some land, or we will all be drowned.' This was the kind of spirits they were. They could bring the rain, but they could not make it stop. One of them dived into the water, down, down, searching for some earth, but before this Hera Hera Hutumy could find earth, it drowned. And still the rain fell and the waters rose.

"The Hera Hera Hutumy climbed higher into the trees, and another one dived down into the water, down, down, down, very far indeed. This Hera Hera Hutumy did find a few grains of earth, but before it could bring these bits of earth up to make land, it, too, drowned. And still the rains fell. The other Hera Hera Hutumy clung to the very top branches of the trees screeching to Miiawa, 'You make some land!' But Miiawa wanted to punish them and simply flew about their heads, her wings making a great noise like thunder. Now the Hera Hera Hutumy saw that Miiawa was surely a greater spirit than they were, and they sang out, just as the waters were rising to their heads, 'Red! Red! That is what we have. Red everywhere.'

"When she heard this, Miiawa changed into the shape of an otter and dived down to the bottom of the water to get earth. This she patted into an island where all the animals and birds were safe until the rains stopped. The Hera Hera Hutumy went away, back to their own place. And everything was as before, except Miiawa was not so happy. Now she knew she did not have red in her forest. She wanted red, and really she was very unhappy.

"Then one day a girl of the People came into Miiawa's forest. This girl's blood was coming down, as it did every moon. And the blood dripped red, red, red, on the forest floor. And Miiawa, seeing this red blood, was so happy that wherever the blood dripped red, red, red, she made red flowers grow, very small red flowers. And she said to this girl, 'I am going to watch out for you. You can come into this forest without fear.' So this was true. Because Miiawa is watching, girls and women go into the forest without fear now. And every year when the little red flowers grow in the forest, all the girls whose blood has come down for the first time are happy and make the Sussuru, Miiawa's Festival.''

Burrum flung out her arms. "Meezzan! Was that not a beautiful story?"

"Yes. Yes. Hurry, come—please?" Zan said. Someplace in the middle of Burrum's tale she had gotten lost, though she had followed the bit at the end about red flowers and blood. Yes, and something about big waters, and animals (she thought) who climbed trees.

"I am waiting for my blood to come down," Burrum said. Zan knew this because Burrum had said it before, and not just once. But the first time Zan had heard the words she couldn't make out their meaning. Blood coming down? Was someone hurt? Then, after a while, she had made the connection.

Strange. Burrum talking about menstrual blood as if it were something beautiful, rather than something you really wanted to hide.

"How happy I will be when my blood comes! And you, Meezzan, has your blood come down?"

Zan shook her head. "No," she said awkwardly. She wondered if she'd ever see red flowers again without thinking of Burrum. She had been in Burrum's company for thirty-six days, according to her calendar. Now she was going to leave her and would never see her again. She wanted to say something fine and moving to Burrum, but when they came to the meadow, she didn't even know how to say goodbye. She couldn't remember ever having heard the word in the People's language. Instead she took Burrum's hands and held them tightly for a moment. "Run back—no, walk— go—to the caves." She pointed along the path. "I will —(she couldn't think of the word for 'stay')—sit here."

"Then I will sit with you," Burrum said, as if there were nothing strange in Zan's having asked to come to the meadow simply to sit there.

Zan shook her head. "No. Run back. Go back!"

"But you will get lost alone," Burrum said. "You know, Meezzan, you are like a baby in the forest. Don't be angry that I say this." She pulled at Zan's hand. "Look, over there!" She pointed to a vivid patch of yellow flowers bending slightly beneath a wind which had sprung up. "The honey flowers are in bloom."

Zan tried to remember from which direction she'd come that first day. It seemed long ago. She had forgotten how high the grass grew, and that there were several mammoth boulders like "her" boulder. A dark cloud passed across the sun.

"Sit—here," she said to Burrum and struck off into the field. What if Burrum had brought her to the wrong meadow? How could anyone tell one from another? No, that wasn't fair. Burrum knew. Zan remembered the little pond in which she had washed her steaming face. What had Burrum called this? Yes—Meadow- with-Watering-Hole.

She glanced over her shoulder. At the edge of the field, Burrum was waving to her. "Meezzan," she called, her hands cupped around her mouth, the wind blowing away her words, "Thunder comes!" She pointed upward. The sky was suddenly dark. Ragged clouds passed across the sun, massing together and throwing deep shadows over the meadow. Zan hurried distractedly from one spot to another. She circled a boulder—hers? No, too small. The meadow grasses were tinged with black, the air became sulphurous.

Zan made go-away motions to Burrum, but the girl didn't move. The grass crackled as Zan pushed forward, sure that the boulder ahead was hers. A splatter of rain fell on her head. Birds moved uneasily between the trees at the edge of the field. Thunder rumbled in the distance. Zan ran forward and there it was, the boulder. The same one, she was sure.

She dropped to the ground, back against the stone, knees drawn up. *Now. Now. Now. Let it happen.* She tensed, remembering how she had been shaken, flung, flayed. *I'm ready.* Green lightning zigzagged across the horizon. She shut her eyes, thinking of Cici, Ivan, Buddy. The names were bittersweet in her mind. But in back of her eyes she still saw the meadow grass, the blurred, dark flights of birds, and Burrum's face with that blunt little nose and the eyes so often fixed on Zan in a rather greedy, affectionate look. With an effort, she banished these images, concentrating on the past. But, of course, she meant the future—or was it the present?

Come on. I'm waiting, I'm here, come on, come on, come on, COME ON . . . Rain struck her hard in the face. Opening her eyes she saw the field, the trees, the sky. Nothing had happened. She rolled over, her forehead against the ground, and beat her fists in a rage on the damp earth. An ache of pain and self-pity filled her throat. Why had she been so sure she could make it happen, just like that, like snapping her fingers. "No," she said. "No, no, no, no."

Minute by minute, the sky darkened. Rain was now

falling steadily. Burrum called to her. Zan could hear her voice, thready, through the wind.

All right. It was only one try. She'd come to the meadow again. And again. And as many times as she had to, make "It" happen. She'd win, finally. She had to believe it. She couldn't believe anything else and go on living. She wiped her face and started back through the wet grass toward Burrum, who was waiting under a tree, holding a large leaf over her head, with another one in her free hand for Zan.

16

Try again. As week after week passed, those words Zan had said so fiercely mocked her. *Try again.* She did. Tried, and tried, and tried to make "It" happen. The field became familiar, an old friend. She could have found her way to it in the dark. The boulder was her lodestone. There, at first, she was careful to sit in a certain way, to arrange her hands just so, to concentrate on the same mental images. Nothing happened. Zero! Zilch! It made her furious.

Then she decided to change her tactics and approach the boulder in whatever mood seized her. She would grip the stone with both hands as if to force herself into it, demanding that "It" happen. Or she would lean supplicatingly, forehead bent to the rough surface, imploring, first silently, then aloud, as if the boulder were alive and willful. "Take me back," she cried. "Take me back!" The next time she might touch the surface gently, almost reverently, bending her neck to its power, making promises to God and boulder and "It" and time. *"If only you will . . . I will never do . . . I will always be . . ."* And then, the humility dry in her mouth, she would beat on it with her fists. "I hate you, I hate you."

All to no avail.

Often, there in the meadow, she visualized her home clearly, could see even small details like the worn spot on the living room rug where everyone crossed to go to the kitchen, or the tiny burn hole in her plaid wool blanket from the time she was experimenting with a magnifying glass. She could see the Woolworth green glass dessert dishes and the big lopsided copper ashtray Ivan had made in shop. She saw everything clearly, yet gradually it all seemed to become more and more unreal, as if all these things were only memories of a dream she had dreamed in a dream.

When she fell into this mood, she squeezed her head between her hands, berating herself. "Idiot! Crazy girl!" But was it crazy to wonder if she would ever see her home and family again?

Often at the caves she would take out her button, safety pin, knife, and key. At once an audience would collect, squatting and watching her every move. Sometimes she resented them. She wanted to be left alone! But other times she found it diverting to teach them something and, pointing to each object, she would name it.

"Nii'uff," they said after her, drawling the word out into two syllables. "Kee." "Baa'tun." "Saf'tee Pan." And she, as Diwera had done for her once, would say, "Eno!" But the little game became disturbing when they reached out to take her things, wanting to pass them around among themselves. She had taught Burrum to leave them alone. Now she taught everyone else. Whenever a hand stretched out, she snatched the four objects and held them behind her in her fist. Finally, she made a little bag out of softened bark to hold them and kept the bag in the special niche in the cave. She was fierce about not allowing anyone to touch it. These things were her only link to her own world.

After a while, Zan developed a special way of looking at her possessions. She would sit on the ground, legs outstretched, bark bag by her side, and slowly, deliberately, bring out the knife, then the locker key, the safety pin, and finally the button. She would arrange them on her right leg in a rough pyramid with the knife as the base, key and safety pin as the sides, and the button as the apex. Each time, she would repeat her actions in exactly the same sequence. In some way, only dimly comprehended, this precise little rite reassured her that she was herself—Zan Ford—not the girl named Meezzan who had discarded her clothes and shoes, who cut her hair with a knife, who wore only a little bark flap around her waist, sucked raw eggs, and shared a bed with nearly a dozen other people. There were some days when she felt divided, half Zan, half Meezzan. Other days she forgot about Zan and was all Meezzan.

There was one long day when she became completely involved in games with Sonte, Burrum, Akawa, Em'-Fadi, Goah, and Naku. They swam to an island to drink the juice of an acid fruit that made them giggly and frolicky. They threw each other into the water and sprawled on the beach, laughing and gossiping. And Sonte hugged Zan, rubbing his nose against her shoulder. All afternoon she was aware of him, his square firm shoulders, the way he drew his eyebrows together so fiercely, so stubbornly. She liked him. Oh, yes.

But, hours later, realizing how she had drifted away from herself, away from Zan Ford, she was struck with terror, then a numb acceptance. Wasn't it true that she would never return home? That what had happened once wouldn't happen again? She was here. Caught like

an insect in a jar with no escape. Why not stop struggling? Gradually she would forget that Zan ever existed.
She would grow up here, have children, get old, die.

But then again, there were hours and days when she
rejected Meezzan fiercely, was apart from them all,
when she drew something invisible around her, not
quite a glass wall, but a keep-away-from-me shield over
her face, in her voice, when the thought of living here
and dying here made her dizzy with despair. She would
think then about her family, about the day she was
mugged, and the morning after when Ivan took her
diary. In one way it seemed remote, like a story she'd
seen on TV a long time ago. But at the same time she
clearly remembered Billy Gold snorting with hysterical
delight over her private thoughts. And, as if the event
were fresh and new, she would feel a clenching in her
gut, and her skin would burn. Then confusion would
overwhelm her.

17

Zan had once thought that after she knew the way to Meadow-with-Watering-Hole she would do nothing but go there every day. But every day there was something else to claim her attention. Burrum laughed when Zan fretted. "Tomorrow," she said. "Tomorrow you will go." If tomorrow came and Zan did not go, then Burrum only said calmly again, "Tomorrow."

There was no sense of urgency among the People. Each day had its rhythm, its pattern, but no one rushed or hurried for anything. As far as Zan could see, the closest they got to work was gathering food and collecting fallen branches from the forest for firewood. The caves required no upkeep, clothing was minimal, and garbage was kicked aside in the cave or piled a distance from the fire.

Adults, as well as children, spent entire days in the water, floating, diving, splashing one another, and catching fish. At night, families would visit back and forth. Often there would be as many as two dozen people around Farwe's fire, talking and telling stories. One night when they had company, Burrum asked her father to sing. Raaniu stood up, crossed his hands on top of his head, and sang about walking through the forest with his daughter. "We go softly in the forest like Wind, Wind hears all that we say, Miiawa hears, We go softly in the forest."

"Do you hear my father sing?" Burrum said proudly, pinching Zan's arm, even though Zan was sitting right next to him.

Zan wondered what her parents would say if they could see how much time Burrum's people spent singing, gossiping, teasing the children and each other, or playing games. Everyone played games. A kind of pickup-sticks with tiny fish bones. Another game like bowling with water-smoothed stones. And the women had a game like a dance in which they sang and tossed a melon backwards over their shoulders to one another.

Grown women playing games! Zan could remember seeing her mother playing only once. Years before, her parents had bought her a pair of ball-bearing roller skates with red leather straps. One day she'd come home from school and seen her mother skating up and down the dark hallway outside their apartment. But the moment Zan appeared, her mother had pulled off the skates and run inside.

One afternoon Zan devised a kind of hybrid baseball-touchball game. Burrum and Sonte and the other young people eagerly took to running around the bases she laid out, shouting and enthusiastically throwing a melon to each other. Although she couldn't get across the idea of teams and competition, for several days Zan's game was what everyone wanted to do. Then they tired of it. The next afternoon they all started out to find honey, but, coming to a long sloping meadow and feeling languid from the heat, they stopped to rest.

"Aii, how cool and fresh Grandmother Earth is today," Naku said, collapsing onto the ground. She and her sister, Noomia, were usually more interested in

painting in Cave-of-No-Name than in anything else. Zan
had never been to the cave, so she had no idea of what
they painted.

Sitting in the grass, Burrum and Em'Fadi wove flowers into chains. A bit clumsily, Zan followed suit. It was
a dazzling, clear day. Everywhere pink and yellow
flowers made gay patches of color. Hills dotted with
evergreens curved upward on either side of the
meadow. Far away were the sharp blue peaks of the
mountains, ridge after ridge of mountains.

"This morning, my sister Meezzan went to Meadow-
with-Watering-Hole," Burrum said, putting on a wrist-
let of flowers and holding up her arm to admire it.
"And so the poor thing did not have any of those little
brown turtle eggs Sonte and I found."

"I don't like turtle eggs," Hakku said. "Nor does my
brother." He and his younger brother, Goah, were
handsome boys with large, egg shaped eyes. They were
inseparable.

"Oooh, those turtle eggs are *delicious*," Em'Fadi
said, patting her belly tenderly.

Akawa, Diwera's daughter, sat down gracefully next
to Zan. The loops of polished nuts and seeds around
her neck swayed with her movements. She looked at
Zan mockingly—or was it friendly? Zan couldn't decide. Akawa was tall, with a proud, almost disdainful
air. She rarely played or sang or shouted with the aban-
don of the others, and often went away on her own. She
seemed, to Zan, to give off a secret inner light. Akawa,
she thought, must be very like her mother, Diwera,
whom Zan never saw without feeling a shiver pass
through her.

"You went to that big rock again, Meezzan?" Akawa
said.

Zan nodded. Whenever she hadn't been to the boulder for a few days, she became uncomfortable and ill-at-ease because she had been eating, and playing, and sleeping well, while far away, somewhere terribly far away, her family was grieving over her.

"What is there at that rock?" Akawa asked, leaning forward, long hands clasped around her knees.

Zan shook her head, smiling slightly. She linked arms with Burrum, partly out of affection, partly to show Akawa that she was at ease. Akawa continued to stare at her.

"Meezzan." Em'Fadi touched Zan's arm. With relief, Zan turned away from Akawa's gaze. "I would go to that meadow with you," Em'Fadi said. This girl never asked for anything directly. If she wanted a fruit some-one else had, she would say, "That fruit smells so good!" and open her eyes wide until she was given a piece.

"Perhaps I will take you," Zan said kindly, although she neither needed nor wanted anyone at the boulder with her.

Puzzling over Zan's repeated trips to the meadow, Burrum had worked out for herself that Zan spoke to the spirits of her family at the boulder. This, she under-stood and approved. She was, on the whole, a very approving, easy person to be with. The one time Zan had seen Burrum truly irritated was when she tried to tell the girl about cars, telephones, hot water, TV, and airplanes. It was all incredibly clumsy, anyway; she had to say things like, "The water comes hot like sun from a hole in the wall," and "People in my place fly like birds in the sky."

Burrum didn't believe her, but more than this, she didn't even want to hear about such things. When Zan persisted in trying to make the girl believe that people flew in the sky, Burrum had turned on her, exclaiming,

"Oh, you make my stomach feel so bad with this foolish talk! I feel sick now, maybe those eggs we ate this morning were bad. Maybe you are going to get sick, too," she added spitefully. And she had stamped away, muttering to herself.

Later, however, she regained her good spirits and suggested to Zan that what Zan had really meant to say was that Beyond-the-Mountains there were spirits (like Miiawa) who could become fish, or birds, or whatever they chose.

Now she draped a necklace of flowers over Zan's neck and hugged her affectionately. Zan yawned and slid down on the ground, hands behind her head. Through half-closed lids she watched Sonte throw a stone to a point beyond the trees. At once, Hiffaru leaped up and threw a stone also, the crushed side of his face turned away from the group. His stone fell short of Sonte's, and although it shamed her a little, Zan was pleased. After Burrum, she liked Sonte the best of all the young people. He laughed at her in a way she didn't mind and taught her the names of trees, birds, plants, and insects. He was quick-tempered and when she forgot things, he would seize her face in his hands to impress his words upon her. But when she remembered well, he smiled gloriously and tugged her hair or hugged her. He was affectionate and teasing with everyone except Hiffaru. Between the two boys there were always sparks.

Tiring of throwing stones, Sonte flung himself down next to Burrum who draped him with a necklace of flowers.

Hiffaru sat down on the other side of Burrum. "Are we seeking honey today?" he said. "Let's go and find that honey."

"I don't want to do that anymore," Sonte said. He

looked around at the others. "Tomorrow, I think, we won't go for honey, either. We'll make a raft."

"A raft!" Hakku shouted, and his brother Goah echoed, "A raft! What a good idea."

"Yes, a raft!" The cry was taken up. But Hiffaru turned his head away aloofly, refusing to be drawn into the excitement.

The next day and for several days after, the young people foraged in the forest for logs that were dry, sound, and light enough to float. They shouldered each log and carried it to the river bank. There, when they had enough, they lashed them all together with vines. Late one afternoon they pushed the raft into the water. It dipped, bobbed, then floated. A cheer went up. They dived into the water, swam to the raft, and crawled aboard.

Sitting low under their weight, the raft slid smoothly down the river. Sun flecked the water. Clouds of butterflies wove through the air. The water flowed beneath them like green silk. For a moment, no one spoke, and for Zan the silence, too, was green.

That night at the fire everyone wanted to hear about the raft, and Burrum told about their trip in detail, not forgetting when Hakku had pushed Goah into the water. "Aii, those boys," the old grandmother said, her hand covering her mouth as she laughed.

A few nights later, Burrum again told the story of building the raft and floating down the river. It seemed that everything was talked over not once, but numerous times, each time eliciting laughter or groans of sympathy. Food, dreams, and animals, sickness, accidents, births, and deaths—all of these were the stuff of conversation. Everything that happened to everyone was passed around. And not only those who were living, but their grandparents, great-grandparents, and great-great-grandparents were spoken of in intimate detail. It was as if everything that had ever happened to those long-dead people was as fresh in the memories of the living as the events of their own lives.

Stories were told and re-told till Zan began to feel that she, too, knew how Aspa, Burrum's maternal great-grandfather, had burned his hand in a fire when he was a small boy. Or how Miiniu, Farwe's aunt, had once, as a girl, leaped onto the back of a deer.

"Mahu is going to tell a story," Burrum said one night, seizing Zan's hand. "Hiffaru told me. Mother, Mahu is going to tell a story!"

"Oh, let's hurry," Farwe said, shoving a last bit of food into her mouth.

It was dark and there was rain in the air, but people streamed in to settle around Mahu's fire. Zan had heard of this woman known as the Teller: an old woman with an erect back and little, fiery black eyes. Looking at no one, the Teller waited imperiously in the center of the gathering till they had quieted. Then she began her story, telling of Olima, the Great Fish Mother, from whom the first people had been created.

Zan saw Diwera in the crowd, squatting like everyone else, listening intently. Zan was surprised; she rarely saw Diwera in the groups of people that went everywhere together. (Once the Wai Wai had come noiselessly on Zan and Burrum in the forest, looked at Zan for a long moment, then walked on. Remembering this, Zan felt a chill of fear.) But for Mahu's stories about spirits, good and bad, about the Anouch'i and the Bear People, Diwera came.

Another time Mahu told Miiawa's story, acting out every part. It was extraordinary. She seemed to shed years, sex, skin, to become the cringing, sneering Hera Hera Hutumy, or a frightened animal close to drowning; then, in another moment, springing through the air, she was Miiawa, a thing of wind, leaves, and water, both spirit and woman.

After the story was told, the old woman appeared very tired and went into her cave, but for a long time Zan and Burrum, still caught up in the magic of Mahu's telling, sat before the fire.

There were stories, and there was music, too. On a night when the moon was full, Ainu, Mai'bu, and Farwe took bunches of grass and held them to their mouths, making high strange wonderful sounds. And Ainu's man, Keyria, brought out a small reed on which he blew like a flute.

The stars were large in the sky, the fire warmed Zan, Burrum's hand rested affectionately on her shoulder. And for that moment Zan was content. She looked from Farwe to Burrum to Keyria, still playing, his thin body drawn up toward the reed, moving with the haunting sounds as if he were, himself, music.

These people! Zan could no longer think of them as crude, unfeeling savages. She knew how they laughed, and played, and sang, and told stories. She knew they had nothing in the way of comfort, but seemed not to need or want anything more than they had. How strange. And how much stranger that, sometimes now, she felt almost the same way.

18

"Meezzan, Meezzan."

Zan slowly opened her eyes. It was morning, and Burrum was whispering in her ear. Zan looked toward the cave entrance, framed by trees. Was it hot outside? Raining? Foggy? Inside the cave, the temperature was always the same, day and night. Ah, the sun was shining. She stretched sleepily. When was the last time she woke, her stomach jerking in panic, as she stared at the stone walls of the cave? She couldn't remember. She only knew she no longer felt uneasy about the cave, the countless rooms, tunnels, and corridors that wound deep into the mountain. Children were never allowed to wander into those areas. It was said that long ago two little babies had been lost there and never found. Even now, on some still nights, the Auuhmaa said she could hear their Tariana crying. "Those poor babies kept me awake!" she said, after a sleepless night, and she reached to hug Lasba, her smallest grandbaby.

In general the adults showed little interest in the depths of the cave, but Foomia, Burrum's young uncle, had a passion for exploring. He'd take a torch and disappear for hours. Once, Zan and Burrum had gone a short way with him. The walls rose in places higher than the torchlight could reach. There was the gurgle of distant water and the rustling of bats. Zan had wanted to go on with Foomia, but Burrum had been uninterested. Half asleep, Zan's mind drifted into those dark passageways again . . . bats . . . and . . . a deep chasm . . . she was falling . . .

"Meezzan, don't go to sleep again!" Burrum shook her. "Meezzan, my blood has come!" The girl pointed to her thighs, which seemed to be smeared with juice. There was a hollow feeling in Zan's chest. Burrum had spoken often of the Sussuru, of her longing to be part of it, of her disappointment that her blood had not come down yet. And Zan had confided her own disappointment. "Ahh, Burrum," she said sleepily, "I am happy for you."

Now Farwe woke and was told the news. She hugged her daughter repeatedly. As Burrum's father, uncles and aunts woke, they, too, were told. The bedding where Burrum had slept was thrown off to a dark unused part of the cave, and fresh leaves were brought in. "Today you go to the Women's Stream," Ainu said. "Yes, you go to the Women's Stream!" She took Burrum by both arms and danced around with her.

Burrum sat down, out of breath, laughing and fanning her face. "When I was a little girl and went with my mother to the Women's Stream, how I longed to go by myself!"

"And now you will," Aunt Mai'bu said, holding little Lasba to her breast to suck.

"Yes," Burrum said. "Yes!" Then to Zan, "One eats only fruit there and bathes in the stream and talks with the other women."

"I remember when my blood came down for the first time," Farwe said. "Do you remember, Mai'bu? Our father dreamed of water flowing in a river from the sky.

When he woke up he felt so happy. He said that since he dreamed such a fine thing on the very night when I had my first blood, it meant I would always have a happy life." She turned to her husband. "Raaniu, did you dream a good dream for your daughter? Surely, you did! Come, tell us your dream."

Raaniu pulled at his ear. "Aii, I have no dream for my daughter," he said. "Do not be angry, daughter. I slept too well."

"I remember my dream," Zan said, as they left the cave and hunkered down around the fire. "Burrum gave me a big yellow egg, but I dropped it and it broke." In the dream Burrum had said, *Oh, no, it will never be the same.* And Zan, close to tears: *But I want it to be.*

"The egg broke? I do not like such a dream." Burrum covered her belly with her hands and twisted away when Zan reached out to her.

"Aiii, an egg breaking!" cried Farwe, pulling at her hair. "You had a bad dream for my daughter. Look how her belly hurts!" Mai'bu and Raaniu stared accusingly at Zan. She was sorry she had mentioned her dream. A dream wasn't real. Yet she remembered now that on waking she had been overcome by a mysterious sense of loss.

"What are these sad faces on this happy day!"

Pointing to Zan, Aunt Ainu gave one of her big laughs. "Everyone knows this daughter of Others is a foolish girl. She climbs trees like a fish on land. She pushes away worms and beetles. Good food. Yes, she is foolish, and I say she does not even remember her dreams properly!"

Burrum had brightened, and everyone looked relieved. "It will be good if our daughter is as clever as her mother," Keyria said proudly, patting Ainu's belly.

Mai'bu found a smooth little pebble and gave it to
Burrum. "Will you make your marks for your blood on
this, niece?" With the sharp edge of another stone, Burrum made a single scratch on the pebble. Mai'bu jiggled
her baby on her hip. "That is the way," she said ap-
provingly.

"Each morning, now, you must make your mark,"
Farwe added. "Tonight, look at the moon. When it
rises again as it is tonight, your blood will come again,
too."

Smoothing the little pebble in her hands, Burrum
turned to Zan. "Miiawa has smiled at me. Before I go
to the Women's Stream let's find some eggs and leave
them at her grove. Then, perhaps she will smile on you,
also." She squeezed Zan's arm. "Don't be sad. Your
blood will come down, soon, I am sure of it."

"I'm not sad," Zan said, pulling up the corners of her
mouth. "See my smile." But it was true that in her heart
she felt envious of Burrum.

For two days, Burrum went to the Women's Stream;
then she told Zan her belly was longing for her, and on
the third day she didn't go, but used the leaves of the
Xongo bush, which were soft and spongy and soaked
up blood.

Those two days Burrum was away were the first Zan
had been without the other girl, and on the second day
she decided to explore the unoccupied caves. How ignorant and fearful she had been at first about the caves!
But since those early weeks she had gone, at one time
or another, into almost every occupied cave, surprised
to find each one different in some way.

Carved out of limestone thousands, or perhaps millions, of years ago by the river that now flowed far
below them, most of the caves were large and spacious.

But some were small, cozy, almost cramped. Some were entered by climbing up into them, some had sloping passageways that led downward to the main room. Some had thick inner walls with "windows" in them. Most extended deep into the heart of the mountain.

One day, high on the mountain, as she and Burrum hurried for home at dusk, a long black stream of bats had suddenly flown out of an empty cave. Zan's questions about the cave and about other empty caves were always shrugged off. Now, with Burrum away, she slipped off on her own, determined to satisfy her curiosity.

Following a faint path, Zan picked her way up the mountain, alternately losing and finding her way again. Finally, she fixed a clump of trees in her mind as a reference point; she had a horror of getting lost. The wind blew the distant but comforting sound of voices toward her. When she found the bat cave entrance, she entered, waiting for her eyes to adjust. Underfoot there was a sudden scuttling, clicking murmur of many creatures. She moved forward, guiding herself with a hand against the wall. A salamander, glistening and slimy red, blinked from a damp recess. She continued slowly on, till gigantic blocks of stone barred her path—great square chunks that might have been hewed by giants. Long ago, the ceiling must have fallen in. Had people lived in the cave then? A family like Burrum's? She thought of them sleeping . . . a child sucking its thumb . . . two sisters with their arms around one another . . . then, without warning, tons of stone raining down, crushing them to pulp. A chill climbed her back. She hurried out into the sun. The wind passed over her like water. She took a long deep breath of air into her lungs. Alive! She was alive!

She went on, looking for another cave. At the crest of a hill, she stopped. All around her, hills rose and fell. Far below, the valley plunged away like a green horse. She heard nothing but the sleepy buzzing of insects and wind among the leaves. A sense of herself as insignificant, no more than a leaf on a tree, came over her. She wrapped her arms around herself. She missed Burrum.

She walked beside a stream winding through a rocky bed. As she climbed higher the stream cut more deeply between its stony walls. The air cooled, ferns and mosses grew thickly over the ledges of gray stone. Rounding a corner, she was suddenly confronted by a huge rock balanced on a high narrow pointed rock base. It rose perhaps twenty feet into the air and looked like nothing so much as an enormous stone mushroom made by a gigantic baby.

Standing beneath this formidable stone sculpture, Zan again felt shaky, vulnerable. Softly, as if her footsteps might unbalance the great round cap and send it pitching down to crush her, she tiptoed away.

She followed the stream until it ran straight into the mouth of a cave. Tall lacy ferns and clumps of thick green moss grew luxuriantly around the entrance. She stepped into a room lit by the rays of the late afternoon sun, the near wall green with algae. Water dripped slowly from the ceiling high overhead, splashing onto the gravelly floor and into the stream. She ducked into a tunnel, walking hunched over; straightening, she found herself in a huge chamber lit by long streaks of light from openings in the distant ceiling. Stone stalagmites rose like cones of encrusted jewels from the floor and stalactites hung like frozen jeweled fingers from the ceiling. Zan was wildly excited by their beauty. She touched one of the delicate stone fingers, half expecting it to melt beneath her hand's heat. The light streaking in through the ceiling made her think of cathedrals, churches, holy places.

"Beautiful," she said. "Beautiful." The walls took her voice and bounced it back and forth. ". . . ul . . . ul . . . ull . . . ull . . ." For a moment the echo frightened her.

The stream that flowed through the center of the room poured into a wall and disappeared. The room itself narrowed at one end to a low passage. Zan stuck her head into the tunneled darkness. She would have to crawl on hands and knees to explore farther. Then, behind her, there was a shout that echoed against the walls like thunder. She pulled out of the tunnel. A black shape, glowing around the edges, rushed toward her. She flung up her hands in fear.

Then she saw that it was only Toufa, an old man with wisps of white hair all over his body and a wispy white beard. "I am Meezzan," she said quickly, confused and shaken by the wild look in his eyes, thinking he was going to hit her, thinking that he didn't remember her, he was so old. "Meezzan," she said urgently. "Meezzan, I am in Farwe's cave—"

Paying no attention, he grasped her arm and pulled her out into the daylight, demanding to know what she was doing in Cave-of-No-Name.

"I do not understand," she said several times, wishing Burrum was with her to explain both to her and to the old man. "I was looking. I did not do anything bad."

"The bones are in there," he said. "The bones are there!"

She shook her head dumbly. Bones? She didn't know what he was saying.

"I am the Keeper. I keep the Death Drum and watch over the bones. I must know all who go here, all, all! Why did you go into this cave? My father was the Keeper, and my father's father, and his father before him, and all my fathers. Their bones are there, as will be my bones. And your bones," he added.

Shivering, she looked at him mutely. She wanted him to let go of her. She couldn't make sense of anything he said. His old man's mouth was wobbling and his eyes were teary and faded with age. She felt a wrench of pity, of sorrow that she had upset him, for whatever reason. She wanted to say she was sorry, but realized she had never learned to say this. Perhaps there were no words for it? Then she remembered what Burrum sometimes said to her. She touched the old man's arm, on which the blue veins stood out like brittle sticks. "Do not be angry with me," she said.

Then he let go of her arm, and she followed him meekly back along the path beside the stream, thinking that there were still many things about the People she didn't know or understand. She thought of snakes, and Diwera, and dreams, and how Ainu had called her daughter of Others.

That night, all these thoughts crowded in on her and she didn't sleep well, but lay awake for a long time, staring over her folded arms into the starry night beyond the cave, thinking of her family.

19

N'ati, the mother of Sonte, entered Diwera's cave without greetings or a gift. Nevertheless, Diwera welcomed her calmly. "Sit by my hearth, N'ati. Come, the fire is warm." When a visitor crossed one's threshold, even if that visitor was panting, that was the time to offer hospitality. "I have only now cooked some of those fat white worms that live in the Enga nut," Diwera went on cordially. "How happy I am that you have come in time to eat with me." She pushed a worm-filled packet of singed leaves toward N'ati.

"My stomach is full of fear now," N'ati said. "There is no room for food." Wearing no necklaces or armlets, scrawny and graceless, she pushed her finger stumps, the marks of her bereavement, through her hair, and rushed straight to the point. Her sister, Yano, whose belly was big with child, was in her time, but the child was stubborn and did not want to come. All through the night, Yano had been trying to push the baby out. Now the sun was high in the sky and still the child did not come. "My belly hurts for my sister. She is having pain, so much pain, she walks up and down, up and down, then squats down and screams. Everyone is very frightened. Come!" She seized Diwera's arm. "You must come at once!"

"This is not Yano's first child," Diwera said, rummaging among the roots and herbs on a ledge. She was quite sure the bitter Masi herb she had just found in the forest would do well for Yano. "Why are you so frightened?"

"That other child died," N'ati said, her face twisting. Wailing, she began to recount the unhappiness of that other birth and death. N'ati was older than Diwera and, therefore, Diwera kept her face smooth and did not interrupt. Perhaps Yano was having a difficult birth, but perhaps not so difficult as N'ati said. It could be that N'ati, guarding her sister too well, wished Yano to have no pain at all. Was this not N'ati's way?

Once, long ago, N'ati had had a beautiful young man. N'ati loved Fusiawa so well that she did everything for him. She gave him fish and fruit; she dug the Tinitini tubers he especially liked, although she had to go far from the caves to find them. If he wanted, she would have gladly stuck her hand every day into a swarming beehive to bring him honey. As he didn't have much to do to be well fed, Fusiawa grew plump and lethargic. N'ati's old father, jealous and discontented at not being properly and respectfully cared for anymore, complained that if N'ati could, to spare Fusiawa a few steps, she would make his water for him.

Shortly after Sonte was born, Fusiawa had been bitten by a snake. Perhaps he could have been saved, but he had grown so fat and lazy that without N'ati to tell him what to do (she was away, digging Tinitini for him) he did nothing. By the time she returned, he was stiff on the ground, his legs, arms, and head swollen like rotten fruit. When he died, N'ati, in her grief, insisted that two of her fingers be chopped off down to the base.

Without Fusiawa to care for, N'ati turned her energy and jealous devotion upon the rest of her family— Sonte, her old father, her sisters and their men and children.

Since Diwera's son, Hiffaru, had been promised to Burrum, N'ati had been heard to speak Diwera's name in anger. All this Diwera knew.

"My sister Yano is crying," N'ati said, grasping Diwera's arm so hard that it was painful. "Do you not hear me? Why do you move so slowly? Come! Hurry! My sister needs you."

"Yes, I am coming," Diwera said. "I want to find something else for Yano. Those stinging nettles to rub across her belly. I gathered them only yesterday." N'ati, she thought, had surely spoiled her sister as she had spoiled her man. "Did you not give Yano a bit of Wapa wood between her teeth to help her with her pain?" Diwera asked.

"Yes, yes, but she spits it out. She has so much pain she cannot keep it between her teeth. Come!"

Holding the nettles, Diwera followed N'ati quickly down the path. If, indeed, Yano was in pain and need, then she must not delay.

Yano had prepared her birthing spot near the river in a secluded place. Diwera approved of the place she had chosen. The child could be washed quickly when it came, and the cold water would make the infant cry out. There was nothing more satisfying than the first healthy scream of a newborn.

There were a good number of women attending Yano, and a few men squatting silently beneath a tree, among them Yano's man, Huopi. There was a fine bed of fresh grass laid down for Yano, but instead of squatting there, singing to her child to come into the world,

Yano beat her head against a tree, moaning shamelessly. "The Wai Wai has come to help you," N'ati said, plucking at her sister's upraised arms. "Here is Diwera. Come, sister, come, Yano, turn your face. Speak to Diwera."

Diwera set down the bundle of nettles. She took Yano's arm and led her to the bed of grass. Yano looked at Diwera with big, fearful eyes. She was dripping with sweat, and her skin was a poor color. Diwera spoke calmly and gave her the crushed Masi herb she had brought. It had a bitter taste and Yano screwed up her nose. "Eat it, chew it well, mix it with your saliva and swallow it slowly," Diwera said, her voice dropping into a rhythmic, reassuring singsong. She gestured to the other women to come closer. They clustered around Yano, forming a wall.

At Diwera's direction they rubbed Yano's arms and legs briskly, warming her flesh. Color slowly came up into Yano's face. She finished the last of the crushed herb and seemed calmer. When she again began shouting as the infant pushed to get out, the women rubbed the stinging nettles across her swollen belly to draw away the pain.

"Oooo! Oooo!" Yano screamed without shame. Chanting, they again drew the stinging nettles down across the tight flesh, calling on the pain to come out of Yano and into the nettles.

Long before the sun was gone, a perfect boy child was born. The birth cord had been cut and tied, when someone noticed that the child wasn't breathing. Diwera scooped the infant into her arms and sucked at his nostrils. A gush of liquid poured into her mouth. The child screwed up its face and cried, "Ahh. Ahhh, ahhh, ahhh," making everyone laugh with pleasure. The men beat their hands against their thighs, and the father took the child into his arms, holding him up proudly.

That evening, from all the caves, from up and down the mountain, people gathered around the fire outside N'ati's cave to see the new infant. A large circle was drawn around the fire by the new father, who chanted as he dragged a stick through the earth. *In this circle my son will live, and in this circle my son will die. Sun comes in the morning and Sun sleeps in the night. My son will live in this circle and Sun will rise for him. Moon comes in the evening and Moon sleeps in the day. My son will live in this circle and Moon will rise for him.*

Zan was there with Burrum's family. The men sang, loudly, lustily, praising the new mother. As they sang, the child was passed from hand to hand, its thin limbs wavering in the air. Even Lishum held the infant for one moment, pressing his lips solemnly against the round forehead before passing the child to Zan. As she kissed the baby and handed him on to waiting arms, a chill of pleasure crept into her stomach.

Later, the new father called on the women to sing. "Sing your songs, you women. We men will listen and learn them, and sing them, too!" This caused an outburst of delighted laughter. At that moment, turning to say something to Burrum, Zan saw Diwera in the crowd, staring straight at her.

Unconsciously, Diwera clenched the fingers on one hand. For many moons she had been watching Meezzan, trying to understand, to penetrate the girl's otherness. This Meezzan was strange. Different in her ways, different in her Ta. She moved like a child who hadn't yet learned how the earth fits her feet. She knew nothing of what a person should know to live. She was different, too, in her flesh, bigger than others, with heavier bones. Her skin color was not pleasant and soft like good earth sifted through the fingers, but covered with those little spots that she named "frek'ulls." She had them everywhere, on her back, her face, her arms. Yet, alarming as all that was, Diwera had at first sensed some purpose, like a bright fire, in the girl. She had thought perhaps the spirits called to the girl as they called to Diwera herself. She had even thought once of taking this girl to live in her cave to teach the ways of Miiawa and the forest. But she had counseled herself to move like the hawk, which flew so slowly, in circles, diving for its prey only when it was sure.

So she had circled Meezzan, and watched, and waited. As the moons passed, doubt and fear grew in her belly and often awakened Diwera from sleep. At such times, looking over at the sleeping form of her daughter, Diwera would sigh deeply, her thoughts turning from Meezzan to herself as a girl, then again to her disappointment in her daughter, and at last again to Meezzan.

Zan tried to stare back at Diwera, as if unaffected, unafraid. She wanted to say something brave and forthright. *Why do you look at me all the time? I don't bother you. Why don't you leave me alone!* But under the impact of that steady, measuring brown gaze she was forced to look away, flushing hotly with a shame and fear she didn't understand. And it came to her again, as it had before, that she was still a stranger in a strange land in a strange time.

20

When the first pale loop of Fire Moon appeared in the night sky, Sonte, Goah and two other boys went to live by the river with nothing but a bit of fire. No one could approach them, not even their mothers. They were learning to be men and could eat only seeds and roots. They could not speak, cry, or make loud noises. They could, however, sing. Therefore, every day the men who had lived the longest and were most deeply respected went to the river where the boys had made a hearth for themselves. Standing hidden among a thicket of trees, they sang men's songs. After each song, they waited for the boys to sing back to them. Cupping their ears, the old men would cry, "What is this? I cannot hear anything. Are those the voices of men, or the buzzing of insects? What! I am listening for the men's songs, but all I hear is the chatter of the Tan Tan bird, that foolish bird who can only say, tan, tan, tan, tan, tan, tan!"

The boys would sing again, singly and together, at the top of their breath, carefully pronouncing the words. If they made mistakes, the old men would cry out, "Whose son is singing that way? Teach your tongue to sing those songs properly!" And they would walk back and forth among the trees, their hands clasped behind them, singing in their old men's voices.

When Fire Moon had grown fat and round, and the old men were satisfied that the boys knew the songs, they told the women, "Now it's time for your sons to have honey."

The next morning, before dawn, Burrum and Zan joined the other women and girls and small children. "That honey tree is far away," Burrum said, yawning, "and we want to get there when the bees are still drowsy. Then they are dull and forget how to fight." The sky was dark. A few stars glinted silver. Mist wreathed the trees. N'ati led the way, holding a smoldering brand. "We will go now, to get honey for my son, Sonte, and for the others," she said. "You, Lishum, you, Manawa, you other children, don't go off the path." Quietly, yawning, their breath steaming in the cool air, they filed down the mountain, stopping once to drink from a stream bubbling out of a mossy place.

As the dark faded and morning light filtered into the forest, the children yawned less, let go of their mothers and sisters and ran back and forth along the straggling line. The women talked and laughed. Zan walked with Burrum and they, too, talked quietly of different things, of Lishum, of Meadow-with-Watering-Hole, where Zan still continued to go, and of the Sussuru, which was no longer so remote. Zan wondered again about the Sussuru, Miiawa's Festival. Why was it so important? Why, whenever she spoke of it, did Burrum's face light up?

The path wound uphill along a narrow stone ledge overgrown with stunted trees. They came across a huge peccary whose foot had been trapped between two stones. The piglike creature had probably died several days before. Its bloated body, the size of a bull, was a vile grayish green. "Oh, you of the first race, how ugly you smell," Burrum shouted. She grabbed Zan's hand and they ran past the corrupted animal, holding their breath and exploding into relieved laughter when they could no longer smell it.

The women and children emerged onto an open plateau broken by great slabs of red rock. They crossed two open fields and climbed another hill. On the crest of the hill, the honey tree, a hollow tower, scarred and battered, rose above the other trees. The wind creaked through its ancient, leafless branches as the women danced around it, knocking on the thick trunk and calling to the bees to come out. They built a fire of grass and leaves, feeding it lavishly till smoke encircled the tree. Burrum thrust a stick into a hole in the tree and brought it out dripping with honey. "The honey! The honey for my son," N'ati cried in delight. Everyone dipped a finger into the honey and licked off the sweetness. The next chunk was wrapped in a leaf for carrying back to the boys. Smoke puffed into the air. A low moan emerged from inside the tree. "The bee people are talking," Lishum said. The moan grew louder. From high above their heads, the bees spilled out, a black-gold stream pouring straight for the honey seekers. Zan had a brief moment of fear before she realized that the bees, drunk on smoke, were too groggy to find their targets. To everyone's amusement they managed only to sting Lishum on his upper arm. Lishum scratched the stinger out with his fingernail and went right back to the honey.

On their return, the women carried the chunks of leaf-wrapped honey to the boys, who devoured it and then plunged into the river to bathe. After this, surrounded on all sides by their families and friends, the boys went back to their caves.

Only a few days later, the Season of Rains began. Day after day, morning and afternoon, in an unbroken rhythm, rain poured from the darkened sky, while wind bent the trees and sent birds flying like leaves through the air. Whitecaps foamed over the river. Nothing could be heard but the pounding of water on trees, rocks, and earth. Between morning and afternoon, the storm would break, and for a while the sky would be washed clean.

Then Zan, emerging from the cave, or perhaps a hollow tree where she had sheltered from the rain, would drink in air that was sweet enough to taste. Every day, the sweetness of the air and the water surprised her afresh. Sometimes, lying on the bank of the river, drinking, she would suddenly recall the metallic taste of water at home and how it often came out of the faucet stained a dingy yellow.

But she didn't like the daily rains. She couldn't get used to being wet and then dry, and then wet again. Burrum, however, was overjoyed. "Rain Moon and Moon of Tears. That is all, Meezzan!" Then the red flowers would bloom in the forest, and Burrum would take part in the Sussuru. Hardly a day passed but that she mentioned the festival.

Early one afternoon before the rain, Zan, Burrum, and the other young people, with Lishum and Ai'ma following them, went out searching for the Gikko, a queer, twisted tree with clusters of long sausage-shaped fruits. After plucking the fruit, they broke them open to expose the fat seeds, which they sucked hollow.

When the sky darkened and the wind sprang up, bringing the rains, they tore off the thick, flat Gikko leaves and, covering their heads, hunkered down beneath the trees. After the rain stopped, the air was cool, even though the sun had emerged. Zan shivered. "A fire. Let's build a fire," she said, and everyone scattered to find dry wood and tinder.

As he often did, Lishum trailed Zan, helping her gather twigs and leaves. A branch, split down the middle, was stuffed with plant fibers and placed on the growing heap of twigs. Breaking off the tough-looking stem of a bamboo-like plant, Sonte threaded it through the split branch, then pulled it vigorously up and down through the crumpled fibers. Nothing happened. Hiffaru took over. His arms flew up and down in a blur of motion. The plant tinder burst into a little shower of sparks, which he quickly blew up into a fire.

"That is the way to make a fire," Hiffaru said with satisfaction.

Sonte's face darkened. He stalked off and pulled himself up into a tree.

"Come down here by the fire," Burrum said coaxingly. "Sonte, come and sit with all of us."

"The fire is good," Zan added, hoping Sonte would come back at her call. But he turned his face away, whistling as if he were perfectly indifferent to all of them. Since the boys' ceremony he had become, if anything, more stubborn than before, and more openly hostile to Hiffaru. But that went both ways. Right now, Hiffaru looked delighted to have irritated Sonte.

Throwing more wood into the fire, Zan stretched out her hands. Next to her, Lishum stretched out his hands, also. When she shifted, he shifted. When she stood up, he stood up. Each time he imitated her, he threw her a mischievous, sparkling glance.

"Lishum, little fish eyes, I have a brother like you," Zan said.

"I know this," he said.

"Yes, you do. I have told you this before."

"Tell me again," he said. "I want to see your little brother." He looked around. "Meezzan! Where is he? At the caves? Who is his mother?"

"His mother is—Bernice."

"Burr-neess!" He chortled over the name. "Burr-neess! Where is she?"

"Yes, where is she?" his cousin Ai'ma said in her deep voice.

"She's at my home," Zan said.

Lishum folded his arms across his chest, regarding Zan seriously, then shook his head. "Meezzan, here is your home, your cave! No Burr-neess!"

"I have another home," she said. "You know this. I told you this, also."

"I forgot." He sounded dubious. "Where is it?" Frowning, he looked around. "Oh, at the caves, yes, now I know!"

"No, not there, foolish little fish. Another place," Zan said. "Far away."

"Far away? Where is that? Where is far away?" It was difficult, perhaps impossible, for Lishum to understand. His whole world was contained by the river, the caves, the forest, the meadows and streams and swamps he was already beginning to know well, just as Zan had learned the streets of her neighborhood when she was a small girl. But even then, when she was as small as Lishum, she had already known that the world was crowded with people. It had never surprised her when she went shopping with her mother to go on thronged streets, or into stores crowded with strangers, to see everywhere countless, unknown people. Lishum, on the other hand, knew everyone in the world. Why not? Didn't they all live in the caves? And hadn't everyone always lived in the caves since the first People were created by Olima, the Great Fish Mother, who had swum out of the river to cast them forth from her belly?

That Zan came from another place where there were other people was actually incomprehensible to the little boy. He had heard of Beyond-the-Mountains, but it was only a phrase. It was not real like Place-of-Night-Sun where, someday, when he was very very old like his Auuhmaa, he would go to meet all of the people whose spirits had left their bodies. He decided that Zan was teasing him.

"You don't live far away, you live in the cave, with me and Burrum, and everyone," he said, settling the discussion. "Look what Akawa has! I want some ants!"

Akawa, her neck set at its usual proud angle, long arms moving gracefully, was prodding a huge, reddish ant mound with a stick. Dozens of large, shiny red ants rushed out to repair the damage to their home. Akawa selected one to eat.

Licking his lips, Lishum hunkered down next to her and captured an ant. Holding it up in the air between thumb and forefinger, he sang out in his high voice, "Little brother ant, I will eat you now. May your Ta be happy in Place-of-Night-Sun. Do not be angry with me, I am hungry." With that he bit off the ant's abdomen, tossed away the rest and crunched happily. "Oh, little brother ant, you taste so good." He reached for another.

Burrum had also gone to the ant mound. "Meezzan, this is for you." She held out an especially large red ant. Holding back laughter, the other young people watched Zan. Although she was no longer overcome with revulsion when someone ate a slug, Zan continued to refuse the offerings of beetles, ants, grubs, or worms. And everyone continued to be amused by her refusals. None of them could understand her distaste for such good food. Now she was about to refuse again, automatically, when something stopped her. *I'm going to eat that ant*, she thought. A strange feeling took hold of her, a feeling all green and cool and lovely, as if her bare feet had grown from the soil, and her skin from the trees, as if she belonged to all of them and to the rain-wet soil and to the ants, too. She felt that she belonged in a way that made it right and good to eat the ant. Taking the insect from Burrum and bringing the struggling creature to her lips, she said, "Little brother ant, may your Ta be happy in Place-of-Night-Sun." She bit off the abdomen and chewed bravely.

"Meezzan ate the ant, Meezzan ate the ant," Lishum chanted, dancing in delight around her. Ai'ma joined in with her deep voice. "Say it's good, say that little brother ant tastes good."

Chewing hard, Zan swallowed. The ant tasted slightly acid and watery, like an unripe blackberry. Hunkering down near the mound, she picked up another one and handed it to Sonte, who had left the tree. "These ants are very good," she said, as if she ate them every day. "Eat more, there are many." Then, impishly, she added what Sonte had told her so often, "You must thank them, you know, or else they will turn to poison in your belly!" She selected another ant for Burrum. She felt almost foolishly delighted with herself.

"Give *me* an ant, Meezzan." Lishum leaned on her shoulder. "I want you to give me one," he said jealously.

After Lishum, she saw Em'Fadi watching her with big, begging eyes, so Zan picked out an ant for her. Then it became a playful, teasing ceremony in which everyone—the inseparable brothers, Goah and Hakku, Hiffaru, Foomia—each had to have an ant selected by Meezzan. They were so absorbed that no one noticed Diwera passing a little distance away. The Wai Wai had heard the laughter and had seen the group by the ant mound. At once she picked out Akawa, part of the group, yet slightly separate, as always. Aii, that Akawa. Diwera's thoughts took a familiar path. The girl would neither swim in the water, nor fly in the air. She would take an interest neither in having a man, nor in learning all that her mother could teach her.

Hidden from the young people, Diwera saw how they hovered around Meezzan, like bees around a flower.

For many moons now she had been watching Meezzan. The girl had come to the People after Moon of Berries. She had been with them in Llachi Moon, Moon of Bear People, Beaver Moon, Grass Moon, Moon of the Long Night, Egg Moon, Bird Flight Moon, Fire Moon, and Rain Moon. Now it was Moon of Tears. So many moons! And still, whenever she saw the girl, Diwera felt as if there were thorns in her belly. It was the powers of the girl. The powers that Meezzan gave to no one, no matter how politely, how sweetly they phrased their desire. Nii'uff, for instance, was much in Diwera's thoughts. Her son, Hiffaru, often spoke of it. It was sharper than the sharpest cutting stone. It could do many things. It chopped, *tunk! tunk! tunk!* and a root or tuber was cut into bits. Thrown into the air, Nii'uff turned, tumbled, and dived straight into the earth like a diver from a high rock straight into the river. Taken from the earth, it hid away its bright sharpness in its shell, like a turtle withdrawing. In the shell it could no longer cut and dive, but Meezzan had only to give a small tug and out came its tongue, sharp, bright like sun on water.

Besides Nii'uff, Meezzan had other powers, none ever known before to Diwera. These powers the girl often took out and spoke to. Kee, yellow like the yolk of birds' eggs, big-headed, one-legged; Baa'tun, small like a pebble, white as a flower, with tiny blank eyes; and Saff'tee Pan, whose mouth when closed was quiet, but which with a press of the thumb sprang open to show a pointed tongue that could draw a drop of blood.

Often Diwera had come upon Meezzan arranging these things on her outstretched leg. At such times Diwera felt fear and anger that she did not know which spirits Meezzan called with her powers. She had seen the young people clustering about her, staring, asking respectfully to touch Kee or Baa'tun. But Meezzan kept these powers to herself, as if she would lose something by giving them away. Could such a thing be? It was contrary to everything Diwera knew to be true. If she, for instance, gave away a bracelet, a shell, or herbs for sickness, then and only then did they gain their power for good. What one kept for oneself was of little value and brought the keeper no happiness. To give was to enhance one's strength, one's goodness, one's esteem in the eyes of others. If she, Diwera, kept her knowledge and her songs, her chants and cures to herself, then she would not be fit to be Wai Wai. She would be laughed at and scorned. But this Meezzan was not scorned. Her strangeness, her differentness fascinated the young people.

Diwera moved on past the ant mound. *Why are you afraid of that girl?* she scolded herself. *That girl is not a snake.* She rubbed her belly, calming herself. *This Meezzan is only a girl! Am I, the Wai Wai, afraid of a girl?*

Later that day, Diwera again saw Meezzan arranging her powers on her leg. Saff'tee Pan, Kee, Baa'tun, and Nii'uff. Diwera's stomach jerked. She moved closer, yet closer, and for the first time saw that on the big head of Kee there were many tiny marks, like fresh bird tracks, going this way and that way. Fearless, yet somehow deeply afraid, Diwera stared at those marks.

That night she threw many pieces of rotting Lasba wood into her fire, seeking in the green flames the knowledge of Meezzan's powers. Were they powers for good, or powers that would hurt the People? She stared into the flames till tears ran from her eyes, and there she saw many terrible things, but none of them could she understand. She saw towering shapes, roaring flames, things flying through the air like birds, but not birds. She saw people running like ants, here and there, crashing into one another and then running on again. She saw enormous screeching snakes ramming through the womb of Grandmother Earth. And in her head she heard unearthly, inhuman screams.

When the Lasba wood was nothing but ashes, she sat for a long time, gripping her shoulders, her hands cold as the hands of the dead. What did it mean? She had no answers. She knew only that it had to do with Meezzan, and that she must go on watching the girl. For she was the Wai Wai of the People and, like a mother with her children, she must let no harm come to those in her care. In her belly, where everything was told finally, she feared Meezzan, feared what she might yet bring to the People.

21

The setting sun flung long purple shadows across the land; moisture rose from the trees, and birds called in the cooling air. The sound of voices raised in argument brought a crowd to N'ati's cave where Farwe and N'ati were hurling accusations back and forth. No one knew exactly what had caused the outburst. N'ati said she was insulted because Farwe had not come to help her sister Yano at the birth of her child. "Do you know how you have hurt me?" N'ati cried, making a fist and pounding her belly. "You have hurt me here! Your mother's mother was my father's mother's sister, and you were not there."

Farwe did not deny this, but asked why N'ati brought this matter up now, long after the happy birth of the child. Perhaps, she said, N'ati was really upset about something else? Perhaps N'ati was unhappy about the good fortune Farwe's family enjoyed? Farwe's daughter, Burrum, would someday have Hiffaru as her man, while N'ati's son, Sonte, would have to wait for his woman. Moreover, her daughter, Burrum, had found that girl Meezzan who lived with them in their cave with those things she had—Baa'tun with his clever eyes, Nii'uff that cut better than any stone, Kee, and Saff'tee Pan. Perhaps, Farwe said, striving to keep her voice pleasant and her face from crumbling into an angry mask, perhaps N'ati did not like all these good things happening to Farwe's family? Perhaps it made N'ati's son ache in his belly to know that Farwe's family—

"My son's belly is good," N'ati interrupted loudly. "Who says anything about my son's belly?" The cords of her neck stood out like vines. "Who says this thing about my son? Oh, you have made me so angry saying this thing about my son." She turned to the people around her. "Did you hear this? Did you hear this woman say these things about my son, Sonte? Do you see why I am so angry?"

There were murmurs of sympathy and dissent from all sides. Some agreed with N'ati, some with Farwe. Farwe's man, Raaniu, tried to put in a few calming words, but this only upset N'ati even more. "I have no man to speak for me," she cried, and began to lament the way she lived, without a man to warm her, and rub her back, and bring her food when she was sick. She had to do everything for herself! "Oh, I am so angry, I am so upset," she cried, pulling at her hair. "You, Farwe, you have made me feel this way. Do you think that's good?"

Distressed, Farwe looked about her for support. She was always so pleasant. Why was N'ati shouting at her, why couldn't N'ati be pleasant the way Farwe was? Her ears were aching from N'ati's shouts and she wished she were down at her own cave, in front of her fire, talking lazily, singing a little, with her family around her, and everything so pleasant. She couldn't remember what she had said to make N'ati so angry, or why she was here at N'ati's cave.

Of course, Farwe would have been astonished if

someone had reminded her that she had come to boast of Meezzan and to make herself feel good by subtly reminding N'ati that Hiffaru would someday be her new-son.

"What a loud voice you have, N'ati," she said, and once again, uneasily, saw that she had only made N'ati angrier. She scratched her arms and said quite piteously, "I think I touched that Tetee plant today. You know that plant with the little round burrs, it can make one itch all night long." She scratched her arms again. "I want to go down to my cave. My arms are hot like fire."

"Oh, you run away now! You run away from me," N'ati said scornfully. "You come here like that big wasp to sting me, and then you fly away. Paa!" She spit out of the side of her mouth at Farwe's feet.

"Now you are being very bad to me!" Farwe was extremely hurt. She held her belly. "This is very bad." Her tone was mournful. "This is a Quarrel. Yes, you have made this a Quarrel."

"Yes!" N'ati said, with satisfaction. "This is a Quarrel. Good! Now you know what you have to do."

"That boy, Hiffaru, who will be my new-son, will Quarrel for me," Farwe said, and her face cleared. She almost forgot to look solemn and serious, such was the pleasure she felt in reminding everyone again that the son of the Wai Wai would someday be coming to live in her cave.

"Paa!" N'ati spit again and turned her back. Of course her son, Sonte, would Quarrel for her. She didn't have to say it.

The next day, after the morning rains, the Quarrel took place in a clearing Zan hadn't seen before, where nothing but a kind of low yellow grass grew. Almost everyone came for the Quarrel, forming a rough circle, inside which the two boys faced one another.

"Hiffaru, who will be my new-son, will Quarrel for me," Farwe chanted, stepping forward.

"Sonte, my son, will Quarrel for me," N'ati chanted in reply. She stood with her arms crossed over her breasts, very calm, her eyebrows raised scornfully.

The boys approached each other slowly, standing tall, chins high, buttocks tightened, arms folded. Hiffaru was taller than Sonte, well built. The crumpled side of his face with its tiny sunken, lidless eye was like a shatteringly wrong note in an otherwise perfect piece of music. The boys paced forward purposefully, and for a moment, Zan, standing with Burrum, thought neither would stop in time to prevent those jutting chins from smashing together. Then, no more than a foot apart, they stopped.

The crowd was silent. The boys eyed each other. The silence grew, stretching taut as the skin of a drum. Then: "Aiiiiieeee," Hiffaru sang, a wailing, nasal cry like a call to prayer. A shiver passed through the crowd. "Aiiieee, I am here to Quarrel with you," he chanted. "That woman, Farwe, who will be my new-mother, is pleasant. She came to give greetings, she came from her hearth to N'ati's hearth." His voice rose and fell. "N'ati made her feel so bad," he sang. "She called Farwe a big wasp who stings and flies away. She threw down her spittle at Farwe's feet!"

"That is true," Farwe cried excitedly. "Hiffaru says what is true." She was very gay and excited and kept pinching Zan's arm.

Now it was Sonte's turn to relate his version of the disagreement. "Aiiieee," he chanted back, his voice heavier, less pleasing and melodic than Hiffaru's.

"N'ati, my mother, helps everyone. She is such a good woman, she thinks nothing of herself. She has no man to comfort her. Farwe came to her cave to say bad things, to upset her."

And Hiffaru answered, chanting, "Your mother, N'ati, made Farwe's belly hurt with sadness. This is so!"

Sonte swung his head in Hiffaru's face. "Farwe did not come to Yano's birthing," he chanted. "Why did Farwe not come when her mother's mother was the sister of my grandfather's mother?"

"That is so," someone in the crowd called. "Yes, Farwe ought to have gone to Yano's birthing."

"Oh, let them Quarrel," Farwe said, giving Zan's arm another little nip.

When the previous day's disagreement had been thoroughly gone over in every aspect, the insults began. They were mild enough at first. "You are like a child who eats snot," Sonte chanted.

"Your eyes are like frogs' eggs," Hiffaru replied.

Both boys were tense, tight-jawed, and serious as they circled one another, forcefully chanting their insults. Zan couldn't help taking sides; of course she wanted Sonte to win! He and Hiffaru were like prize fighters, dancing around one another, feinting, jabbing, then suddenly—a serious punch!

"May the Diwaddi bird excrete on your head!"

"May snakes cross your path!"

The insults became heavier. "The sight of you is like a white worm who crawls into the stomach and makes me ill," Sonte chanted, scowling.

"I hear you talking, and I know your tongue will rot like a dead tree," Hiffaru chanted. His voice was becoming hoarse.

Louder and louder they chanted. The crowd urged them on, hands slapping appreciatively against bare thighs for an especially well-put insult.

"May your anus burn like fire."

"And your penis curl like a leaf fallen from its branch." They circled one another, faces screwed up, heads thrust forward, words exploding between them.

"You excrete poison stools!"

"Your piss is green and stinks!"

"May the Anouch'i visit you in every dream."

"May all your children be sons."

"May the water you drink pour out of your ears!"

"May the food in your mouth turn to stones!"

As abruptly as it had started the Quarrel was over. Sonte moved away first, turning his back to Hiffaru to show he was through, that his anger for his mother was used up, his capacity for insult worn out. In a moment he turned around again and he and Hiffaru clasped each other's right shoulders so that their arms crossed. Then Farwe and N'ati were brought together. Facing each other, they touched foreheads for an instant without speaking. It was over. The crowd stirred and laughed, and began to talk.

"Is that all?" Zan asked Burrum. It was strange how let down she felt, while Burrum appeared to be totally exhilarated by the experience, running back and forth, talking and laughing and calling to friends.

"Now the Quarrel is finished and my belly is satisfied," N'ati said loudly. And Farwe, not to be outdone, agreed quickly, "Yes, the Quarrel is over. I want to give you something," she added, and taking off one of her shell necklaces she laid it graciously over N'ati's head. Sonte put his arms around his mother and hugged her and the two of them left with their relatives and friends. Others surrounded Farwe who spoke of how well Hiffaru had Quarreled for her. But Hiffaru himself did not stay. He walked away, speaking to no one. As he passed Zan, the tiny eye buried deep in his skull gazed at her, and she was startled to see that his eye was brown, severe, and steady, exactly like his mother's eyes.

22

In the wet dawn, when dew glistened on every leaf, Diwera was searching the forest for the Hauka B'Mawa, a huge, hairy white spider whose bite was fatal. She had risen early from her sleep to begin the search, leaving the cave while Hiffaru and Akawa still slept. She was hunting these spiders to make a paste for a wound in Goah's thumb, a wound that festered and did not heal. It had come from Meezzan's Nii'uff.

Diwera's daughter, Akawa, had seen it happen. Goah had asked Meezzan for Nii'uff. Meezzan said, "No." Goah's brother, Hakku, teasing, had pushed Goah, as he often did, saying, "Take Nii'uff, brother. Are you frightened? Is your belly crying like a little child at night? Brother, I want to see you take Nii'uff." Before anyone could stop him, Goah had snatched Nii'uff by its shining tongue.

Thus, perhaps in anger, Nii'uff had sliced Goah's thumb, cut through flesh to bone. There had been much blood, and Hakku had cried as if it were his thumb that lay open and bleeding. Akawa had packed the cut with fresh leaves of the Hamoia bush. "I could think of nothing else," she said.

Diwera, concealing her pleasure over Akawa's healing knowledge, had nodded briefly. "You did well, daughter. Those little leaves will make the wound heal quickly." She had gone herself to see the boy and been satisfied that she could have done no better than Akawa. That had been many days ago. She raised one hand, fingers spread wide. Then the other hand. So many days! By now the wound ought to have healed, yet it did not. It festered, swollen and smelling of death. The boy's mother said her son did not sleep at night, but raved in pain.

This was why Diwera was out early in the wet forest, hunting for the Hauka B'Mawa, calling softly to bring the spiders to her. As she searched, she had many things on her mind, and in one way or another all came back to Meezzan. In her head she heard the sounds of Meezzan's strange language and, with a sour click of her tongue, she recalled hearing some of these same unpleasant sounds from the mouth of the little boy, Lishum, and the girl, Ai'ma. But it was not only the children who copied Meezzan. She had taught the young people a game in which they pushed and shoved, snatching the melon from one another, throwing it toward some thing called "Ba'sus." Diwera found it difficult, if not impossible, to understand such a game. It was played without singing, where one called out in a loud ugly voice and ran around without sense, afterward shouting Meezzan's words, "Aii'wun, Aii'wun!"

Diwera knew it was because of Meezzan's powers that the young people copied her, learning her games and her words. And there was a deep ugly feeling in Diwera's belly that it was because of Meezzan's powers, too, that so many bad things were happening to the People. Goah's wound. And the rains. In Diwera's memory, the rains had come harder and stayed longer than ever before. The red flowers were blooming in the forest, the time for the Sussuru was near, but still the rains came every day. Often fires were smoky and bedding damp. But worst of all was old Nabrushi, who had lost his footing while climbing an Aspa tree for nuts and had fallen and broken a leg. No one, not even among the First Old Ones, could remember when someone had last fallen from an Aspa tree, which had great wide branches like a mother's arms. It was said by some that a huge bird had flown out of the sky, a kind of bird that Nabrushi had never seen before, and thinking it had come to peck out his eyes he had leaped away from it and fallen to the ground.

The old man had crawled up the mountain in great pain, his face covered with cold sweat, his injured leg dragging. He had collapsed on the ground in front of Farwe's cave. She had sent for Diwera who, grabbing the injured leg with both hands, had pulled with all her strength to straighten the broken bone. That old man, Nabrushi, had groaned and cried in his pain. Diwera had bound sturdy sticks tightly together, one next to the other, put them on the leg, and wrapped all with fresh strips of bark. The men had carried old Nabrushi back to his own hearth, where now he lay, still in pain, his old bones clicking like branches in a wind.

Diwera pressed her lips together. So many bad things. Too many bad things! She came upon a tumble of rocks and, kneeling, called the white spiders to her. She had ready in her hand a little peeled stick with which she would hold down the spiders so she could seize them safely without being bitten. If she were careless or stupid when gathering the Hauka B'Mawa, she would die in great agony.

"Psss . . . whee . . . psss . . ." she called softly. But

the spiders hid themselves from her. She sucked liquid from the stem of a plant, and continued her search. Her feet took her to Meadow-with-Watering-Hole. "Ssss!" She blew out her breath in chagrin. That she had come this far without finding what she sought!

Then, across the meadow, she saw Meezzan rising from the ground, as if rising out of Diwera's troubled thoughts. Leaning her head against a boulder, the girl pounded on it with both hands. Though the wind blew her words away from Diwera, she knew the girl was calling on her spirits, chanting one of her harsh songs. Aiii, she had heard about Meezzan's coming here to a big rock where she put on her strange garments, lay on the ground curled like a child with her eyes closed, and called out to the spirits! Yes, Diwera had heard all this, but now for the first time she saw it for herself.

Head down, the girl came toward Diwera through the high grasses and flowers. Though agitated by her thoughts, Diwera sang out a courteous greeting. Like a startled animal, Meezzan jerked her head up, eyes opened wide, lips parted. Then she smoothed her face and returned the greeting.

"Are you not lonely so far from the caves, without friends or companions?" Diwera asked.

"You, too, are alone," Meezzan said.

Diwera nodded impatiently. She was the Wai Wai. The Wai Wai did not go with others, as everyone else did. But neither did this girl. Sometimes she appeared to be like any other girl, but Diwera was not misled.

When she had first come among the People, Meezzan had not known even how to feed herself from earth and the waters. Yes, she had learned much from Burrum and the other young ones, but what had she done before for food and drink? Perhaps she had no need of these things. Diwera shivered.

"What do you do there? What do you sing?" she said, pointing toward the rock where she had seen the girl ceremoniously pound her hands.

"I go there, so that—I want to go to my home," Meezzan said, using the word for caves. But Diwera understood.

Like Niben, that young man from so long ago, from her grandmother's grandmother's time, the girl surely came from Beyond-the-Mountains. But had she made her way alone over mountains that reached into the very sky itself? So many unanswered questions! Now, Diwera was determined to have some answers.

"Meezzan! What is it like in your place? Do all the people have frek'ulls?"

"Oh, no! Some have skin like yours. Some have skin that is black, some have skin that is red, or yellow."

She takes me for a fool, Diwera thought, but still she remained courteous and calm. "Where is Nii'uff? Do you not have Nii'uff with you?"

The girl shook her head. Her face changed, something passed over her eyes like a cloud through the sky. "It is at the cave," she said slowly. She rubbed her arms, although it was still warm; the rains had not yet come this morning. "Is Goah better?"

Diwera gave her a measuring look. "His wound is very bad. It is green and smells foul. He cries in the night from his pain. Why did Nii'uff bite him?"

"He took it," Meezzan said. "I told him no, but he took it."

Yes, he took your power and thus he was hurt, Diwera thought, and involuntarily she took a step backward, away from the girl. Never before had she known or conceived of anyone with greater powers than her own. The spirits had powers, but one might live a lifetime and never see the spirits. If they did make themselves visible, then it was only for their own purposes, and they soon disappeared again.

"Where is your home?" she asked Meezzan in a deliberate tone. "Where is your place that you came from before you lived with the People?"

The girl twisted her shoulders. Diwera saw that the question made her uneasy. Frowning and looking aside, Meezzan scratched her arm. "My cave—my home—it is far away."

"Yes, Beyond-the-Mountains," Diwera agreed. "Why do you not return?" How good it would be if the girl left the People! The thought brightened Diwera immediately. She put her hand on Meezzan's shoulder. "Do you not want to see your own people?" she said in a warm, encouraging voice. "If the journey is far, we will give you a tantua filled with good food."

"I want to return. Yes! I try, but—" The girl pointed to the rock in the middle of the field, then down toward the earth, straight into the earth. "I must go back to my home from there. It is not easy."

"What are you saying? Do you take me for a foolish woman!" Fear, like white worms, crawled into Diwera's belly. Had the girl sprung from the earth itself? From spirits unknown? Beings who lived below the ground? "Tell me how you came here," she demanded. "Tell me how you will leave!"

"I want to tell you," Meezzan said, "but—I cannot. It is so hard. You are the Wai Wai of the People, I know this." She still spoke haltingly, like a child. "You help the sick. You give them herbs. Burrum says that you are wise. She must be right. You are the wise person, but—I cannot tell you how I can go to my home!" Her face became red and swollen, but she did not cry, her eyes stayed dry, and she broke into a gabble of incomprehensible sounds. Her own language, full of harshness and hard snapping sounds. Diwera felt bruised by the deluge of strange words and she wanted to cover her ears against them.

"Meezzan!" Diwera put all the weight of her position and authority into the one word. And the girl abruptly stopped speaking. She was trembling. For a moment Diwera almost felt pity for her. Then the girl broke free of Diwera and ran into the forest. This rudeness shocked Diwera to her senses. No, no, no, the girl was not of the People! Moon following moon following moon, she had been among the People and still she had not learned their good ways. She would never learn them! Why should she? Her powers protected her!

Distracted and upset by the tide of her thoughts, Diwera turned into the forest to continue looking for the poisonous white spiders. She had not gone too far when she heard a low whistle. High above her, among tumbled rocks, two snakes, each bigger than a man, slowly flowed along the ground, their heads raised. They were whistling. Their enormous bodies were black with shining white spots. "Mother Olima," Diwera whispered. These snakes had white frek'ulls on their black bodies, while Meezzan had black frek'ulls on a white body. And where did these snakes come from, if not from beneath the earth? As Meezzan did.

"Mother Olima," Diwera whispered again. The snakes glided on, their heads raised, whistling. Diwera remained still until they were out of sight, but even then, still hearing their whistling, she could not move. At last the whistles died away. Breath rushed into her lungs. She raised her head and sniffed the air. Soon the rain would begin. She felt dazed, as if awakening from a long sleep. She went on, still looking for the spiders.

In a grove of white trees, she came to a huge fallen tree, moss-covered, the roots rearing like enormous fingers into the air. This tree had been there, in this grove, forever. It was said that Miiawa often came there to rest. This was Miiawa's grove. The trees were bigger and more beautiful than any others. The trunks, white and pale green, rose smooth and straight into the sky. The leaves, like Wind, moved softly, speaking together. Placing a handful of long white Ripari tubers on the great broad trunk of the fallen tree, Diwera called, "Here is a gift for you, Miiawa. I, Diwera, leave this food. Eat it, Miiawa, and when I return, I will bring you another gift. This is true. You may believe this."

Calmer in her mind, she went on her way. As the first spatter of rain pebbled the ground, she found a nest of white spiders. She wrapped each spider she caught in a separate leaf, then put all the little packets of leaves into one big Piishanii leaf, wrapping it tightly with vine and holding it well away from her. Should even one spider free itself, it would spin a glistening, trembling thread and be upon her in moments.

In her cave again, she built up her fire, warming and drying herself. Outside, rain splashed on the ground. She roasted the packets of spiders and pounded the tender cooked flesh into a gray mash. Just as the rains stopped, she carried the mash to Goah to pack into his wound. The boy lay on the family bed, his eyes as large as moons. His father and his brother were with him. At the first touch of the mash on his thumb, the boy cried out. His eyes filled with tears. He held out his hand to his father. "It burns me, it burns me. Father, she is burning me."

"Aii, Wai Wai, my son cries with pain," Goah's father exclaimed. There were tears in his eyes, too, as he comforted the boy.

"Cry," Diwera said to Goah. "Your tears will help

the wound heal. New flesh will grow. Soon there will be no more pain." She turned to Hakku. "Will you stay with your brother? When he cries from the burning, from the pain, take his other hand and press it between your hands. Then the pain will not be so bad." She turned to go, then stopped. "Goah, Hakku. Listen to me. Do not ask again for Nii'uff." She paused, then went on slowly, "Do not ask that girl, Meezzan, for anything. Do you hear what I say?"

Goah nodded; he was in pain and asked no questions. But Hakku, who had been squatting near his brother, half stood up, saying, "My ears hear such a strange thing, Diwera. I would not ask again for Nii'uff! No! You can believe this. But my ears hear you saying not to ask that girl for anything. Diwera, what are you telling me and my brother?"

"Do not ask," she said. "I tell you, do not ask her for anything." She walked out of the cave, ducking at the low entrance, her belly heavy, as though filled with stones. The goodness of asking one's neighbor, friend, companion for what one wanted was a thing sucked in with mother's milk. To ask was to receive, and to receive was to give. To give and to receive was life. And now she, Diwera, had told these boys never again to ask Meezzan for anything. Never before had such a thing been said by one of the People to another.

23

Although the rains continued to fall, the time for the girls' ceremony, the Sussuru, had come. In the forest, the red flowers gleamed mysteriously, tiny red blossoms underfoot everywhere on the dark forest floor. At night the new moon, too, had glowed faintly red.

Now it was the dawn of the first day of the Sussuru. The rim of the sky was edged with pale green. Burrum's breath puffed into the air as she put her arms around Meezzan and nuzzled her neck comfortingly. "Do not be sad without me, my sister. For one moon I will be gone. Then we will be together again." Burrum was sorry to leave her friend behind, yet her sorrow was tinged with a piercing sweetness like the calls of birds at first light. Today was the first day of the Sussuru! How long Burrum had waited for this day, and now that it was here, how happy she was. So happy she wanted everyone else to be happy. She bit Meezzan's neck affectionately, little tender bites like the ones her mother and father often placed on her arms and face before she went to sleep, remembering again how, so long ago, Miiawa had sent this daughter of Others to her. What a good thing that had been!

A little gust of melancholy, like a ripple on a smooth

river, snagged at Burrum's happiness. Not everyone was as happy about Meezzan as Burrum. Some people muttered among themselves about Meezzan's strange ways. They said she was not one of the People. Naturally, this was so! But they also said she might be a daughter of snakes and spirits who lived below the earth. They said she would bring misery and unhappiness to the People. They pointed to Goah's thumb, which had healed but was as stiff as a piece of wood. And to old Nabrushi, who had never recovered from his fall. And to the rains that poured steadily even though this was the time of the Sussuru. For all these things they blamed Meezzan.

Hearing such talk, Burrum was very angry. She did not believe such things, and neither did her mother, her father, or her aunts and uncles. Look how Hiffaru had Quarreled so well for her mother! Look how easily Ainu's baby had been born! And was she not the most beautiful and strongest baby girl one had ever seen? And, above all, had not Burrum's blood come down in time for the Sussuru? These were the good things that Meezzan had brought to Burrum's family!

But there were people—the children of Nabrushi, for instance, and the family of Goah—who said there was a cloud around Meezzan, a cloud one could not see but, nevertheless, was truly there. And in this cloud they said there were many bad things that were dropping down upon the People, one by one.

Burrum stared into Meezzan's face. "While I am gone, you stay here with my mother. Lishum will miss me. You be his sister while I am gone." She rubbed Meezzan's back once more, then turned away as Farwe called, "Come, daughter. Hurry."

Farwe plucked a smoldering brand from the fire.

"Come, Burrum, come, girls of the Sussuru," she cried, her voice ringing through the clear morning air. Soon the other girls and their mothers joined Farwe and Burrum. Em'Fadi, the quiet one, was there. Bahii, a small child; and Noomia and Naku, the sisters, husky girls with brisk manners. "Are all the girls of the Sussuru here?" Farwe asked. "Are all the mothers here?" But Em'Fadi's mother was dead, so her aunt escorted her.

"We're here," Noomia said, and her sister Naku added, "We're ready!"

"Then sing, girls of the Sussuru," Em'Fadi's aunt said, and she broke into song in which they all joined. Thus, singing, they filed down the mountain, passed through a meadow, and into a grove of tall white trees, like those trees in Miiawa's grove. Set in the middle of these trees was the Sussuru hut, made of bark and branches with a narrow low entrance and a hole in the roof to let out the smoke of the fire. Farwe dug the torch into the ground, and the four women and five girls set to work repairing the damage wind and rain had done to the roof and the walls of the hut. Large fresh leaves were laid across the roof. Branches were woven into the walls and, inside, the floor was brushed clean of last year's debris. Fresh beds of leaves and grass were laid for each girl, and in the center of the hut, the hearth was ringed by a newly laid circle of stones. Wood was gathered and stacked for the fire. The girls and their mothers laughed and talked as they worked, stopping often to eat fruit and nuts. The mothers were solicitous, for they knew what lay ahead for their daughters. "Have more fruit, daughter," Ahera, the mother of the little Bahii, urged. "Come, eat this sweet fruit, so your belly will not be hungry tonight."

At last all was done. The torch passed from the hand

of one mother to the other. Farwe, reclaiming it, touched the glowing tip to the kindling and the fire blazed up. "Remember, the fire must not die," Farwe chanted. "The fire must burn day and night. If this fire dies, the moon will fall from the sky. Daughters! Do not forget the fire!"

The. women gathered near the entrance to the little hut with last-minute admonitions. "You must not talk."

"You must stay by the fire without speaking."

"Daughters, above all, don't cry, don't weep. Otherwise you will die young."

"Yes, yes, we hear you, mothers," Noomia and Naku cried together.

The girls were eager to be left alone. Only Bahii, whose blood had come very young, looked sad to see her mother leaving. Burrum put her arm around the child and led her to the fire. The girls looked at one another and smiled. Now they must not talk again for a very long time.

That night they slept only in snatches, all of them sitting up to be sure the fire didn't go out. Outside their hut they heard the sounds of night: leaves rustling, wind in the trees, animals prowling; mysterious and terrifying sounds. Not one of the girls had ever before spent a night away from the warmth and comfort of parents and relatives. In the light of the fire the girls looked at each other's shadowed face, eyes glistening and large, and thought of the spirits who wandered in the night, of the Anouch'i, and of Tariana with eyes of fire. But no one said anything. They must not cry, they must not fear; they would soon be women and had to be brave. The child, Bahii, huddled tightly against Burrum, but even she did not so much as whimper.

Their first day alone they ate nothing.

On the second day they drank only water. Their mothers prowled outside the hut, calling to them, "Are you guarding that fire? Don't you see the sky is darkening? Build up the fire, daughters!" Wood was shoved inside the hut, but none of the girls answered the calls, or gave thanks for the wood. They were hungry and tired and didn't smile as often. That night they took turns staying up to tend the fire. Noomia and Naku took their turns together.

The next day fruit was left inside the hut, but not enough to satisfy their hunger. They left the hut only briefly, one at a time, careful that no men or boys were about, for if now they looked at men, forever after their legs would tremble when they climbed trees.

Each day the mothers left a bit of fruit, just enough for a few bites for each girl. Each day their mothers called to them from outside the hut, teasing them, taunting, and testing. "Daughters! The moon is fleeing the sky. What! Have you let that fire die?" But the girls were brave and proud and didn't answer, although their bellies longed for the comfort of their mothers' arms and their mothers' voices. Yes, they longed for that, but none of them, not even little Bahii, gave way to her longing and crept outside to her mother. No one spoke. No one cried. Burrum stroked Bahii's arms and smiled at the child to give her courage. Noomia and Naku tended the fire, carefully rationing the wood.

The girls lay on their beds with their faces on their arms, or sat around the hearth poking at the embers, watching the sparks fly up through the hole in the roof. Once each day they shared the fruit, eating it slowly, tasting the sweetness on their tongues and then in their throats.

The days passed slowly into the nights, and the

nights again into the days. Each morning and each afternoon the girls heard the rain on their little roof of leaves and looked at one another, and sighed, and smiled, and threw wood into the fire. Ah, how good the fire was when it rained, yet they could not speak of it. Sometimes they put their arms around one another, leaned their heads together, and dreamed silently. They had dreams while they slept and dreams while they were awake.

The quiet Em'Fadi cried out many times in her dream-filled sleep. "Mother! Mother!" she cried. Each one of the other girls, awakened, felt Em'Fadi's orphaned cry as if it were her own. "Mother," Em'Fadi cried again. Bahii, grinding her teeth against tears, crawled over to Burrum and locked her arms tightly around her neck. Burrum, without speaking, stroked the child's back over and over.

Burrum dreamed many dreams. She dreamed of her mother's mother's mother who had come to this very Sussuru hut, and of all the girls before her who had crouched by the Sussuru fire. She sensed their presence in the fire and in the air and in the earth beneath her feet. She felt the unnumbered generations of girls before her, of mothers, entering her body, becoming part of her as she was part of them. *This is what it means to be a woman.*

She dreamed other things, as well. She dreamed of a butterfly lighting on her shoulder and speaking in her ear. As she dreamed, she did not know if she was the butterfly or the butterfly was her. She dreamed that she swallowed a stone that began at once to move in her belly like a child. She held her belly tenderly and thought, *This is what it means to be a woman.* While she slept she dreamed, and while she sat before the fire she dreamed. Strange and beautiful dreams such as she would never dream again: of rivers and birds, of fruit and bears, of mothers and great trees that reached into the sky and down into the earth.

And she dreamed, too, of Meezzan who smiled at her and said, "Yes, you are my sister," but even as she spoke, Meezzan became a green frog sitting on many poisonous white eggs. And this frog, Meezzan, still spoke, saying, "Sister, sister, I have here something delicious for you." She showed Burrum the poisonous white eggs and shoved them with her bent frog's legs toward Burrum's mouth. Burrum leaped back and woke with such a shout of fear that Bahii leaned toward her and anxiously stroked her face. All that day, Burrum could not forget that dream. The green frog, Meezzan, and the poisonous white eggs. Aii, her stomach ached with this dream!

One evening, the mothers came into the hut, saying, "Daughters, it is time. The new moon is here!" The girls thought this was another test of their strength and turned their heads and refused to answer. Laughing, Farwe and Ahera and the other women took their daughters by the arms and led them outside. "Look up. The new moon has come!" Raising her eyes, Burrum saw the thin young moon, like a baby's new tooth. "Now you may talk," Farwe said, "but softly, daughter, softly at first."

"Mother, I had so many dreams!"

"Yes, yes, I, too, had dreams. Aii," Farwe sighed, "that is such a long time ago, but I still remember my dreams. Yes, such dreams! Such dreams." She took her daughter inside the hut and walked her around the fire. The other mothers did the same with their daughters. Then they told the girls to sleep one more night in the hut with the fire burning.

In the morning the mothers were there again to take their daughters into the forest to adorn them. All day they worked. They squeezed the red juice from Urucuru seeds and dipped little leaf brushes into the juice and drew designs on their daughters' bodies: wavy lines like water on their breasts, circles like the sun on their arms, tiny fish on their bellies, and the crescent of the new moon on their backs and legs. They picked curly young Bassai leaves and tied them in bunches below the girls' knees and around their arms, ankles, necks, and waists. They put clusters of the red flowers of Miiawa into their hair, behind their ears, and tucked into their mingaus. At last, toward dusk, the mothers were satisfied and following their daughters in single file, they went back up the mountain to the caves, where the fires were burning. There everyone waited to see how beautiful the girls looked, how proudly they walked, how happy they were that they had been strong, that they had fasted and dreamed and were no longer girls, but women.

As they moved along the path, from deep in the forest came a long haunting call like a cry torn from a throat aching with pain and loss. The girls looked at each other, their eyes widening. "Menari!" they whispered. The secret Menari, an instrument known only to a few chosen women, its voice heard only at the time of the Sussuru. Hidden in the forest, it called and called, its voice like the wind in the soft wet evening.

24

From new moon to new moon, for twenty-eight days, Zan had been without Burrum. Once she had followed Farwe and heard her and the other women call out to the girls inside the little hut. She had listened to the women's admonitions and felt a strange delight at the girls' silence. But afterward she had felt lonelier than ever to think that Burrum was inside that hut with four other girls, while she was outside.

The rains had come every day, and for the most part she had stayed close to the cave and the family, sleeping, watching Ainu's new baby for long peaceful hours, and playing with Lishum. She became very close to the little boy. In the mornings, he went with her to the river to wash, and together they picked fruit and brought wood for the fires. Seeing the two of them with one another so often, Sonte teased, "Who is that man with you, Meezzan? Who is that strong man with the deep voice?"

Lishum wrapped his arms around Zan's legs, "Sonte! Listen to me. Listen to me! When I grow up, I will be Meezzan's man."

Slapping his thighs in glee, Sonte cried, "Yes, I hear you. Now let me hear you sing the men's songs, little man!" Everyone around laughed. But, unruffled,

Lishum continued to go wherever Zan went. Only when she went to Meadow-with-Watering-Hole did she slip away alone.

She still made regular visits to the meadow. She had left her clothes hidden in a hollow tree near the boulder and always put them on at once. Sometimes she wore the little bark bag with her objects, other times she left it in the cave in its niche. But at least once every day she took out the button, key, safety pin, and knife and arranged them in the triangular pattern, whispering to herself, "I am Zan Ford."

Since the day when Goah had cut himself, she had been adamant about not letting anyone near any of her things, especially the knife. She no longer played games with the knife, or cared to impress anyone with it. In the beginning it had been safety (she thought); then, seeing the awe it engendered, she had used it, half knowing that it protected her sense of superiority. Now she used it only to cut fruit, or her hair, or sometimes to idly whittle a stick.

Faithfully, she made the scratches in her calendars. She already had five pieces of wood thick with slashed marks that added up to more than forty-one weeks. Burrum's aunts were puzzled by her calendars. They often picked up one of the pieces of wood and drew their fingers over the six little marks slashed across by a seventh. Zan had been unable to explain a week. The People had no names for days, neither did they count beyond raising their fingers. Yet each woman kept a lunar calendar, and Ainu had noted the moons of her pregnancy by stringing a pierced shell for each moon on a bracelet she wore until the birth of the child. (Only two days before the child was born, she had, with perfect assurance, gone about making her birthing bed.)

One day at the river, Zan stared for a long time at her

reflection—Meezzan. Half naked, barefooted. Hair tangled. The thick, crowded marks on her calendar marched through her mind. Would she still be here when the Sussuru was held again? Ainu believed she would be. Earlier, seeing that Meezzan missed Burrum and felt unsettled, Ainu had said, "Meezzan, calm your belly! The Sussuru comes to all girls, your turn will come also." And laughing one of her big, comfortable laughs, she had added, "I will be your mother for your Sussuru."

"Ainu, you are good!" Zan had said, pinching Ainu's arm affectionately. It was true that she would have been happy to be part of the Sussuru. She had wondered so often, with a tinge of envy, what Burrum was thinking and doing in the little hut. Every night, Zan had looked at the moon; she had watched it wax, grow full and beautiful, slowly wane, then disappear altogether for two nights, till at last the little new moon showed itself again, pale and fresh. Then she knew that the Sussuru month was over.

The day of the girls' return, Zan waited with the others. At twilight, the air was silvered by a distant cry, strange and haunting. She shivered and without knowing why held out her arms.

"The Menari!" Ainu held her baby daughter in the air, her face alight.

"Oh, listen," Mai'bu cried. "Listen! Listen!" Kneeling, she hugged Ai'ma. "Listen, daughter!"

And Zan, standing with the women, longed to cry out herself, Oh, listen to the Menari!

Laughing and crying, imploring and exulting, the Menari sang. *Hear me. I am I . . . I am you . . . I am the Menari . . . hear me . . . oh, hear me!*

Then Zan saw them coming, the women behind, the

girls ahead. Adorned with leaves and flowers, they came slowly up the path, hands on one another's shoulders, their movements rhythmic, faces radiant, singing to the Menari as they came. *I am I, I am you, I am the moon*, the Menari sang, and the girls sang back, *We hear you, O Menari, we hear you singing in the forest* . . .

The last light of the sun illuminated their figures; light sprang from their heads like sprays of water, and all around them the air was golden, quivering. Up they came, singing, proud. They stopped before Farwe's fire and there, arms around each other's waist, danced around the hearth.

They sang and danced at Farwe's fire till the sun was gone; then they moved on to the next fire, and the next, and on to each fire. With each stop the crowd grew. Everyone was there, men and women, the old ones, the boys, and the little girls who watched their older sisters and cousins with envious eyes.

Eyes glistening, bodies bedewed with perspiration, the girls pounded their feet upon the earth in exultation. Their sisters and brothers danced with them, lifting their knees and stamping their feet; their mothers danced, shedding years as they twirled and shook; and their fathers and uncles danced, raising their arms and throwing back their heads to sing. Feet thudding, hands slapping rhythmically against flesh, mouths open in song, they danced till they fell back, exhausted, their places taken immediately by others. Only the Sussuru girls danced on and on through the night, their throats taut, their beatific faces turned always toward the forest and the haunting, distant music of the Menari.

As the hours of the night passed, the wild dancing and exultant singing called to Zan, drew her even

closer, until at last she, too, began to dance. Burrum's
arm went around her waist and they danced together.
Bending, shaking, stamping, on and on they danced.
Zan's face was flaming; cold sweat filmed her body like
another skin. In the center of her self there was a deep
ache, as if she, the daughter of Others, had long ago
lost the sweet taste of life and only now knew it was lost.

The fire blazed in the center of the circle of dancers;
the earth resounded with stamping feet; heat and excitement mingled like smoke; and the silver voice of the
Menari untiringly twined with the ecstatic voices of the
swaying dancers: voices that cried and called, voices
like the voices of birds, the voices of animals, the
voices of the river and the trees and the wind. Somewhere inside herself, Zan briefly understood everything
and began to cry and sing in a voice she had never
heard, a voice that was part of the dust and the heat,
part of the night and the bodies, part of the air and the
wind, part of all that was and all that would ever be.

25

Waking, Zan looked at once, as she always did, toward the entrance of the cave. The last shreds of a blue morning mist floated above the ground. For an instant, she, too, seemed to float above herself as she recalled again the ecstasy of the Sussuru night. "Aii, Burrum, my sister," she said softly, turning. But Burrum was not curled up next to her. Nor was Farwe sitting up in her place, smiling and nodding. Rather she and Burrum and the old grandmother were bent over Lishum. He moaned and thrashed out with his arms.

"Burrum—?" Zan said, rising. The girl threw her a swift, terrified glance.

"My head hurts," Lishum cried. "There is a bird inside my head. Oh, he is pecking at my eyes. Burrum! Auuhmaa! Meezzan!" he screamed, flailing about. "Make the bird go away."

Farwe put her face against her son's. "How hot he is! He is hot like the sun!"

"Lishum, Lishum, don't you want to get up?" Burrum said. "Come, we'll go down to the river and bathe. Here's Meezzan, we'll all go together."

"No, no, make that bird go away. Oh, he is pecking out my eyes. I'll fall from the tree like old Nabrushi!

Burrum! Meezzan! Why don't you take him away!"

"Yes, yes, Lishum, he's going, he's flying away," Zan said, squatting down next to the child, but he continued to scream and moan.

His lips were swollen, his skin flushed and puffy. Several times that day he vomited a yellow-green, foul-smelling bile. Even after it was cleaned up with hand-fuls of grass, the acid odor lingered in the air. He gib-bered nonsense, screamed, and once bolted upright and staggered toward the back of the cave. "Come away," Burrum cried, but before she could reach him he fell in a heap. Raaniu carried his son back to his bed and lay down next to him, holding the boy in his arms.

Zan stayed by the child all day, feeling angry and useless. If only there was something she could do. If only she had an aspirin! She slept uneasily that night, waking with Lishum's moans. Several times she heard Farwe and Raaniu whispering to each other and to the child. In the morning Lishum whimpered that his neck hurt, he couldn't move his neck. He spoke wildly of the Bear People, he thought the Bear People had come in the night and were eating his neck. The family hovered around him. His mother stroked his face, his uncles brought him water.

He seemed to sleep for a while and they left him with the old grandmother, so that they could bathe and find some fruit. When they returned he was still asleep, no longer thrashing violently about. Farwe was pleased. "My son sleeps. Soon he will wake and be well." But the day passed and Lishum couldn't be wakened. "Aii, I am frightened for my son!" Raaniu exclaimed.

Farwe pinched the boy, gently at first, then more violently.

"Lishum!" Zan shook his arm, determined to wake

him. "Lishum, do you hear me? Wake up!" She shook him harder. "Lishum!" He slept on. "Lishum!"

Burrum tugged Zan away.

"Aunt Ainu has gone for Diwera," she said. "The Wai Wai will help Lishum. Shhh, do not scream, Meez-zan. The Anouch'i will hear you and find my little brother."

When Diwera came, she knelt by the child and ran her hands over the body. His limbs twitched and jerked, but his eyes stayed closed. Diwera placed her mouth against his and sucked in mightily.

"What is she doing?" Zan whispered.

"She is sucking his throat, so his throat may grow fresh again."

Diwera straightened, sprinkling the child with invisible water. "Come, Miiawa, daughter of the forest," she chanted, "you are beautiful, come and refresh the body of this sick child with your cool hands, with your green hands like little leaves. Come, Miiawa, who lives along the streams and among the cool trees, come sing, *pri, pri, pri,* and refresh the child's hot body." She sprinkled the invisible water on his face, his hands, and his chest. After this she gave Farwe a leaf full of black powder and told her when to give it to Lishum, and how to hold up his head so that he would swallow the powder.

Through the rest of that day and the night and the next day, Farwe gave Lishum pinches of the black powder on his tongue. But when it was all gone, he still slept. Farwe began to cry. "I do not want my child to die." She pulled at her cheeks as if she would strip the flesh from the bones. "I do not want to lose my son!"

Raaniu clutched his belly. "If my son dies, I will die inside here."

Now the First Old Ones were sent for. Four women

and two men, the oldest of the old. Their legs trembled as they walked, many were half blind, and rarely did any of them leave their daughters' caves. They were old and wise, wise in ways unknown to those who had not attained such a great age, wiser even than the Wai Wai who came to watch them try to cure the child.

The old ones squatted around Lishum. They touched his fevered jerking limbs with claw-like hands. They pushed back his eyelids to see his senselessly staring eyes. They talked among themselves and at last concluded that the Anouch'i had stolen the child's Ta.

"Aiii," the Auuhmaa cried, tears falling from her single good eye.

"Let us find the Anouch'i and ask them to return the child's Ta," Foomikii, an old man, said loudly.

"Yes, what need do they have for such a young child?" Bai agreed. "Let us find those Anouch'i."

They went outside, followed by the family and Diwera, and lay down on the ground with their ears pressed hard to the earth, still wet from the morning rains. "Who hears the Anouch'i?" Taomi said shrilly. She sniffed the air. "I smell the birds. I smell the animals beneath the earth. I hear them talking, but I do not hear the Anouch'i."

They struggled to their feet, groaning because their bones were stiff with age. "Let us look for the path of the Anouch'i," Meetil, the oldest of the old, said. He raised a quivering arm. "I know the path for Sun," he chanted. "I know the path for Moon, I know the path for Night, I know the path for Day. Animals have their paths, and Miiawa has her paths. The fish swim in their paths. Where is the path that leads to the Anouch'i? Where are the tracks of the Anouch'i?" he asked in a quavering voice.

They overturned stones and peered into the leafy branches of trees. They panted with exertion, sweat covered their bodies, and their eyes bulged with fatigue.

"Come, Anouch'i, come, we are not afraid of you!" Meetil cried tremblingly. Spittle stood at the corners of his mouth, his legs were visibly shaking, and his eyes seemed to stare into something unseen. His chest heaved up and down. "Anouch'i, Anouch'i, we are not —not—not afraid—" All at once, his legs gave way and he fell, striking the ground heavily. "The Anouch'i have found me," he gasped. "They have struck me in the eye. They have struck me in the chest. Oh, my eye, my chest, oh, oh—" He lay on the ground, unable to rise.

The other old ones stood around Meetil, shaking like trees in a storm, their hands trembling around their faces. "Thou, O Anouch'i, are greater than we," Bai wailed. "You have taken away the child," she cried thinly. "You have struck down this man." She tottered into Farwe's cave, wailing praise of the Anouch'i, tearing off her necklaces and bracelets and throwing them into the fire. She tore hair from her head and threw this, too, into the fire.

"Now, Anouch'i!" she cried, raising her veiny arms. "I have given you things. I have given you everything. Give me back the child. You do not need the child's Ta, Anouch'i." The other old ones crowded in after her, tearing off their ornaments, seizing hunks of their hair and throwing all into the fire. Then Farwe and Raaniu, Burrum, Ainu, and all of the family, and Zan, too, tore off everything they wore, tore out hair and threw it into the fire.

"We are giving you everything," Farwe moaned. "Now give us back our little son."

"Give him back, give him back," they cried, and caught up in the delirium of wailing and crying, Zan added her voice to the others, pleading with the Anouch'i for the little boy.

But the Anouch'i did not give him up and, shaking with exhaustion, the old ones had to be fetched back to their caves by their sons and daughters. Near tears, Zan ran out of the cave. She had believed—she had *wanted* to believe in the old ones' power and knowledge. She pushed her forehead against a tree, rubbing it back and forth. Maybe Lishum would get better anyway. Maybe in the morning he would sit up smiling and grab her arm, demanding that she play with him. *Right now,* he would say. *I want to play now, Meezzan!* He would grab her, grunting fiercely, and . . .

A hand, hot and heavy, came down on her shoulder. "Meezzan."

She shook her head. She didn't want to talk to anyone . . . Lishum would grab her arm and she would fall down on the ground, pretending he had overpowered her . . .

"Meezzan." She was spun around. "Look at my eyes," Diwera said. She put her forefinger against Zan's breastbone. "Hear me. If the child dies, you must leave the People." Her finger poked fiercely into Zan's chest. "Listen to what I say. If the child dies, do not stay here. Take your powers and return to that place where you belong. Go away from the People." Her lips tightened. "Leave us! Leave us!"

26

In the morning, Raaniu, who had slept all night with his arms around Lishum, woke to find himself embracing a lifeless body. He shook Farwe's shoulder. "Wake up, mother of my son! Your son has left us. His Ta has left us." Tears fell down Raaniu's cheeks. "Your son has gone to be happy in Place-of-Night-Sun."

Farwe reached for the dead child and rocked him at her breast as if he had been an infant. "Lishum," she called softly. "Lishum, Lishum . . ."

Now, everyone was awake and crying. "Let me kiss my brother," Burrum said, stroking his hair. "Meezzan, come and kiss my brother."

Dazedly, Zan bent over the child's body and put her lips to his mouth. There was a terrible pain behind her ribs. Only days before, Lishum had been alive, laughing, crying, speaking, touching. Now there was only this—thing. This—body. Unresponsive, Clammy, stiffening. He was—*dead*.

She understood.

But that it had happened to a child, to Lishum—it was unfair!

"My cousin is so cold," Ai'ma said in her deep voice. "I don't like Lishum to be so cold!"

Tears filled Zan's eyes. Lishum. She rocked Ai'ma back and forth. How could it be?

Oh, she understood what death meant. Breath stopped, heart and brain, kidneys and liver, arms and legs and eyes all stopped working and pumping and being. Yes, that was it, but, really, she didn't understand it at all! Why had it happened? It was wrong! She wanted to cover her head and crawl into a corner.

But there were things to be done and no one could hide in a corner. One by one they kissed the dead child. Now, Farwe lay him down on the bed of leaves and crawled on hands and knees to the hearth, where she rubbed ashes in her hair and smeared her face and body with soot. "Come, take the ashes," Burrum said. Her hands were burning hot on Zan's arms. "Protect yourself from the Anouch'i. They have found our little brother. We must not let them find anyone else." Faces and bodies disappeared beneath the ashes. Only eyes glowed large and wet from the sooty masks.

"Come, Keyria, Foomia," Raaniu said in a loud voice. "Come, my brothers, come, Miiniu, we will take this child's body away. Vulture will devour this useless shell." The four men picked up the child, one at each limb, and carried him from the cave.

Something hard and frantic was pumping in Zan's throat. Lishum had said, *When I am grown, I will be Meezzan's man!* Now his body was to be eaten by animals. She clutched Burrum. "Where are they going? Oh, what are they doing?"

Burrum's face was streaked with sooty tears. She put her mouth to Zan's ear. "Hush, hush, they are taking him to Cave-of-No-Name." Zan's heart slipped sideways in her chest. She remembered the old man, Toufa, his agitation, her confusion. "We must not let the

Anouch'i know," Burrum whispered, "else they will come and steal his body!"

The bedding on which Lishum had lain during his illness was thrown into a far, dark part of the cave, and fresh bedding was gathered. The men returned and once again all smeared themselves with soot and ashes.

Farwe and Mai'bu took brands from the fire. Ainu put her baby down on the bed and, leaving Ai'ma to care for the infant, everyone else followed Farwe out of the cave. They climbed up the path, joined along the way by other families. The rain fell. The path became slippery. Here was the hill where Zan had stood the day Burrum was at the Women's Stream. She remembered her naive pleasure in exploring all alone. Lishum had wanted to come with her, but she had slipped away from him.

Now, with people packed densely behind her, with everyone here except Lishum, she again followed the stream coursing between gray ledges, again came suddenly upon the enormous mushroom rock, hurried past it, and came to the soaked, green entrance of Cave-of-No-Name.

Entering the cave, they followed the stream into the cavernous, high-ceilinged room bejeweled with stone formations. Here, Zan thought, they would stop, but they continued on, moving to the end of the room where it narrowed into a low tunnel.

Ahead of Zan, Burrum entered the tunnel on hands and knees and disappeared into the darkness. Zan followed.

Acrid smoke from torches filled the air. Zan's throat burned. Soon her hands and knees were scraped raw. Crawling behind Burrum, pressed by people behind her,

Zan sensed the narrowness of the ledge and the awful depths to her right, but she could see nothing.

"Keep close to the wall," Burrum instructed. Her voice sounded oddly hollow. "Do not be afraid."

Zan crawled slowly forward. From deep inside the mountain came the measured beat of a drum, as if the heart of the mountain were pounding. It seemed to her that it was pounding out Lishum's name. *Li-shum . . . Li-shum . . . Li-shum . . .* The beating of the drum drew her on, beating through the earth, beating in her head. The ledge widened, sloped downward. She was able to stand again.

Her legs tottery, she followed Burrum into a large rounded chamber already half filled with people. More people crowded in. Torches flickered. From somewhere in the center of the room came the incessant drum beat. Bones and skulls were heaped in the corners and along the edges of the walls. A large opening in the ceiling let in a wash of smoky light that fell across a platform of rock, where Lishum's body lay.

People swayed and sang, groaning, keening, "Little son, you are gone. You have left us." On hands and knees, Raaniu beat his head against the earth. And next to him, Farwe mourned, "Oh, let me go to Place-of-Night-Sun! I am tired of suffering in this world. I want to see my little son, I want to be with him in that happy place."

The heat and smoke stabbed into Zan's eyes. She looked again and again at Lishum on the platform. Had he always been so small, so shrunken?

And still people crowded into the mourning chamber, crying and singing, pushing Zan back to the wall. Suddenly, a huge red fish leaped toward her, a fish from a dream, glittering mouth open, eyes bulging from

his head. A cry caught in her throat. Behind the red
fish, smaller fish, red and white, with fins like wings,
swam toward her out of the dense smoke. She flung out
her arms and sagged against the wall. The fish were
painted. Above them birds were painted; beneath the
fish, water. Zan rubbed her fingers over the wall. Fish
painted over fish, birds over birds. Generations of fish
and birds, faded, smoky, ancient beyond thought. Then,
a half-lifesize figure. A female body with the head of a
fish. Round breasts, arms upraised, legs bent at the knee.
The fish's head, wise and mysterious. The figure triumphantly dancing atop a mountain painted over the
curves and bumps of the wall. *Olima,* Zan thought.

Burrum pulled her away from the wall into the center of the room, where the wispy-haired old man
Toufa sat cross-legged, beating on a drum made from a
giant turtle shell. Now there was nothing pathetic about
him as he bent with dignity over the drum, bony shoulders curved, hands moving like dancers over the shell,
eyes drawn deep into his head.

In the confined space, the mournful voices and the
pulsing beat of the drum reverberated through Zan till
she felt her body dissolving with grief. Burrum's fingers
dug into Zan's arm. "When the Death Drum is quiet,
when we have stopped singing our sorrow, when we
have all left, then the Vulture with White Eyes will fly
down through the ceiling and clean Lishum's flesh so
that Ta may go free."

Zan's throat ached. She remembered the time she
had seen Lishum lying in the rain, laughing, simply
laughing with joy as the rain poured down on him. And
other times, when for long moments he had been deep-
eyed and reflective, hanging onto his mother's breasts
or rubbing his cheeks against his father's face.

Pressed on every side by the hot, quivering bodies of the mourners, with the smell of smoke and death in her nostrils, the drum beating in her ears, Zan felt raw and aching.

When at last they left Cave-of-No-Name and came out into the waning light of day, she was exhausted. In Farwe's cave she lay down and fell into a stuporous sleep. Waking only moments later, she thought at once of Lishum. She turned her head. In a moment wouldn't she see him, belly poked out, calling her? She staggered from the bed into the wet, soft evening. Were the vultures already tearing his flesh?

Under a tree, Burrum squatted, her face streaked with soot. Her uncle Keyria was tightly binding the base of her little finger on the left hand with a bit of vine. The finger was white, drained of blood.

"What is Keyria doing to you?" Zan said, squatting down next to Burrum.

"Put your finger here, niece," said Keyria, pointing to a flat stone. Burrum laid her finger on the edge of the stone. With the flat of his hand, Keyria gave her a tremendous blow on the upper arm. "Now you will not feel it so much," he said, and began sawing through Burrum's finger with a sharp stone.

Horror sucked Zan hollow. She grabbed for Keyria's arm, but Burrum stopped her.

"No! Meezzan, do not touch him." Burrum's lips were white, bloodless.

Keyria grunted as he pushed the cutting stone forcibly through flesh and bone. Without lifting his eyes, he said, "Meezzan, Nii'uff would be good for this."

Zan moaned, a dry sickness in her mouth. Burrum's eyes were glazed. She didn't cry out. The severed finger dropped to the ground. Blood gushed from the wound.

Keyria handed Burrum a clump of grass to put on the stump and told her to hold her hand up in the air. He stroked her hair and spoke to her in a soft voice. "Are you comfortable, niece? Do not walk around. I will bring you fruit to eat." He picked up the finger and took it away.

Burrum looked at Zan. "Meezzan, do you not know? It is for my brother. Thus, I mourn him forever."

27

For hours that night Keyria played on his reed, a thin melancholy sliver of sound, and Raaniu, squatting before the fire, sang softly, almost to himself. Both Burrum and Farwe nursed mutilated hands.

It was very late before the family settled down to sleep. Raw with the pain of Lishum's death and Burrum's mutilation, Zan slept only fitfully, dreaming of stifling tunnels.

Waking before everyone, she at once felt Lishum's absence. No matter that a dozen others slept on all sides of her. Lishum was gone, and the cave seemed empty. Zan crept out.

She went down to the river. The sky in the east was a clear green, in the west dark as crows' wings. She ate berries and chewed a handful of sweet grass, then climbed a tree to look for a bird's nest. A wind sprang up; far away rain marched across the valley. Holding onto the tree with both hands and rocking slowly, she thought of Lishum.

Then, from her perch she saw Diwera going into the forest and she remembered the Wai Wai's terrible words. *If the child dies, go away from the People. Leave us!* Zan clapped her hands fiercely over her ears,

but the words would not be blotted out. Climbing down
from the tree, she hurried into the forest after Diwera.
Pain and grief made her bold. She would make Diwera
take back those words. She would meet Diwera's eyes
without flinching and tell her, *Diwera, why do you
blame me? I loved him too! You tell me to go away, but
I have nowhere to go.*

And Diwera would say, *Of course I did not know
what I said! I was full of grief myself. You loved him
like a sister, everyone knows this. Those were foolish
words I spoke!*

As she set foot on the forest path, the rains came,
splashing leaves, pounding the earth. Beneath the wind,
the huge trees bent, groaning. Soon Zan was soaked.
The wind and rain obscured all sound. Twice, three
times, she called Diwera. "Diwera . . . wait . . . I must
talk to you-ooo . . ." Each time the wind swallowed her
voice. Rain fell steadily on her head, mud splashed her
legs, her hair stuck to her shoulders. Diwera moved at a
fast, steady pace. Through the dim wet tangle of trees
and vines, Zan barely kept the woman in sight. But she
was determined not to turn back.

Ahead of her, Diwera ran across a log bridging a
swollen stream. By the time Zan had cautiously followed on the slippery log, Diwera was out of sight. Zan
ran, stumbled, ran again, her face and arms whacked
by wet branches. Far ahead, blurred, blending with the
trees, she caught a glimpse of Diwera. She followed her
into a field swaying with reeds growing high over her
head. But she lost her again as the field gave way to dry
soil and stubbles of grass pushing up through rocks and
stones. She ran straight on anyway, leaping over stones.
Abruptly she was standing on the rim of a ravine. Far
below, the rain-swollen river boiled over rocks. On the

other side of the ravine, the cliff wall was sheer, layers of rock exposed by the water that had gouged out the channel. "Diwera? Diwera!" Zan called into the rain and the pounding of the river. "Diwer-aaa!"

Below her, Diwera suddenly appeared, a tiny figure zigzagging down the cliff wall.

Crouching for balance, Zan began descending the ravine wall, slipping and sliding, clutching at plants to steady herself. She fell, picked herself up, went on, sliding the last few feet on her back. At the bottom of the ravine, ferns and creepers grew thickly along the banks. A series of stones resembling a natural bridge led to the middle of the river, where an enormous wedge of rock jutted high into the air. There, on top of the rock, Diwera stood, her back to Zan, arms upraised, braids streaming into the wind and the rain.

Standing on Asking Rock in Place-of-Fear, rain and wind blowing across her uplifted face, Diwera called on the spirits to help her in her troubled time. Had she offended the spirits? Neglected some promise made to Olima or Miiawa? Was this why they had sent Meezzan to the People? So that Lishum, a child, would be taken from them? So that the rains, unlike any within memory, would pour from the sky without cease? So that Nabrushi, that good old man, would become too fearful to leave his daughter's cave?

The night before, Diwera had dreamed of three hills. The sun set below one hill. The moon rose above the second hill. And from the third hill, the old Wai Wai, Yooria, spoke the name of Meezzan. Waking, hearing that name resound hollowly in her head, Diwera knew that all these bad things came from Meezzan and her powers. She knew that this day she would go to Place-of-Fear.

"Olima, mother of us all, answer me," she implored, raising her wet face toward the east. Dimly, through the furious pounding of rain on water, and water on rock, she heard the spirits answer, ". . . err meee."

Once, long ago, she had come to Place-of-Fear with old Yooria. Here, no one but the Wai Wai dared come. Here, when all else failed, the Wai Wai came to call Olima and the spirits who lived in air and water. Always they answered in half-heard words, a mockery of one's own voice, reminding one that there was no power as great as the power of the spirits, that the spirits spoke in their own time and in their own way.

"Your daughter calls you," Diwera cried. "Speak to her. Tell her."

". . . errr," the spirits echoed from the corners of the ravine.

Diwera's mind darted like a bird before a storm. *Olima, what must I do about Meezzan? Why has there not been a girl I can touch and say, You will be the Wai Wai when I am gone, when my flesh is loosened and eaten by the vultures. Meezzan's powers are so great. Show me a way to protect the People. Olima, send me a sign.*

She looked up into the gray swirling sky, and then down into the angry waters. If a single bird flew across the sky, it would mean one thing. If the sky was darkened with birds, it would mean another thing. Fish breaking the water, frogs with yellow eyes, or a herd of Pinudri deer coming to drink—each of these things might guide and direct her thoughts. She saw nothing except rain gushing from the sky as if it would never stop.

"Olima!" she cried from the depths of her confusion and, crossing her arms over her breasts, she gripped herself in a frenzy of longing for life to go on as it

always had. Closing her eyes, she again implored the
spirits for a sign. All around her she felt their presence,
behind her and over her, in the turbulent air and in the
rushing waters. Oh, let them speak! She would listen
and learn. She opened herself to the spirits and, in the
midst of her reverie, through the sound of rain beating
on stone and water, she felt them touch her on the
shoulder. An ecstatic shudder passed through her body.
Her lips moved in wordless thanks. That touch, like the
wings of a great bird, carried her upward, up, up, up,
up into the air where in a blinding vision she saw the
whole world spread beneath her, forest and mountains,
river and streams, the world of the People, the land
below and the sky above, the stars and moon and sun
all rising and falling . . .

Diwera . . .

Her name was being called by the spirits! Above
the drumming of water came, "Diwera! Diwera!"

Opening her eyes, she saw Meezzan standing before
her on Asking Rock, and her ecstatic vision was blotted
out by a wave of terror. None but the Wai Wai could
come to Place-of-Fear! Yet, here stood Meezzan. And
nothing struck her down!

Diwera saw Meezzan's lips move, she heard her
voice say, "I followed you." Her own lips felt numb, as
if she had poisoned herself with raw Pana. How great
must be the powers of Meezzan! Greater than Diwera
had feared. Greater even than the powers of the spirits
who lived in Place-of-Fear. A groan welled up from
deep in Diwera's belly.

Meezzan plucked hotly at her arm. Diwera's eyes
blurred; she trembled suddenly and was bathed in sweat
as her head echoed with words and voices: the spirits
were speaking to her, giving her the answers she had

sought. Her mind was split as if by lightning and, at last, she understood everything. This Meezzan was not flesh and bone, not one who had come wailing bloody from between her mother's legs, but a spirit sprung full-grown in the shape of a girl. A spirit come to challenge Diwera. The knowledge made Diwera gasp for breath as if her chest were being slowly crushed beneath a great rock.

"Go!" Diwera tremblingly commanded the Shape of Meezzan. "Go! I know what you are!" But the Shape went on breathing its hot breath and foul words into Diwera's face. Then Diwera knew what she must do. Her flesh shrank from the Shape, but with a cry of mingled fear and defiance, she thrust it away from her, sending it toppling over Asking Rock and into the angry waters. The Shape of Meezzan cried out, but Diwera leaped onto the stepping stones and did not look back.

28

The rushing waters tumbled Zan swiftly downstream as if she were a fallen twig. Sucked under, she struggled to the surface, choking and coughing, only to be scraped against a rock and pulled down under the water again. The river pounded, pulling her under, filling her eyes and mouth and lungs.

Going to drown. Die.

She clawed her way to the surface, gulped air, was pulled down again. The first numbing shock wore off. Her mind started working, giving her directions.

Don't panic. Hold your breath . . . you're going up . . . look for something to grab . . .

Surfacing, her head banged against the thick exposed root of a tree clinging to the ravine wall. She flung out her arms and embraced the root desperately. Half in, half out of the water, she had strength enough only to hang on. The river surged by, sucking greedily at her dangling legs. She pulled herself slowly along the root, inching toward the shore, where she fell on her belly.

Zan sat up, shaking. Clinging to bushes, half crawling, she made her way up the ravine wall. At the top she looked down at the river.

Blood trickled down her legs from scrapes and cuts. On her hip there was an egg-sized lump already turning blue. She scrubbed at a thin line of blood.

She pushed me in. Tried to drown me.

Keeping to the top of the cliff she walked back to the spot where she'd followed Diwera down into the ravine. She realized the rain had stopped. A fresh wind blew the sky clean. The sun sparkled off the big rock jutting out of water.

Pushed me in. Just shoved me. Backwards into the water.

She walked away. Thoughts came in chaotic waves, then receded, leaving her blank, only to rush in again. *Wanted to kill me. Kill me? Unreal.*

Why would anyone want to kill her? Yet she had been shoved into the water. Deliberately. The fact was there, inescapable.

"I might be dead now. I could have been drowned." The sound of her own voice saying this inexplicable thing was too much. She couldn't cope both with the enormity of what had happened and with finding her way back to the caves. She concentrated on the latter. She might have followed Diwera for an hour, or for two hours. She might have been in the water for five minutes, or for fifty minutes. It was impossible to know.

Doesn't make any difference. Just get back to the caves.

She talked to herself about the path, which direction she ought to take, describing the field she had crossed and what she remembered of the forest trail. But as soon as she stopped talking, she began thinking about Diwera.

All the time she had been speaking to the woman, she had felt that Diwera didn't really see her. Her eyes had been strange, glittering in a fixed way. And then she had shouted, "Go," or "Go away," or something like that, and before Zan could even take a step, she had shoved her into the river.

"She really did," Zan said to herself. "She really did that." Her throat ached. She longed for someone to hold her head and comfort her. Whenever Zan bruised herself, Farwe would say, "You poor child! You poor thing!" and hug her as if she were as small as Lishum.

Lishum. A chill shook her. She had forgotten. She sat down on the ground, her head against a tree, eyes closed, arms around herself. But she couldn't rest. She saw Lishum's body in the smoke-filled cave. Then Burrum's bloody finger stump. And water, the horrible torrent rushing over her face, buffeting her as if she were a bit of debris.

Lishum was dead. And she might have been dead. An awful loneliness came over her. "Ohhh!" she cried. "Ohhh!" She needed to touch someone. She rocked herself back and forth, aching for the caves, for the fire, the jostling and laughter of the family.

She pushed on. The sun was low in the sky. After a while, surprised and grateful, she realized that the afternoon rains hadn't come. She thought she was moving in the right direction. How long had she been walking? She tried to think clearly. It seemed to her she ought to have been back at the caves by now. Was she walking in circles?

Scared, she sat down again to think. She must have slept. Perhaps she had slept the other time she rested, too. Confused and exhausted, she went on, stopping to eat some berries. She realized that she had eaten almost nothing all day. Birdcalls filled the air. The sun set. The sky darkened. Soon all light would be gone.

She moved on, knowing she ought to stop because she would never find her way in the dark. The moon rose, splashing the forest with light. Suddenly, among the rocks above her, as if framed in a window, she saw the profile of an animal with long tusks jutting down its upper jaw. The head, shining in the moonlight, was golden with tawny hair. The great cat puffed like an ox, now loudly, now softly. Zan leaped away in terror, ran down a slope and splashed across a stream. Completely out of breath, her sides aching, she pushed her trembling legs to the top of a hill.

Can't go on. Exhausted. Stupid to keep looking for the caves.

She would sleep and go on in the morning. As she climbed a tree, ants stung her on one leg, then on the other, then on her foot. She tried to pick them off, but they stung her hands. She had stepped on a nest and they were coming out to sting her all over. She ran again, brushing off ants, letting her feet go where they would. *Run all night. Run forever. Never stop.*

She smelled smoke and ran harder. Smoke was curling into the moonlit night air. She heard voices, singing, people laughing. In a moment, she was on the path up the mountain. A crowd milled around Farwe's fire. Diwera, too? Zan moved behind a tree, quiet, watching. She circled around and slipped unnoticed into the empty cave.

Zan lay down on her bed of grass, then got up and reached into the niche in the wall for her little bark bag. The niche was empty. She put her hand into the crevice again, searching thoroughly. Nothing! She knelt down and felt on the floor, and found the bark bag almost at her feet. She knew, even before she reached in, that it was empty. She tied the bag to her waist and crawled around on the floor.

Who could have done it? Farwe? Burrum? Keyria? No, not the family. Outside, laughter splashed through the night. A needlepoint of pain and fury touched her spine. Only yesterday, they had been weeping, sobbing, grieving over Lishum. Now they could sing, laugh. Her mouth was dry. Too much had happened for her to comprehend. Her ribs began to ache, as if in delayed reaction to the battering they had taken in the river. For the first time since the beginning, she was truly afraid for her life.

29

Late that afternoon, Diwera had come back to her cave. Mumbling chants, she knelt before the fire and threw in handfuls of secret herbs. The fire blazed with brilliant colors, giving off a strange, musky odor. Hiffaru was piercing polished dried nuts for a necklace, his thoughts anticipating Burrum's admiration of it. He believed his mother was so absorbed that she was unaware of his presence. This was often the case. But, presently, she drew him to her, saying, "Listen to me, my son. The Shape of Meezzan is gone. This afternoon the rains did not come. The Season of Rains is over, and now bad things are finished for the People."

"Where is Meezzan?" he said. Earlier he had gone to see Burrum and she had asked him if he had seen Meezzan.

His mother's hands held him fiercely. "Hiffaru, my son. Do not ask anything. I tell you the Shape of Meezzan will not come again. Now her powers must be offered to Olima. My son, I may not touch those things. It is not for me to touch those powers." Her brown eyes gazed at him, drawing him closer. How tenderly he loved his mother! She was the only one who did not flinch from his shattered face.

"I will help you, Mother," he said. And later, when dusk had fallen, he went down the mountain. Many people were singing and talking outside Farwe's cave, making Farwe and Raaniu laugh so that the grief they felt would not poison them like the bite of a snake. No one noticed as Hiffaru went into the cave, found the little bark bag, and emptied it into his hands. And no one noticed when he left.

Where the river ran swiftly, he climbed to the top of a high rock and, one by one, dropped Kee, Baa'tun, and Saff'tee Pan into the water, each time calling, "Olima! Olima! Take this power far away from the People. Olima, do you hear your son calling you?"

He had only Nii'uff to drop into the water and was raising his hand when something stopped him, a feeling in his belly that confused him. He wanted to go on holding Nii'uff. To *have* it. Never before had he felt such a longing. His body went hot all over, and hottest of all was the hand that held Nii'uff. So many times he had seen Meezzan use Nii'uff, seen it cut, *thunk! thunk! thunk!* It was like a living thing when it twirled in the air and dived into the earth. He had seen Sun in Nii'uff as Sun was often in the water, dazzling the eyes, making little suns sparkle in the air. He had seen Nii'uff hide as Turtle hides. Yes, he had seen all these things, but he had never, like some others (like Sonte), sniffed about Meezzan, hoping she would give him Nii'uff. He was too proud! He had always had better things to do. Yet, all the time he had dreamed of Nii'uff.

Hiffaru leaned out over the water, knowing how Nii'uff would spin and plunge in its fall, but again his fingers refused to give it up. *Throw Nii'uff into the river, my son. Give Nii'uff to Olima. Your mother, the Wai Wai, tells you to do this.* Never before had he disobeyed his mother. Yet he took a step backward, away from the water, then another step. Then, again, he went forward and held out his hand, but at the last moment he retracted it and swiftly walked away, his belly clenching as if he were hungry. Yes, he was hungry! Hungry for Nii'uff. The knowledge of this hunger and of what he had just done shamed him deeply. He moaned as if in pain, but even as he did he was thinking of ways to conceal Nii'uff from the others.

It was dark when Hiffaru stopped again near Farwe's cave. A half moon was slowly rising in the east, casting a glow over the scene before him. There were still great numbers of people about, but no one paid any special attention to Hiffaru. He was always on the edge of gatherings, rarely in the center. Glancing swiftly around, he saw Bahii and Em'Fadi, Goah, Mahu the Teller, Sonte, and Sonte's aunt Yano with her baby in her arms. Perhaps his mother, too, was somewhere among them. Aiii! What would she say, what would she do if she found out that he had not given up Nii'uff and its powers to Olima?

Pushing aside these troublesome thoughts and opening Nii'uff, he laid the bright tongue flat against the flesh of his arm. Cool, cool as water, and like water it shone in the moonlight.

He pressed the point firmly against his arm, drawing blood as Nii'uff bit him. He pressed the point against his arm again and again, dizzy with wonder. Nii'uff took little bites and blood welled up in tiny spots along his arm. Nii'uff was his! He would never give it to anyone. His breath trembled at the thought. It would no longer matter that he was ugly. It would no longer matter that they whispered the Anouch'i had got him on his mother, that the heel of the Anouch'i had slipped, crumpling half his face like a leaf. No, none of that would matter because everyone would want what only he, Hiffaru, had.

In the joy of these thoughts, he forgot that he would have to conceal Nii'uff, and he nearly laughed out loud, imagining how people would say respectfully, *Oh, Hiffaru has Nii'uff. How fine Nii'uff is!* He would smile and bend his head, but he would not give Nii'uff to anyone. No, not anyone! Then he thought of Burrum, as he often did. Aiii, when she saw that Nii'uff was his and that everyone respected him, then at last she would forget about Sonte! Drawing his forefinger tenderly over the sharp tongue of Nii'uff, Hiffaru saw a sweet vision in his mind: Burrum leaning against him, as they admired Nii'uff together; and Sonte appearing and Burrum saying, *Who is that boy who calls himself Sonte? I don't remember him. He makes me tired. I wish he would go away.* Yes! Yes! Burrum would forget Sonte and think only of him, Hiffaru. Again, slowly, as though he were caressing his mother's face, Hiffaru drew his fingers along the blade of Nii'uff.

Kneeling by Farwe's fire, feeding wood, Sonte peered into the pale darkness beyond, where a few minutes before he had seen Hiffaru. Something about the protective hump of Hiffaru's shoulders had caught his attention. Sonte had always been more aware of Hiffaru than of anyone else, except Burrum. He knew how Hiffaru looked at Burrum, knew how Hiffaru looked at him. Whenever he thought of Hiffaru someday lying with Burrum, a cold, hard feeling gathered in the back of his head and in his belly, and he would push away his mother's hands and speak to no one.

He had been glad to Quarrel with Hiffaru for his mother! In the way of the Quarrel he should not have

felt anger, except as he felt his mother's anger toward
Farwe. He should not have derived pleasure from the
Quarrel, except as it came from defending his mother.
Yet the moment he had seen Hiffaru facing him with
his one tiny, flat eye, like the eye of a snake, he had felt
pleasure and rage quaking through him. He had spit out
his insults as if they came straight from his belly. Sonte
had been ashamed and had told no one, not his
mother, not Burrum. Thus the shame had stayed with
him, lying hard in his belly like a stone.

Now he stood up and slowly edged his way through
the crowd toward Hiffaru. "Sonte, my son." His mother
took him by the arm. "Is your belly well, my son?"
Lishum's death had upset N'ati very much. All night
she had had bad dreams and had awakened this morning crying that she had seen her man, Fusiawa, once
again laid out on the platform waiting for Vulture in
Cave-of-No-Name. Sonte and Yano had both been
needed to calm his mother.

"I am well, Mother," he said, patting her hand.

"Mahu will tell a story," his mother said. "Come and
listen, my son."

"Soon, Mother." Again he moved toward Hiffaru,
close enough to see that Hiffaru held in his hand something that gleamed like fire sparks. At once, Sonte knew
what it was. *Hiffaru has Nii'uff.* A hot stream, like raw
Pana in the throat, poured into his belly. Often, he had
seen Hiffaru's eyes on Nii'uff, and he had known that
Hiffaru wanted Nii'uff as much as he himself wanted it.
The wanting crept like poison from the belly, to the
throat, to the brain. Yes, Sonte knew that poison feeling well—to want and not have. To ask and not get.
Was it not this way with Burrum?

"Hiffaru," he said. "Nii'uff is fine, is it not?"

Hiffaru's head jerked up. "You speak foolish things." He tried to hide Nii'uff. His small eye darted from Sonte toward the gathering around the fire. "I do not know what you mean."

"No, you are the foolish one!" Sonte said. "My eyes tell me you have Nii'uff! I am surprised to see you with Nii'uff. I did not know Meezzan gave it to you." Sonte spoke calmly, but the poison foamed like angry waters in his belly. "I would like to have it now."

He held out his hand. When one asked for something, then, of course, one expected to receive it. Only Meezzan did not do this, for she was a daughter of Others. But Hiffaru did not give him Nii'uff.

"Listen, Sonte, my friend," Hiffaru said. "You do not want Nii'uff. Paaa!" He spit to one side, as if to show that Nii'uff was a thing of no consequence.

Sonte scrabbled his toes in the dirt, his arms crossed over his chest, trying to appear uncaring. "It would make my belly happy to have Nii'uff. It would make my mother happy to see her son with such a fine thing!"

Hiffaru scowled. "Go away, Sonte. Do not ask me for Nii'uff. It is a bad thing! Do your ears hear what I am saying?"

"My ears are open. They hear you. Now let your ears listen to me!" Sonte's voice rose so that people around the fire looked up. "You have called me friend," Sonte went on loudly. "If I am your friend, then let me keep that bad thing for you." Again he held out his hand. "Give me Nii'uff, Hiffaru, and I will give you something, of course. Tell me what you want." He touched a necklace of tiny shells on his chest. "My mother, N'ati, made this necklace for me. Let me give it to you." He began to remove it.

"Aiii! I do not want your necklace," Hiffaru said sharply, walking away.

Sonte grabbed his arm. "What is this? What kind of man are you?" The poison churned in his belly and his brain. Was Hiffaru always to have everything he was denied? Hiffaru would have Burrum—then let Sonte have Nii'uff! "Give Nii'uff to me. You, of the ugly face, give it to me!"

Hiffaru was shaking. He had dreamed of the power Nii'uff would bestow on him, but truly he had wanted no one to know the shame of keeping it. Now Sonte had said everything in his loud voice for everyone to hear. Burrum, her mother, her father, and all people who knew him—all the People!—had heard Sonte say that Hiffaru had Nii'uff. They had all heard Sonte call him "ugly face." Hiffaru raised the hand that held Nii'uff. Sonte's perfect face mocked his eyes.

Hiffaru meant only to make Sonte leave him alone. He did not want to look at his face anymore. He did not want to hear his voice anymore. He only meant for Nii'uff to bite Sonte as it had bitten him (but perhaps a little harder). From the corner of his eye, he saw Burrum watching Sonte in a way she never watched Hiffaru. In that instant Nii'uff moved like a living thing in his hand and its shining sharp tongue darted into Sonte's belly. Sonte made a queer sound. Hiffaru's mouth dropped open; he pulled away Nii'uff, and Sonte fell against him, slipping slowly to his knees while blood from the hole in his belly smeared Hiffaru's body.

30

"My son, my son, my son, my son," N'ati sang dully. She sat on the ground with Sonte's head in her lap, smoothing the hair away from his face. His eyes were rolled up into his head, showing only the whites. Blood and foam leaked from his mouth.

On her knees, Diwera bent over Sonte, packing the wound with handfuls of leaves and grass to stop the bleeding. All around was pandemonium. People staggered in every direction, clutching their hair, breaking into shrieks of terror. Never had one of the People struck a fatal blow against another.

"My son, my son, my son," N'ati mourned, kissing Sonte's face repeatedly. Burrum and Farwe clung to each other, weeping. Nii'uff lay on the ground, bloody, untouched. No one dared go near it, as no one went near Hiffaru, who crouched, trembling and rocking, his arms over his head.

As she finished doing what little she could for Sonte, Diwera looked up and saw before her the Shape of Meezzan, kneeling and crying, wringing its hands over Sonte's body. Diwera's eyes bulged in horror. Her limbs trembled. Had she not seen with her own eyes the Shape carried away by the river? Now it had come back! Were its powers limitless? Her belly jerked in terror. Beyond a doubt, she knew it was the Shape of Meezzan that had made her son keep Nii'uff. The Shape of Meezzan had driven Nii'uff, held in her son's hand, into Sonte's belly. The Shape of Meezzan had made that deep and terrible hole in Sonte's flesh, through which his life was pouring out.

Staring at the fearful Shape, its mouth open and wailing as it bent over Sonte, Diwera knew that she must drive it away once and for all. She must destroy the Shape before it destroyed the People. She must turn the power of the Shape against itself. "Aiii," she groaned as she forced herself to reach over and pick up the stained Nii'uff. Her hand shook and she gripped her wrist with the other hand for strength. Crying out in a hoarse voice, she flung Nii'uff at the Shape of Meezzan, calling upon it to depart from the People forever.

The Shape screamed and fell back. It screamed and screamed, and the screams were taken up by others. Cries echoed and re-echoed. Men and women ran senselessly about in panic and grief, colliding with one another, crying out their terror. A man banged his head against the cliff face. A woman chewed on her arm. The screaming and wailing grew in intensity. Diwera stood up, crying out her own anguish.

"Come! Stop! Mahu! Raaniu! Fosia! Listen to me. Listen. The Shape will not harm you anymore." But the screaming only grew louder. Diwera's voice could not pierce the clamor. People trampled through the fire; children wailed hysterically; at her feet N'ati chanted her grief over her stricken son. And Diwera knew despair.

Someone grabbed her arm. "Mother. Mother!" It was Akawa. "Mother, we must tell the Keeper to beat the Death Drum."

"The Death Drum," Diwera repeated. And, as though she were the daughter, Akawa the mother, she said almost pleadingly, "But that drum is beaten only for those who have died." Sonte still lived, though the breath escaped his mouth only in shallow puffs.

Akawa's hand tightened on Diwera's arm. "They are all afraid. They are screaming and running around. Their minds have fled. We must stop them, Mother. The Anouch'i are among us! The People will come together for the Death Drum. They will stop and listen when they hear the Death Drum."

Diwera stared at her daughter in confusion and triumph, shame and joy. She had thought Akawa shallow, vain, unfit to be Wai Wai! "All this is the doing of the Shape of Meezzan," Diwera said, her hands stretching wide to indicate the hysterical people. Two women ran past, screaming, and a man with a child in his arms fell to the ground, writhing and choking. Diwera felt herself trembling again. "I have made the Shape die," she said harshly. "I took its power into my hand, and I used it against itself!"

"Yes, Mother, yes," Akawa said. "But tell me that I may call for the Death Drum!"

"Aiii." Diwera bent her head. Grief bruised her. Grief for Sonte. Grief for Hiffaru. Grief for herself, who had had to raise her hand in anger and fury.

"Mother," Akawa pleaded.

Diwera nodded. "Go, then. Go!" She watched Akawa hurry away. The girl would find Toufa, the Keeper of the Death Drum. Akawa was right. Now was a time to beat the drum. Soon, Sonte would die. But already something else was dead, something that had died when Hiffaru plunged Nii'uff into Sonte's belly. Never again would the life of the People be the same.

"Olima, Olima," Diwera cried. Then the sound of the drum was heard, and Diwera knelt next to Sonte and joined Farwe in chanting her grief and sorrow to the solemn slow rhythm of death.

Running down the path, Zan, too, heard the hollow beat of the drum. Down the mountain she ran. The moon, like a huge, half-closed eye, seemed to follow her into the forest. She ran to the only refuge she knew— the meadow. Her feet took her unerringly through the high, damp grasses to the hollow tree, where she threw on her clothes and, like an animal seeking shelter from a storm, flung herself down next to her boulder, burrowing as close as she could to its familiar presence. She was too far away now to hear the drum, but it seemed to beat in her head, telling her that Sonte was dead. The blood sticky on his belly . . . his eyes gone into the back of his head. *The knife . . . oh, the knife . . . he's dead . . . it hurts to think . . . hurts . . . hurts. . . . oh, help me, help me, helpmehelpmehelpme . . . please . . . please . . .*
Her mind sank and drowned. Her heart beat like the drum. Her skin and bones, blood and flesh drew together like a beam of light, narrowed, intensified, concentrated, her total self no more than a terrible thrusting need to be removed from the pain and fear and grief. She felt nothing in the ordinary way, neither the ground beneath her, nor the stone against her back. The moon no longer shone for her. Her bones were cracking, her skin peeling like bark from a tree. She cried out, but no sound came. Burning streams of silver poured through her eyes. Then there was darkness and she was like a speck of dust flung through space and time forever . . .

31

Zan's teeth were anesthe-
tized. Numb. That was the first thing she noticed. Then
the noise. A jet plane moved through the darkening
blue sky like a prehistoric fish, its shriek trailing behind
like a barbed tail. Car horns barked. "Hey, Ed," someone yelled, and all up and down the length of J Street
and inside Mechanix Park, street lights popped on, one
by one.

"Maud-ee! Peter! You come home, you hear me!"

Sirens. "Aaa-yaaa, aaa-yaaa, aaa-yaaa . . ."

Dogs barking.

A blast of music.

Trucks rumbling on the highway, engines whining
high for the steep grades.

Cars. Thwap! Thwap! Thwap! Thwap! Thwap! Endlessly.

The ground vibrated with noise. The air was shattered by noise.

And the smells. The stink of buses and cars. Oil and
smoke. The odor of rotting garbage. The smell of cats.

And lights. Street lights glaring into her eyes. Headlights. Lights from the apartment buildings across the
street. Harsh punishing lights.

After a while, she spoke to herself. *Get up now. You*

made it. You're here. Up. Up on your feet. She pushed herself to her hands and knees, swayed there for a moment, then collapsed to the ground on her back. Her arms and legs were still weak from the blackness. The storm. "It." She felt raw, bruised. Tears leaked from her eyes, wet her cheeks, ran into her ears.

She tried not to let his name come into her mind, tried not to see the blood, the leaves packed into the hole in his belly. But she saw. She heard. She wanted to howl desperately, blot out the unending noise, the voice in her head, the images behind her eyes. The knife, bloody, coming at her. Acid jetted into her belly. Had she screamed? She couldn't remember. She had fallen onto her side, rolled over, scrambled and crawled away, sobbing, panting, stumbled to her feet, and run. It was all a blur in her mind. Running through the forest. Moonlight. Wetness of branches and grass. The drum. Thum . . . thum . . . thum . . . thum . . .

She pushed her head back and forth against the ground. Oh, Lishum. Oh, Sonte.

Burrum, what are you thinking now?

A man walked by on the other side of the park fence, singing in a drunken voice. "Oh, bury me not on the lone prairie . . ." He laughed. She heard his footsteps fading.

Her teeth were still numb.

Come on, this won't do. It's not like the other time, you know. Here you are. Home. There was a sensible little voice somewhere in her mind. She tried to listen to it, obey it.

She stood up, staggering, off balance, almost falling, but catching herself against the boulder. Slowly she walked through the park, out the gate. She flinched as a car roared past, tires screeching as it took the corner.

For a long time she stood on the sidewalk, pressed against the park fence, trembling, unable to cross the street. Cars passed with sickening regularity. The glare of headlights. Tires on pavement. Snatches of talk and music from car radios. ". . . weather tonight is fair . . ." ". . . ba-bee ba-bee . . ." ". . . users of Corona Cigars know . . ."

A gang of boys, baseball bats over their shoulders, passed her. A man walking a little dog on a long leash. A woman in a black coat and a turban who peered at her, then hurried on, her coat pulled tightly around her.

Zan was dizzy, nauseated. The lights spun in her eyes, spun in her head.

A woman stood at the curb, waiting to cross. She carried a brown paper grocery bag in her arms. Zan stepped behind her and followed the woman across the street, her throat acid. She stepped up on the sidewalk. Safe. The woman walked away. Again Zan tried not to let Sonte's name come into her mind. She rubbed her hand over the rough brick of a building. She started toward home.

32

Talking to herself, whispering, Zan made her way slowly through the half-darkened streets. *C'mon, it isn't that bad* . . . "Yes, it is—I feel so—strange." *Okay, just keep walking, keep going toward home* . . . "Yes—okay—" She dragged her hand along the buildings she passed, scraping her palm. The pain was good. It was real. Her sneakers, untied, flopped loosely on her feet. *Turn the corner here, third building* . . . "I know that." She hadn't forgotten where the family lived. "I'm not that far gone," she told the sensible little voice. A man, passing, looked at her oddly.

She stopped in front of her family's building. The kitchen fronted on the street. She looked up. Light in the window. Behind her, cars passing steadily. A knot of kids, boys and a few girls, down at the corner beneath the street lamp. Laughter and talk drifted her way. "Henry's got it . . . Henry's got it!" "You cheapskate!" "Naw, it's Henry—" She went up the steps. "Henry, Henry," a half dozen voices yelled. The air, clammy, stung her nostrils and her throat.

She negotiated three flights of stairs like someone very old or very feeble. Picking her way up, one stair at a time, leaning her head against the wall, stopping to draw in deep breaths. She wondered at herself. Hadn't she thought so many many times of these very moments? Imagined racing up these stairs, flinging open the apartment door, crying out her arrival. I'M HOME! HEY, EVERYONE, ZAN'S HERE! She wasn't sure now how long she'd been gone. Toward the end, she had neglected her calendar, some days forgotten to scratch in her marks. But close to eleven months, she thought. Eleven months. Almost a whole year.

The halls smelled of vinegar and coffee. Voices leaked out from behind each separate door. Little families in little apartments. Closed off from each other. She rounded the landing and started up the last flight. Faster now. Stronger. Eager at last. It was true then. She was home. Maybe she hadn't believed it till that moment. She stood in front of their door. Brown chipped paint. Three shiny locks. She turned the handle. Unlocked. That meant they were home. Her father, anyway. She stepped into the hall.

The smell of cheese baking. TV sounds from the living room—bright, chattery, fast. Pots rattling in the kitchen. The mirror over the telephone table. She was shocked to see herself. It had been so long. She stared. Was that Zan? Dirt on her forehead. Tanned. Freckles everywhere. Tangled hair. And her eyes—wide, staring, leaking tears again. She was home. From the TV came a burst of laughter and applause. "Ha, ha, ha, ha, hahahahah . . ."

She touched the telephone and the polished surface of the table. *Go on in there and let them know you're back.* The sensible little voice again. *Go on, this is what you've been waiting for. Them, too.*

She took the few steps that led to the living room. Kim and Buddy were lying on the rug in front of the TV, chins in hands, feet up in the air. Buddy's red head shocked her. For how long had she been mixing him and Lishum in her mind? Her face grew hot with guilt, then, pain. Lishum. She dropped to her knees and hugged Buddy, dragging him off the floor, squeezing his sturdy, squirming body against her. "Buddy, Buddy, Buddy . . ."

"Shh, it's the good part," Kim said, not looking up.

The kitchen door swung open, and her mother called, "Enough TV, you two. Come in for supper."

Zan's throat thickened. "Mom! Mom, I'm home."

"So I see," her mother said pleasantly. She walked over to the TV and snapped it off. "Enough, I said. Zan, looks like you're squeezing the life out of poor Buddy. Go wash your hands, kids. And watch the noise. Dad is having a nap in the bedroom. Zan, come in the kitchen and help me."

Halfway back to the kitchen, she paused and looked at Zan, who was numbly following her. "Where've you been all day, anyway?" She shook her head, half smiling. "What in the world have you been up to? You're a mess." She plucked at Zan's shirt with a faint air of distaste. "What're all these awful-looking stains? And your hair—what'd you do to it, honey? It looks like you combed it with an egg beater." She stared at Zan. "Have you been out in the sun all day?" Her smile wavered, she shook her head in a half abstracted way as if shaking off unpleasant thoughts.

Where have I been all day? Where have I been all day? She had heard wrong. She must have heard wrong. It was that awful pain her head, the noises, the glaring lights of the house, the walls that she felt pressing in on her. She followed her mother into the kitchen.

"Mom, you must have worried. I have so much to

tell you. I missed you so much . . ." The tears, leaking again.

Her mother was busy at the stove. "That's sweet, honey. Get out the milk. Pour the kids each a glass. Let's get them fed first. Ivan should be coming home any minute."

And now Zan knew something was wrong. Gone nearly a year and only, *That's sweet, honey. Get out the milk.* She smoothed her hand over the gleaming stainless steel face of the refrigerator. The door swung open at a touch. Shelves stuffed with food, all there for the taking. *That's sweet, honey. Get out the milk.* She felt dazed, confused, sick. Was she being punished? Maybe they thought she had run away—all this time. They were mad. Punishing her. *Pretend it never happened. Let her see if she likes that!*

"Mom, don't you care?" Her voice was so thin. "Why are you so indifferent?" She was still staring dazedly at the shelves of food.

But her mother was pulling the pan of macaroni and cheese out of the oven. "Oooh, this is hot. Hand me that spatula—" The macaroni pan banged onto the table.

Zan closed the door. Inside her, things were spinning and jiggling, whirring and whirling. It was all happening in her head. Faster and faster. Crazy, whirling, spinning, faster, faster—*STOP IT.* She leaned her burning forehead against the cool metal of the refrigerator.

"What's the matter?" her mother said, looking up. "Is something wrong?" She dropped a wedge of baked macaroni onto a plate.

"I think so. Yes. I've been away. You act so—"

"Don't tell me it's the diary thing still bothering you. You ought to know, honey, you can't leave things lying around this apartment. And, anyway—I didn't read it, but I took a quick look—some of the things you wrote in there, you'd have been better off not to. Know what I mean? It's better to keep things to yourself, sometimes. Are you listening, Zan? I feel like I'm talking to myself. You seem like you're a million miles away."

"Yes, Mom. I heard you. I heard everything." Her voice strong for a moment, then fading out. Because the spinning and whirling were starting again. She couldn't stop it. Couldn't stop what she was thinking. "Mom—what's the date?"

"Date? Same as this morning. Twelfth, I think."

"And the day?" Things going faster and faster in her head.

"Saturday, naturally." A touch of impatience in her mother's tone. "What's this, a game? A riddle?"

"Saturday. The twelfth. Of October?"

"All right, Zan, you're behaving very strangely. Have you got something you want to tell me? Where were you today, all day? Did you do something you shouldn't have? You look a little funny, too."

Today, all day. Saturday, the twelfth of October. The sounds of the house throbbed along her skin. The same day. It was the same day. "Mom, there's something—" She groped for words. "Something happened—" She leaned her head against her mother's breast. She hadn't done that for years. She put her arms around her mother, held her tight. "Mom, listen, this'll sound crazy, I know, but it's true." She spoke fast, pleadingly. "I went into the park, you think it was this morning, but really it was months and months ago, almost a year ago, and I was caught up in this kind of storm, like a force, and—"

"Zan, I can't understand one thing you're saying."
Still pleasant, but an edge to her voice. "Now, *is* something the matter with you?" She pushed Zan a little
away from her and looked at her searchingly. "You
look off, somehow. Your color's wrong. Your skin
looks awfully dark! I bet you're getting sick." She put
her palm to Zan's forehead. "I'm sure you have a little
fever. Your eyes . . ." Her voice trailed off and she
smiled crookedly, almost in bewilderment, then seemed
to pull herself together. "Lie down, honey, if you're
getting something, maybe we can nip it in the bud." Her
voice grew brisker. She gave Zan a little turn toward
her cot. "Hop in now. I'll get you some juice."

"Yes, I feel sick," Zan said. She lay down on the cot
near the wall. It was narrow, hard. The room was too
warm. She was sweating.

Ivan came in, whistling, bumping her cot as he
passed. "I'm starved. What's to eat? Hey, Mom, you
should see the stereo Billy's grandfather said he'd buy
him if he passed all his classes this term."

Zan pulled the blankets over her shoulder, closed her
eyes. Her father called from the living room. "Supper
ready yet?"

"Five minutes," her mother said. And to Ivan. "Set
the rest of the table. I guess we'll eat together, after all.
Might as well. Cici's out. Zan doesn't feel well."

"Oh, cripes," Ivan groaned.

Under the blankets Zan was sweating profusely. Her
throat was tight with fear and her mind was skittering
every which way, like those crazy cars at a carnival that
bump into each other. *It's just like always . . . they
haven't changed at all . . . maybe I never left . . . she
said it was the same day . . . maybe I'm crazy . . . made
it all up . . . what if none of it ever happened . . . none*

of it was real? Real. The word echoed mockingly. *STOP THAT.* Then off again, in another direction. She had left the knife. Why had she left the knife? It had brought so much grief, terror, pain, already! But what else could she have done? The knife thrown at her, her terror . . .

She curled up under the blanket with her knees up to her chest, hands in a ball beneath her chin. Remembering . . . something . . . someplace . . . she had curled up like that before . . . Then it came to her, the first night at the caves, when she had slept outside in terror, almost crazy.

Her father came into the kitchen with Buddy and Kim hanging onto his hands. She wanted to cry out, *Daddy! Dad! Dad!*

"Picked up a bug somewhere, Zan?" he said, and sat down at the table with his back to her. She closed her eyes, didn't speak.

She slept poorly that night, wakened by dreams of running through the forest, running and running, behind her Diwera, and ahead of her the ravine . . .

She stayed in bed the next day, and then for three more days. She was sick, trembling and weak. She got out of bed only to use the bathroom. Her toes curled on the hard ungiving floors. She breathed in the stale apartment air. Listlessly, she drank a glass of milk and ate a piece of soft white bread. She couldn't seem to stay awake for long. Burrum came to her in her dreams, calling her, *Meezzan, Meezzan, my sister* . . .

And Sonte, smiling a little in his prideful way, telling her she had confused the words for egg and smooth stone. And Farwe, crying, *Oh, your poor thing!* as she examined the insect bites on Zan's back. Ainu, tickling the baby's stomach. Keyria, playing his reed, eyes

closed. And old Mahu, the Teller, spreading her with-
ered arms and, through some magic or art, creating
Miiawa. Goah, his huge eyes clogged with tears as he
looked at the blood gushing from his thumb. And
Akawa, long, tall Akawa. Hiffaru, standing apart, looking at everything, at everyone, from that small eye. And
then coming out of the cave, seeing the knife in Hiffaru's hand . . . the hole in Sonte's belly . . . screaming
. . . and Diwera shouting . . . the knife flying through
the air toward her . . .

Over and over she dreamed of that last night and
woke each time, moaing, certain that it had all happened. Until the doubts came again. Had she dreamed
it? Imagined it? Made it up?

One morning she sat up in bed. "Cici. Aunt Cici,
could you come here?" Cici was in the living room with
the two children.

She came at once. "Feeling better, Zan?" She wore a
thick, black turtleneck sweater, jeans, and sneakers.
"Want to talk? Don't be surprised if I babble—Kim's
baby talk is getting to me." She winked and sat down
on the edge of the cot.

Zan clutched her arm. "Cici, listen—you know the
morning I had that fight with Ivan? Over the diary?
And I ran out of the house, I was so upset and
everything—"

"Sure." Cici stroked her arm lightly. "I remember I
used to keep a diary, too. Oh, the things I wrote in it!
Half of them lies, you know, things I *wished* would
happen to me. My mother found it once, and what a
fit she had! Thought her youngest daughter was going
straight to hell in a handbasket. And—"

"Cici!" Zan began spilling it out, all of it, at once:
the rock, the shattering storm, "It," finding herself in
the meadow, Burrum, Sonte, the forest, the caves—

Cici laughed and bit her lip, moved just a little back from Zan, clasped her hands in her lap. "Honey, I didn't know you had such a vivid imagination. You know, you sound feverish. I bet you really are sick and not just upset over that diary—"

"You don't believe me."

"Believe what, Zan? I believe you're a better story-teller than I ever thought before. Hidden talent, eh?" She poked Zan lightly on the shoulder. "Look, you got yourself awfully upset over your brother reading your diary, and I don't blame you for that. Not one bit. I'll stick with you on that! Ivan really went too far that time."

"Cici. You don't believe me." *Forget it. Keep it to yourself.* Zan lay back, turned her head. "I'm tired, Cici. Thanks for talking."

"Sure, hon. You rest. Rest your mind. Try to feel better."

The next morning her mother took Zan's chin in her hand. "Zan. Look at me. Now, listen to me. You're not sick. You have no fever, no sniffles, nothing, except that hangdog look in your eyes! Okay, that's enough. A diary isn't worth all this. There are people with *real* troubles in the world. Now you get up and—"

"It's not the diary, Mom. It's not. It's what I tried to tell you. I was somewhere else in time, I mean, cen-turies ago, no, thousands of years ago with cave pe—"

"And stop that babbling," her mother said evenly, "or you'll have us thinking we've got a mental case on our hands." She smiled to soften her words. "Honey, you take things too hard. You've got to learn to have a thicker skin. Now, I've gone along with you for four days, but this is it. You're up and out and to school, this morning. Got that?"

"Got it," Zan said. Her voice was okay, her own, not

weak. She was furious with her mother, furious with Cici, furious with herself. Lying there sniveling, feeling sorry for herself. Her mother was right about that. Feeling sorry because she felt so guilty, so sick and guilty, and at the same time, scared. Scared that she'd made it all up. *Did I? All imagination? Could I have?*

Her jeans and shirt were still crumpled under the cot. Her mother always refused to pick up after her. She dragged them out to take to the hamper and felt something in a pocket of her jeans. She pulled out the little bark bag. Her breath escaped in a long trembling sigh.

She tucked the bark bag carefully into her pillow-case, drew the blanket over the cot, covering her pillow. She carefully examined each of the other pockets. All empty. The bark bag was enough. She had been there. And there was one person, at least, who would believe her. Who would understand.

Mr. Oberdorfer.

She went to school, stepping out carefully into the streets, memories and grief sitting under her ribs like small hard stones. It was all so strange! Her feet, confined in shoes, clumped unforgivingly over dead cement sidewalks. There was no fragrance in the air. And at school, the water tasted like rotten eggs. The noise shocked her. The classroom walls pressed in on her.

At lunch hour she couldn't eat the cardboard pizza served in the cafeteria and went to find Mr. Oberdorfer. He was sitting at his desk in the empty classroom, finishing a sandwich. A little red thermos cup of coffee steamed in front of him.

"Mr. Oberdorfer, could I speak to you for a minute? Please."

He wiped his mouth with a paper napkin and indicated a chair. She didn't sit down. She had meant to prepare the way, but she plunged in. "Do you remember the river of time you told us about?"

"River of—oh. Yes, of course. Einstein—"

"Well, I did it."

"Did it?"

"I stepped across," she said clearly.

He blinked at her and smiled faintly, brushing crumbs off his suit jacket. "I beg your pardon?"

"I stepped across. I crossed that time bend. Saturday —last Saturday, it happened to me!"

"Saturday," he repeated politely. He nibbled at the fingernail on his little finger.

"Yes, Saturday. I was in the park," she said, noting how pink his fingernails were. Did he polish them? "Mechanix Park. I was there, and then I was somewhere else. I was with the People. And—and it was just as you said."

A feeling of dread seized her. Mr. Oberdorfer nibbled earnestly on his fingernail. She pushed on. "It's all there. Everything. You said so, and it's true. All there—" Her voice faltered. Mr. Oberdorfer wasn't laughing at her, or getting angry, or irritated. But he didn't hear her. She saw it on his face. The politeness. The slightly glazed vagueness.

Delicately he flicked a bit of fingernail off his tongue. "I'm sorry—uh—Alexandra, but I'm not sure what the purpose of this visit is."

"I'm referring to what you said in class last week," she shouted, suddenly so angry that she was shaking. Damn them! Damn them all! Why couldn't they hear her? Why couldn't they listen and believe? "I was sitting right there when you said it!" She pointed to her seat. "And you told us, you told me, that time has no beginning and no end. Do you remember that?"

He sat up straighter. "I know what you're referring to. Our discussion of time as related to history. Why are you so angry? What a funny girl you are, Alexandra. Did you take everything I said literally? Did you really think I meant—"

"Yes! No. That is, I only sort of believed it. But then it happened to me."

"It happened to you," he repeated in a humorous voice.

"You said you believed, you *really* believed that someday someone would find out how to go back on that river of time, and—"

"Well, yes," he said, and now he was smiling at her, almost affectionately, inviting her to laugh at her own silliness. "Yes, I do believe that. But that's for the future. Something that will happen when we humans have greater control over senses that we're not now even aware of possessing. Perhaps when we poor creatures have evolved to a higher stage. But as for right now—" He shook his head, still smiling. "I didn't mean to upset you. I remember you were very taken with the idea."

"Yes," she said, backing away.

"That's gratifying for a teacher. Often we feel we're talking to a class full of blank faces and blanker heads."

"Yes," she said, again. She was at the door.

"Keep up the interest and the good work, Alexandra."

"Yes. Thank you."

"Any time," he said, generously.

That was Thursday. She found it difficult for the rest of the day to breathe and behave normally. However, she tried. She made it through the day. She made it through Friday, and then through the weekend. She went on trying every day for another four days. Went to school, saw Lillian, smiled, sat in classes, made squiggles in notebooks, wrote meaningless words and answered foolish questions.

One night she got up late when everyone was sleeping. Only a small night light burned in the bathroom. She sat on the covered toilet seat for a while, shivering and thinking. Oh, the people here! They didn't see or touch or sense one another. They didn't listen or hear. They ran from rain, lived without stars, and had never learned to whistle like the birds. Madness. Madness. Madness.

She went to Ivan's room and knelt by his bed. She shook him, whispering, "Ivan, wake up, wake up! I want to talk to you." In the crib, Buddy snored.

"Huh?" Ivan raised himself.

"No one will believe me," she said urgently. "Maybe you—" She told him. Finally, light began to leak into the bedroom from the street outside. "I didn't make it up. It really happened. It happened to me, Ivan." She wanted him to believe. She wanted to share it. The wonder. The pain.

He nodded slowly, and for a moment his eyes were as pure and open as the eyes of children, as the eyes of the People. They said, *I believe you.*

She threw her arms around him and cried in the language of the People, "This is a true thing, my brother." But before the words were finished, he had shoved her away, his face had closed against her, and his lips were twisting into a safe, mocking smile.

"Boy, you are something! One minute you want to kill me, the next you're hugging me!" He turned around and punched his pillow. "Are you crazy, waking me up in the middle of the night? Who wants to hear your weird-o dreams, anyway! Go on back to bed. And you'd better not go around talking gibberish in front of anyone else, or the little men in white coats will come for you."

The next day in school she began to feel as if she were suffocating. The air was killing her. The walls were bending, threatening to topple and bury her. The clock on the wall ticked without cease. Tick . . . tick . . . tick . . . tick . . . TICK . . . TICK . . . TICK . . . TICK . . . TICK . . . TICK . . . They were all dead, ticking away, they had all been dead forever, they would all die, why did she care, what did it matter . . . TICK TICK TICK TICK TICK TICK TICK TICK TICK TICK . . .

"STOP," she screamed. She ran out of the school into the street and kept running, knowing she was running toward something she could never find again.

33

Nov. 1, Friday.

Just had my first session with Dr. Davenport. Excused from last hour of school to go to him. Psychologist. He looks like Dustin Hoffman. Short, homely-nice. He told me, "You can say anything to me, Zan, I just want to help you. Want to talk about what happened in school last week? Why you screamed, and all the rest?"

"Freaked out," I said, to see if I could shock him. Couldn't. "Because it all seemed so wrong," I said. "The walls and the clock and—"

"Yes," he said. "Go on."

I didn't know where to start. Except I did know, really. Start in the beginning, my sensible little voice told me. So I did. With the diary first. Then the rock. I got as far as the part about meeting Burrum and Sonte for the first time when I saw it in his face. Didn't believe me. I stopped talking. What was the use?

"Any more?" he said. Super calm, as if I were explosive, and might go off BOOM! any moment.

I nodded. "Some."

"You don't have to tell me now, if you don't want to. I want you to be relaxed, feel at ease. We'll talk about everything. We'll work on this thing together. So you can feel good again and smile and have fun and do things girls your age do, and not be bothered by clocks and—"

"You don't believe what I told you," I said.

He pulled at his lip. He kept tugging at his lower lip the whole time. "You're imaginative," he said. "Imaginative people are often under a strain. A kind of special burden. Of course we all have fantasies, it's nothing to be ashamed of. But we have to recognize them as fantasies. Recognize the difference between fantasy and reality."

Yes, Dr. Davenport, I hear you. But you didn't hear me. Not even when I told you about the bark bag. About my locker key and knife which I don't have anymore. You said these things could be explained. That I had lost them, probably, that day, which would be natural, being upset and so forth. That I had made the bark bag (yes, I did, Dr. Davenport!), but *naturally* that I had made it here in the park, under stress so that I didn't remember doing it and instead had "integrated" it into my fantasy. You like those words. "Stress." "Integrate." "Fantasy." "Reality." You must have said them a dozen times each.

So, now we've met. And, as you said, we've gotten to know each other. And we both know the point of my going to you. To get my head screwed on straight so I'll stop telling stories to Ivan in the middle of the night, stop screaming in school, stop saying things were different *there* when every sane and sensible person knows there is no *there*. There is only *here*. Here. Here, forever.

Nov. 5, Tuesday—session #2 with Dr. Davenport.

"You know, Zan, your family is very distressed about you. Your mother blames herself that she wasn't more severe with your brother when he violated your confidences—"

"I didn't *confide* in him," I said.

"No, no, I meant when he read your diary. By the way, how do you feel about your brother? Are you jealous of him? Do you feel that the family pays more attention to him than to you?"

"No," I said. "Not especially."

"Well, how about telling me more about that day at school, or about this place you think you visited? Whatever you want. Let's talk about things."

So we talked. I tried to tell him that something real had happened. I told him that I was sure my mother noticed I was changed the day I came back.

"How's that, Zan?" he said. I can't help liking him. He leans toward me as if he really wants to know what I'm thinking.

"I was away almost a year," I said. "If you knew me before, *you'd* know something was different, too."

"A year changes people," he agreed. I thought for a moment, Oh God, he's going to listen to me. Then he went on, "But, Zan, you went nowhere in fact, only in your imagination. No time had passed. You yourself agreed it was the twelfth of October when you left your house, and—"

"Yes," I said. "Yes, Saturday, the twelfth of October."

I'm to see Dr. D. twice a week. I'm to go to school, except if I feel too bad, then I don't have to go. It's odd how they all sort of tiptoe around me now, just because of one good scream. And yet none of them know what it meant, they really don't know, and they can't hear me when I try to tell them.

Nov. 12, Tuesday.

Had my fourth session with Dr. D. I'm getting the picture now. It's like a game, isn't it? I mean, school and the family and the whole thing with the doctor. It's all a complicated game and everyone has a part to play. Trouble was, I stopped playing my part. So now they want to help me so I can be good and play the game the right way again. And stop upsetting people.

Almost every time, Dr. Davenport reminds me how my parents are worried about me. It's true. Every day, Dad asks me, "How're you feeling, honey? You okay?" He's nice to me. Mom, too, of course, and Cici. Even Ivan, though he's sort of embarrassed by my being nutsy.

Nov. 21, Thursday.

I don't know what I'd do if I couldn't write things down. Get them off my mind. Here I am in the park, sitting on my boulder, my fingers frozen, writing like some kind of nut. But I have to do it this way. Too worried that they'll find stuff around the house, read it, and there goes that. Then they'd find out that I DO BELIEVE AND I ALWAYS WILL BELIEVE THAT I LIVED WITH THE PEOPLE.

So, no more diary under the mattress. Not for me. Too chancy. Sometimes I do write little things down on scraps of paper at home, but I'm really careful not to let any of them out of my possession. Mostly, I write here, not in school either because kids are always reading over your shoulder or snatching your papers. And when I get through writing, where does it go? That really bothered me for a while. Then I got the solution,

and it was so simple and so funny, too, that every time
I go to the bank I have to laugh. A safe-deposit box to
hold my scribbles! Seven dollars for a year, less than
one hour with Davenport costs my parents. I keep the
two keys to my safe-deposit box right on the chain with
my new locker key and my house keys. Mom noticed
them the other night, and I said something vague about
a gym locker and she seemed satisfied.

Nov. 28, Thursday.

Okay! I'm through. Through with Dr. Couch. Nine
sessions and here I am, certified normal again. I
thought he might want to stamp it on the back of my
hand—NORMAL—in blue ink. I could show it every
time Mom and Dad get that worried look in their eyes.

The last couple times I kept thinking, What's going
on here? Why am I sitting here talking to this nice man
when he doesn't believe a word of truth I tell him, and
it's costing my parents, besides. I couldn't see that it
was helping me, either. I knew he didn't believe me
from the first time, and I knew nothing I said was going
to convince ME that I was super upset over my diary
and had imagined the whole thing about the People.
And the money bothered me. I heard Mom and Dad
talking about taking out a loan. And they were doing
some fighting over money, too, but trying not to let me
hear.

So, today, when Dr. D. said to me, "You *can* help
yourself, Zan. I've told you before, I'm not a Freudian,
I don't believe in looking for long-ago traumas. God
knows we've all suffered them. I believe in helping
people here and now. I want to help you feel better,"
and, etc, etc, etc. I broke in and said, "I do feel better.

I feel *all* better. I'm fine. I'm okay! I'm not going to do anything like that screaming thing again."

He looked sort of surprised, then pleased, as if he hadn't really thought he could bring it off. "And what about the caves?" he said in a kind of testing voice.

"I know now it was all my imagination," I said, the way he wanted me to. "Because of the diary, the violation of my privacy. It freaked me out, I couldn't handle it."

He was nodding seriously, yes, yes, yes. I kept on telling him what he'd told me in these past weeks. "It kept working on me, I was really upset, and I can see now that I made up the whole cave thing as a sort of escape—"

"Yes, I thought as much," he said. "You know, the human brain is a *fascinating* mechanism!" He sounded really happy for a moment, then he got serious again and stood up and came around his desk and shook my hand, saying, "Zan, it's been a pleasure. You're a sensitive, imaginative person, and I hope you do something, someday, with that imagination. Now, if you start feeling like the walls are coming in on you, and I guess we all get those feelings, sometimes, then you feel free to call me up. Okay?"

"Okay, Dr. Davenport." We shook hands again, and he walked to the door with me and squeezed my shoulder for a moment and then closed the door, and that was that.

So there we are. Zan is cured. Zan is normal. Hip, hip, hooray.

Dec. 17

Woke up this morning thinking about Burrum. I do that a lot. Think about Burrum and Sonte and all of them at night, and in the morning, too, when I wake up. I'm pretty good now about not letting them get into my mind during the day. Pretty good at smiling and talking and being "myself" again. That's what they call it. "Zan's herself," they say. "Zan's settled down."

Dec. 20

My period has started. I was in the bathroom getting ready for bed, and I noticed a stain in my panties. Blood. The first instant I was nearly sick with fright. Any time I see blood now, even a scratch, the first thing that comes to me is Sonte. Then I realized what it was. And this marvelous feeling went right through me. I thought, Wow, Zan, you made it! I started to laugh like an idiot, really happy laughing. I felt so good I wanted to think of a million funny things to make me go on laughing. Instead, I thought of Burrum and the Sussuru, and it came to me that I'd have to make my own Sussuru. If I didn't say or do anything, nobody would ever know except me, and there wouldn't be any celebration.

So I called my mother. She came into the bathroom and closed the door. "Mom," I said. "Guess what? I just started bleeding."

"Bleeding!"

"My period," I said. "Mom, my period."

Her face got bright, kind of full of color, and she glanced toward the door, like she thought Ivan and Dad would overhear. But the next thing was, she hugged me. "Honey. You're on your way to being a woman, now. And I guess I should talk to you about things."

I hugged her back. "It's okay, I know about things." It felt so good to hug and to know she was happy for

me that tears came into my eyes. And Mom saw them
and got worried. "Now, Zan, now, honey, you promised
us, you told me you wouldn't take things so hard, so
emotionally."

"It's okay, I'm just glad," I said.

"You sure?" she said.

"Sure."

Then she went out. So that was my Sussuru.

Feb. 18

Cici's moving out. Everybody's crying and carrying
on. Cici says she has to have a place of her own, she
can't go on like this, it's driving her crazy just looking
after the kids and not having her own life, and lots of
other stuff. Mom is worried about Cici living alone, and
what will she do with Kim if she works (babysitter,
Cici says), and will she (Mom) have to quit her job,
too, because of Buddy. I'm going to get my bedroom
back, which means privacy and a place to keep things,
even something locked if I want it. But I don't care. I
don't want Cici to go, either. She's *family*. It makes me
sick to think of Cici going. I get that screaming feeling
in my head again. So I came out here to the park to sit
on the rock and write with my clumsy mittened fingers.
Write it out so it won't hurt so much inside, so it won't
go round and round in my head.

How sad life is sometimes! There are days now when
I do forget *them*, when I forget I knew something else,
when I think, this is it, this was always it, this way, no
way else. Then I remember. Little things. Sun on the
water. Eating a piece of fruit. A song. Holding a bird's
egg. And I see how it is here, harsher, hurried, frantic.
So much sadness. And yet I guess our lives are ordi-

nary, just like the lives of most families, maybe in some ways even better.

March 18

Makes everyone uncomfortable when I sit around, and they ask me what I'm doing, and I say, "Thinking." Thinking! What's *that* mean? They want me to *do* something. So I make brownies. Call Lillian. Take Buddy for a walk. Visit Cici and Kim in their new apartment.

March 25

Did a comp for English. Topic: "An Imaginary Journey." I had to write about *them*. I gave myself an "imaginary trip back in time." It was as if, for a little while, I was there again. I told about the People, how they lived in caves, what they ate, what they wore, about the Wai Wai and the Sussuru, the honey hunt and the raft and—oh, everything I could think of. Miss Schecter handed it back with "good's!" written all over it. In my last paragraph, I wrote, "The journey changed her. She had seen another life, another way of being. She had undergone great pain and great fear and even greater sorrow. She had seen people whose eyes were unveiled, people who lived with almost nothing, lived with the wind, sun, dust, and rain, open to each other, ignorant yet wise in so many ways. They had not known words for hate, evil, kill, or war. They had not known how to strike one another in anger, how to cause pain and harm. They lived quietly, joyously, with demons and gods, with animals who spoke to them, with acceptance of themselves as part of the circle of life and death, and life again."

Miss Schecter made great big red brackets around this and wrote, "Zan! Splendid! I never knew you had this talent! Please come see me!"

She wants me to write more. But I have no more to write. This is the only thing I could have written. I tried to tell her. I had a foolish little flicker of hope that she would realize why I could write that way. No. She couldn't hear me, either. She kept saying, "But, Zan, I know if you try—you showed so *much* in this composition."

Keith Manning, who was there to talk to her about his marks, winked at me.

April 30

It's so hard to be the way *they* were. I'm trying. With the family. With Lillian. With Keith. We went to the movies Saturday. He's got this big shambling way of moving, almost clumsy, and a huge laugh. I make him laugh when I don't mean to. "I'm weird, aren't I?" I said, half teasing him, half testing him. "But that's why I like you," he said. That gave me such hope that I wanted to tell him about the People, but I didn't. I didn't dare. I've learned my lesson about that. But, still—can't I be open? Touch and comfort, laugh and cry and speak my mind and *be there*, not hidden, not secret, not withholding? I try. That's all I can do, isn't it? Try.

May 30

My belly hurts today. Not bellyache. Just a hurting belly. Feeling things in my belly, like the People did.

Must be the weather. I miss them. I dreamed about B. again, and S., too. Today I saw a woman standing in the gutter, talking to herself. People laughed, hurried past her. I saw her eyes. Mad eyes. Open, blazing. I shivered. I hurried on, just like everyone else. Am I going to be like everyone else? Afraid. Forgetting everything. Oh, please don't let me forget! Please!